WHAT HAPPENS IN Sorrento

Prologue

MUSIC VIBRATED THE WALLS, the deep base thumped and echoed in my brain. Bodies smashed up against each other, jumping, grinding, and dancing as DJ Precious Petrol made the hours-long wait to gain entry worthwhile. I raised my hands above me, spinning, absorbing the music, the sweat, the laughter, the crush of bodies all around. This was what life was made for. I loved it.

Fun. Far away. Free.

I spied my friend Clara, tongue deep with some unknown guy. A good thing. Her asshole boyfriend had never deserved her and made good on his promise of always being toxic by making her walk in on him with another woman.

Bastard.

"Maddie!" Evelyn, my second-best friend from college waved for me to join her at the bar. We were over in Spain on a vacation. Having just graduated from college, we deserved a vacay and what better place to go than Spain where the water was warm, and the men were hot.

I joined her, my mouth dry from the smoke machine used in the club and from overexerting myself as a dancer, which I was not by any stretch. Eve bounded against the glass bar, sliding a shot glass of tequila toward me.

"Bottoms up, bitch!"

I downed it and it burned my throat. "This is so much fun!" The music grew louder, a *dof dof dof* that you couldn't help but move with. "I don't know how I'll get up in the morning to clean all those rooms at the hotel." It was a bit of a pain having to work during my vacation, but if it enabled me to travel to Europe with my friends it was worth it. "I'm going to be so hungover." I downed another shot Eve slid my way. My eyes watered.

We both laughed. "Omg, yes! You poor thing, but at least we can say we danced the night away at Exile and enjoyed our last few days here in Ibiza."

"True." I ordered two more shots. I was going to be legless by the end of the night. But there was something about Spain that made you a little wild. People from all walks of life partied hard here, and we'd seen a few celebs on vacation walking about Barcelona just last week.

"I wonder who owns this nightclub. I bet they're raking it in." This was my first vacation overseas. In fact, my first vacation anywhere. Being in the foster system back in the US until I turned eighteen didn't allow financially for European vacays. Not like my two best friends. Trust fund babies, but still somehow had turned out normal and nice. My only family really.

"They are rich babes." Eve gestured toward the restrooms. "Just before I saw some chick almost leave her Dior bag in the bathroom."

Not uncommon, seeing the oddest thing done by rich people who didn't know what it meant to struggle. I ordered a beer, smiling at Eve, who shook her ass at a guy who walked past, eyeing her like a lollipop to lick. "Did you see Clara getting it on with some guy? He was fucking hot."

"I'm happy for her." And I was. It was about time she moved on and found her independence again. "What better way to get over someone than to get under someone else?"

Eve lifted her third shot of tequila in agreement and tapped it against my glass of beer.

"Guys! Guys!" Clara joined us, her lipstick a little smudged across her cheek.

I wiped it off and cleaned her up as best as I could. "I'm leaving with Pablo." Clara wiggled her brows. "He's asked me to go back to his place, and I'm going to go."

"Are you sure?" There are a lot of crazies out there, and she hadn't known him a night. Nor had Clara been in the dating scene at all. She was pretty green when it came down to it.

"What if he tries something you don't like?" Eve asked.

"He won't. He's a teacher." Clara reached for the man who certainly looked like he wanted to teach my friend a thing or two. I doubt it would be academic. "What teachers are cray cray?" Clara asked with a small smirk.

I could tell she was looking forward to reclaiming a part of herself that her ex asshole stole.

"She has a point, Maddie." Eve waved Clara off. "Go. We know your location by your phone. Do not lose it, and text us when you can."

"Okay, I will. Byeeee."

Clara danced off toward her Spanish hunk, and boy, he was good-looking. Handsome enough to tempt anyone to disappear into the night without knowing a single thing about him. A little pang of jealousy spiked through me. I so wished I'd had at least one romantic fling while on vacation. For the last two years, I had prioritized my advertising and marketing degree, determined to remove myself from ever being vulnerable again. To land a dream job that would give me security for life. I was so close now for that future to become reality I could taste it, and there was no way that I was going to let getting into a relationship get in my way or cloud my judgment. In another two short years, I would graduate with a masters. Nothing must distract me.

A fling, though, that I would do. Still, dick eluded me the last month. Was I giving off prude vibes? Maybe I wasn't as hot as I thought I was. I had a nice body, was intelligent with nice skin. I sipped my beer. God, I needed a man. "I hope she has a great lay."

Eve laughed, her green eyes sparkling with wickedness. "Oh, so do I. Her vibrator needs a break for one night."

I chuckled, glad that the little buzzing sound so often heard through the thin walls of our college accommodation in NY may soon cease for a night or two. "True."

The music morphed into a melody, and the lights dimmed, giving the club a dark and mysterious air. A guy Eve had been dancing with earlier joined us and snatched her back onto the dancefloor. I sat on a barstool, surrounded by hundreds of people, and yet alone. My friend's happiness made me smile. This summer had been one of the best of my life, and our month-long party was ending tomorrow. I didn't want to feel down about it. With luck, I could be back in Europe soon if I landed the job I wanted, which had great benefits and pay, including generous leave. I reached for my beer and frowned. A hand covered mine, stopping me from picking it up.

I looked to see whose hand was on mine. My mouth gaped, and my heart did a ridiculous lurch.

All that was holy, who the hell was he? I did a double take, snapping my mouth closed. The stranger had a cocky, confident grin that sent heat directly between my legs. He was hot, and he knew he was fucking hot and the kind of effect he had on women.

He tilted his head, his dark-brown eyes slipping

over me like a physical caress. Goosebumps rose on my skin, and I swear I could hear my heartbeat hitting my chest. The urge to run my fingers through his dark hair bombarded my thoughts and I fisted my hands to stop myself. I bit my lip, breathing deep to stop the erotic imaginings of how else I could clasp his hair and when.

"Is something wrong?" I managed, glad I didn't sound like a starstruck idiot who was drooling at the hot dude still holding my hand on my beer. I may be desperate for dick, but I didn't want anyone to know it. Especially him.

He stepped close, wagged his finger before my nose. "I saw someone drop a pill in your drink. They saw me coming, and before I could get over here, they bolted. Don't drink that." He leaned on the bar and yelled at the bartender for another.

Fuck. My chest squeezed at the implication of what I escaped. "Wow, thanks." Horror images of being date raped filled my mind and a shiver wracked my body. I hadn't even seen anyone beside me.

The bartender poured me a beer, and I didn't know where to look. I really wanted to look at my rescuer standing so tall and handsome at my side. His dark hair and sun-kissed skin shouted Italian, not to mention his long, dark eyelashes. But his accent was more British than Italian. Maybe he was here on vacation too.

"Here you go." The bartender threw a napkin beside the drink and went off to serve others.

I took a sip, swaying to the music. "You're my knight in shining armor. Or is that Armani?" I teased, smiling at the quirk of his lips. His mouth screamed sin, and his lips were fuller than a lot of women I'd seen here in Ibiza who were addicted to filler.

I swallowed, feeling out of sorts and well out of my league. No American girl from multiple foster homes and a university scholarship pulled these types of men at bars. I certainly had never had such luck, but maybe tonight, that fortune was changing for the better.

I may get dick after all...

He glanced at his clothes and shrugged, unimpressed with what he wore, as if it were a common everyday thing to be dressed so expensively. Maybe he was a drug lord, a high-flying CEO, or a rich boy. Even if he were all those things or none of them, the way he was looking at me right at this moment made my heart beat fast and my mind scrabble not to speak like a blubbering fool.

"You're not from around here?" A statement more than a question.

I shook my head, sipping my new beer to delay the inevitable of telling him he was wasting his time. I was leaving the day after tomorrow, and our paths would never cross again. "New York, as a matter of fact. I'm in Europe for a working vacation this summer. And you?"

"A weekend break before I go back to work, although I mixed my weekend with work." He raked me with a gaze that left my skin prickling with awareness. Heat licked my body, and I shivered. As tipsy as I was, this highly polished man liked what he saw, and so did I.

"Where is work normally?"

"Rome. I fly back tomorrow morning."

"Right." I bit my lip, forcing my breathing to calm the hell down. Why did I feel like I'd run a marathon? My body felt aflame. The thrumming warmth between my legs did not help. Did he know I found him gorgeous? That merely being beside him made me want to do things no good girl ought?

He stared at me with dark, hooded eyes, and I wanted to ask if he was thinking the same dirty, sexualized thoughts I was. Maybe my drought between men had been too long this time, and I was hornier than I thought.

Damn.

I smiled to hide my nervousness, but it didn't help. He read me like a book and reached out, taking my hand. He pulled me through the nightclub, the dancers moving out of our way as we walked in the direction of a roped-off VIP area.

Of course, he was a VIP. He certainly gave off that vibe, and I should have known. Without saying a word, a bouncer lifted the rope and allowed us to enter the room. I looked around at the people who occupied the tables and lounges. I was certain I'd seen Heather Scott from the hit TV series *Situation Unsure*. Surely, I was seeing things.

The Roman god glanced back at me as we walked, entering another room. It had a glass wall, where I could see the people in the nightclub dancing and drinking, enjoying their night. The music was a little muffled in here, but the atmosphere was heavy with expectation. Black leather booths sat against the walls, yet they were empty.

We were alone…

He pulled me inside and closed the door, the snick of the lock loud even with all the noise surrounding us. "Do you know what I want?"

I nodded, knowing what he meant. I could feel what he wanted, words were irrelevant. He stepped close to me, his warm, hard body pressed against mine. I sucked in a startled breath, my hands sliding up his shirt.

The shirt was soft, well made, Armani was quality. Yet corded muscles, hard and flexing beneath my palms, were in contradiction to his attire.

He stared at me, his eyes piercing right to my soul, reading me like a book and knowing what I wanted. I wouldn't be here with him if I wasn't up for being naughty. Without saying a word, his large hands cradled my face before his mouth crashed onto mine. Our tongues tangled, teased, and beckoned to be wicked. Heat dropped low in my belly, running all the way to my clit. I moaned, wrapped my arms around his neck, and kissed him back. He tasted of fruit and wine, delicious and as intoxicating as the alcohol I had consumed all evening.

He pressed against me, his cock thick and hard in his pants. I surged against him, undulated against his body. My skimpy dress no barrier to our need. I reached down, fondled him. I gasped through the kiss, feeling his size. He was so thick, for a moment I felt hesitant, then he sucked at my tongue, and I knew I needed him inside me.

He was walking satisfaction, and I needed him to scratch that itch.

I had never been with a man like this before. Never been so brazen. But something told me that if I were to have a one-night stand on the last night of my European vacation, I wanted this man to be the one who popped that cherry.

"You're beautiful," he murmured against my ear, biting my lobe.

His hands reached for my dress, yanking it up with such force the stitching ripped. I didn't care. All my thoughts, wants, and needs were focused on having him inside me. Thrusting his sizable cock into me, filling me to completion. I grew wet at the thought. The sweet ache between my thighs begged for gratification.

He grabbed the crutch of my panties and tore the little strip of fabric away.

"Yes," I gasped as he ran his fingers along my cunt. Stroking, teasing…

"You like that, New York?"

I liked the name he bestowed, a little mystery to go with our tomfoolery. A finger slipped into me, and I gasped. I pressed down on his hand, wanting him deeper, faster, harder.

It wasn't enough. I wanted more. So much more.

He wrenched my leg onto his hip and pressed me

against the glass wall. I remembered where we were, seeing the people dancing but inches from the glass.

"They can't see us. We can only see them."

I sighed, relieved not to be on show for everyone in the nightclub. His large hands slipped about my ass, squeezing my cheeks, hauling me up into his arms. I wrapped my legs around his waist. My breath hitched at the wild, untamed light in his eyes. It promised satisfaction, hot, uncensored sex. No commitments, no names.

His wild gaze met mine. A dark light burned in his eyes that warned me of the pleasure to come. An indulgence I was more than willing to relish. He did not scare me. Only the thought of not fucking him and having this memory did.

"Do it now. Please," I begged, the juices of my desire running down my legs.

"My pleasure." I thought he would thrust into me. Claim me. Instead, he pulled a condom out of his pocket, slid it on and then pushed into me, with a slow, torturous stretching that was too much. I dug my fingers into his shoulders, threw my head back and screamed.

I came.

"Fuck you're sweet, but you screw like sin, New York."

His words made my orgasm rip through me with such a force that I saw stars. I convulsed against his rigid, large cock, quivers shot out to every fingertip and toe. I rode him, took what I wanted and savored the pleasure for as long as I could.

He was my first one-night stand. First fuck in a club.

I could get used to such satisfaction without commitment.

He thrust into me. I gasped at the pressure, the first sweet ache building again for more deliciousness to come. He was big, not just his dick, but him. Tall, broad, strong arms. He took me against the glass wall as if I weighed nothing at all and never lost his stride. I was consumed by him, at his mercy and trying not to lose myself in his overpowering ways.

"You're so wet for me, beautiful."

I was, there was no denying that. So lost in his ministrations I couldn't answer, merely nodded. "Keep fucking me," I managed, my words breathless.

He growled and devoured my mouth. The kiss was devastating. Deep and consuming. His teeth nipped my bottom lip and I yelped. A wicked grin twisted his lips before his tongue licked along where he bit, soothing the hurt.

His hands clasped my ass as he thrust into me. Good God, I couldn't catch my breath. He hit a spot within me that begged to be stroked, satisfied.

The man was a master.

My body shook. The need to come again beat through me. I could feel it coming, so deliciously close until he pulled out and set me on my feet. The change in position made me sway and I leaned against the wall as he dropped to his knees.

Holy fuck, he wouldn't.

He did.

He set my leg on his shoulder and bared me to his gaze. If I thought his eyes couldn't darken more with desire, I was wrong. They were liquid heat, pools of sin that taunted me to join him in his vice.

His tongue glided along my sex. I sucked in a breath, moaning as his mouth suckled my clit before he slipped one finger into me. "Oh God," I breathed.

His answering moan shot pleasure through my core. He fucked me with his mouth, ate me like a man starved of sustenance.

Who did such a thing to a person they'd only just met! I couldn't reconcile the highly polished man who saved me from drink spiking to the wicked Italian god on his knees worshipping my cunt.

I undulated against his mouth, rode him like a woman possessed. No fear, no shame. Who the fuck was I?

"Oh yes, please. Fuck yes," I mumbled words, incoherent with a tinge of begging, but I didn't care. He owned me, played me like a musical instrument and I was his sheet music.

"You taste so good." His words, muffled by my sex, made pleasure slice through me. I was so close to orgasm, one that threatened to be even stronger than the last.

Just before I combusted into a million pieces, he stood, wiping his mouth and chiseled jaw of my juices. "Turn around."

I did what he commanded without question. Expectation ran through me, making me malleable. His cock pressed against my ass. He tipped my hips, pressing against me and took me from behind. I groaned, my face against the glass, the air of my breath frosting the wall.

It was too much.

I couldn't catch my breath.

Couldn't breathe.

Think.

My pussy fit him like a glove. His corded chest pressed into my back, his fingers pinching the skin on my hips. He slipped one hand down my stomach, slicing over my sex to roll my clit with his thumb. I jumped at the touch, his fullness in me, along with his wicked fingers driving me beyond coherent thought.

"Where have you been hiding, New York?" His words kissed my cheek. His hand circled my throat. His tongue flicked out, teasing the underside of my ear.

"I cannot get enough… I've never…" Why couldn't I speak? I fought to clear my mind, attempted to get my words out. "I've never done anything like this. I've never been so audacious."

He growled, the sound dark and full of warning. "You're mine now."

I wanted his words to be true, but then, this was a one-night thing, a moment in time that would pass like everything else. Would I see him again? I did not think so. The realization made me bold.

He relentlessly took me, and I gave myself up to his

dominance. My orgasm teased at the fringes of my sex, so close and yet wickedly aloof. He tipped my hips to a different angle, and that was all it took. I came hard, my body rocked to its core by the gratifying tremors that shot through me. My legs shook and my knees threatened to turn to water.

"I'm coming," he rasped, his cock swelling within me.

I pressed against him, my body drinking in his seed. His rapid heartbeat thumped against my back and matched my own against the wall.

"Fuck, New York. You're amazing."

I leaned against the wall, the cool glass chilling my brow. I forced deep breaths into my lungs, trying to calm my pulse. He slipped out of me, and I shuffled down my dress, ignoring my torn panties that lay at my feet.

Our eyes met and I was rocked by how fucking handsome this man was. I lay my hand against his jaw, needing to feel his stubble against my palm, pinch myself I hadn't imagined having the best sex in my life with a stranger.

His cocky grin was addictive. It also told me he was a player, a man who was used to getting what he wanted whenever and wherever that was.

"Have dinner with me. Tonight. I know a great restaurant not far from here. It's quiet and we can talk."

Was he wanting this interlude to be more than a one-night stand? Not that I was complaining. I would love to see him again, tomorrow night would even work, my last night in Ibiza. Go out with a bang and have him on a bed, which promised to be even better, hotter than against a wall.

"I'll have to tell my friend where I'm going first or she'll worry, but I can meet you outside in ten minutes?"

He nodded, running a hand through his hair that had fallen across one eye. He was a disheveled god, his suit a little ruffled, his lips swollen from my kiss. He reached down and shoved his large cock back into his boxers before zipping up his pants. I licked my lips, tasting him still.

God, he was so hot.

My body heated and I felt myself grow wet at the thought of fucking him again.

He leaned forward and kissed me, the embrace slow and tender. The opposite to the raw, dirty kisses we shared while fucking.

"I'll see you out front in ten."

I left him, making my way through the VIP room. My legs shook and I forced myself to raise my chin and not look sheepish and utterly smug. I found Eve at the bar with the same guy who stole her from me, ordering another round of shots. I downed a vodka she lifted before my face.

"I'm heading to dinner with a guy I just met. I'll meet you back at the hotel tomorrow morning. I think I'll be sleeping at his tonight."

"You hooked up with someone?" Eve's eyes sparkled with excitement.

"I did and he's so fucking hot. I think I may have found my vacation fling. A little late, but better than never."

"What happens in Ibiza stays in Ibiza," Eve's guy friend shouted, laughing.

I picked up another shot glass, downed the vodka, the sharpness of the drink bringing tears to my eyes. "Later, Eve. I'll tell you everything in the morning."

"Make sure the story is a good one."

"Oh, it will be." I moved toward the exit, dancing through the crowd, my mood carefree, my night looking up, even if it was my last.

I paused at the sound of a woman's shriek followed by men shouting. Madness erupted near the entrance of the club. Men shouted and fists were unleashed. The music continued as the all-in brawl spread through the nightclub like cancer. I fell to the floor and crawled toward the wall, trying to get out of the growing melee.

I hunched on the ground, trying to protect myself as everyone went crazy, before a foot, attempting to kick some other random clubber connected with my face. A polished black Massaro loafer was the last thing I saw before everything went black.

TWO YEARS LATER

"WHAT HAPPENS IN SORRENTO, LADIES..."

The view from our Airbnb lounge balcony overlooked the Amalfi Coast. A welcome surprise none of us had been expecting, but then with Eve's father having booked the house for us, it wasn't surprising he only wanted the best for his only daughter.

The expanse of the ice-blue water, Mt. Vesuvius imposing and grand in the hazy distance told of ancient Roman civilizations, of grandeur and history that had survived for thousands of years no matter the changes time brought with it.

"Two years. Can you believe it's been that long since we were in Europe last?" Not that we made it to Sorrento after Ibiza, but still, it had been in our plans. The sun dipped in the western horizon, kissing the ocean, announcing dusk would soon be descending on the area.

Such a pretty burnt orange that you didn't often see living in New York. Concrete, noise, pollution, and people. Lots of people was all you ever saw in that city, although it did have its good points too.

"If that brawl in Ibiza taught us anything, and Maddie only just making it out of the nightclub alive, it's to live in the moment and not take life for granted. And now that we're here, celebrating my cousin's engagement to Banker Bob, that's exactly what we're going to do." Eve rolled her suitcase into her room.

"So who is Emma marrying again?" I asked, seeing the hotel a little farther down the road from where we were to attend the engagement party tonight. "By the looks of the hotel, Banker Bob is fancy." I went back into the lounge room and slumped onto the plush cushions. We had been traveling for hours, and my eyes were itchy and sore from lack of sleep. I closed them a moment, needing a little rest.

"His name is Robert Venguard, a banker or stockbroker, something along those lines anyway, but he's from London, and they wanted a destination wedding. My family will only be here two weeks, but us ladies, we get to enjoy Sorrento for two months. It's going to be so much fun. I can't wait to hit the beach."

I smiled, but my summer was destined to be a lot different than Eve's and Clara's. They weren't working like I would be, but it was a little annoyance that was necessary to enjoy Europe with my two best friends. A few hours a day working at the coffee house wouldn't be so bad, and the majority of time I could be at the beach as well.

"This is what you're going to wear tonight, Maddie. I insist."

I opened one eye to see what dress Clara was holding up. The latest Gucci crystal-embroidered mini dress in black. I'd seen Clara wear it before in New York and she knew I had salivated over it then. "That's very short for an engagement party. I don't want everyone to see my panties, Clara." Even though the thought of wearing it made me giddy.

"Oh, don't be silly. It's the latest fashion and it'll suit your long, slim legs. You'll look divine."

I held up my hands, resigned to do as I was told. "Fine. Thank you, darling. It's beautiful and will ensure I won't eat or drink anything for the evening for fear of spilling anything on that dress."

Clara tsked tsked me. "Don't be ridiculous. You'll eat, and these dresses, no matter their price, are to be worn and enjoyed. Don't panic if you do get it dirty. It can be cleaned."

"What time is this engagement party starting? Do we need to hurry?" I started for my room, needing to shower for the first time in twenty-four hours. Hopefully it would wake me up a little. Not to mention there may be handsome single Italian men at the party who may make my night a little more fun. If I'm going to be wearing Gucci, I better shave my legs and armpits too.

"At eight," Clara clarified. "It's supposed to be decadent inside, Emma wanted floral, so expect lots of flowers. The Dudley-Fairfax has gone out of its way to accommodate their every wish. Only the mega rich stay at the chain of hotels and there are only a select few around the world. It has a huge, terraced garden that overlooks the ocean. In her last call, Emma mentioned that's where we'll be dining for the night before moving down onto the lower terrace where there's dancing planned. It supposed to be the prettiest view in Sorrento."

"Sounds lovely. I'm so excited," Eve shouted from a nearby room.

I grinned, excited and awake again at the thought of the night to come. One for the books that would probably never happen again. Not for me at least.

Several hours later we were ready. Eve had ordered a taxi to take us up the hill to the hotel, even though we could have walked, but with all three of us wearing heels, and Eve wearing her new Jimmy Choo's, that was a trek she wasn't willing to make.

Once there, an usher escorted us through the hotel lobby, marble and mirrors, black registration desk that gleamed with not one handprint welcomed us. There was a scent of vanilla mixed with the smell of salt in the ocean air. The lobby led into a breakfast room that overlooked the ocean, although we were escorted to another part of the hotel for the private family event.

Hundreds of guests were invited. I swallowed,

having not expected an engagement party to be so grand. I knew Clara and Eve were trust fund babies, but how big were their trusts if this is how their family members lived as well?

Clara was right about the flowers—peonies, gardenias, and hydrangeas were everywhere. A waitress carried a tray of champagne nearby and we each procured a glass. I sipped the wine, a delicious flavor that again spoke of no expense spared. Clara introduced us to the many family members who were in Sorrento for the nuptials, before we made our way to our table. It seemed the florist had been given carte blanche for the table decorations too, so much so that I couldn't see the person sitting opposite to me. The starched, white tablecloths, black chairs, and crystal candelabras that the flowers climbed up through was one of the most beautiful layouts I'd ever seen.

"It's a lot, I know, but Emma wanted it as beautiful as it could be for her wedding, and Robert does everything Emma wants." Clara smirked.

"She's very lucky, but it's not too much. It's just perfect." I sipped my champagne, thanking a waitress when she came around and filled our water glasses. Eventually, everyone was seated. Clara introduced Eve and me to those at the table we'd not met before. All of them welcoming and diverting. The night was off to a good start.

"Where is the bride-to-be and groom-to-be? There's no one at the main table?" I asked.

Clara ripped her bread roll in half and glanced at the

main table. "They'll want to make a grand entrance." Clara rolled her eyes but grinned. "Emma was always one for theatrics."

I laughed and grabbed a bread roll myself, a little sad that I would have to slice into the whipped butter that was shaped as a shell. "This hotel is amazing." I glanced at the menu on the table. Dudley-Fairfax Hotels Inc. They weren't in the US, not yet at least. Maybe they would open a hotel one day in NY or LA. If they catered to the rich, those would be the locations to settle on.

The sudden clapping and shouts of congratulations startled me from buttering my bread. I jumped, my knife clattering to the table and hitting my plate with a bang. I ignored the few looks I gained and joined in with the clapping.

The bride wore a silk ballgown in a floral design, the bodice fitted with a wide neckline and voluminous skirt. The semi-sheer, spaghetti-strap, floor-sweeping gown was utterly fitting for the location. Casual but elegant. Perfect.

"Emma looks beautiful." Even I could hear the awe in my voice.

"She should. She's wearing an Oscar de la Renta."

My brows raised. This was quite the event, considering it was just the engagement party. Their wealth and kindness also meant I was invited to that affair too. I couldn't wait to see the Valentino dress Emma had hinted to Clara she would be wearing. Although the wedding wouldn't be for several more months and in Capri.

The engaged couples' attendants walked in after them. All dressed impeccably, and no doubt designer garb. It was like watching the runways during the Paris fashion.

I took a sip of my champagne and choked at the sight of one of the groomsmen. I turned toward the table, picking up my napkin, trying to smother the noise, but my body refused to cooperate. My hand tightened around the soft linen.

No. It could not be. Of all the places. Of all the chances…

Under control of my body functions again, the blood drained from my face when he stood behind the table, facing the guests. I shut my mouth with a snap. I'd never seen him smile before. He'd looked so different from the last time we'd met.

Fleetingly but entertaining as that had been.

In the VIP room at Exile in Ibiza two years before…

Holy fuck, my one-night stand was the best man!

VIP boy stood and tapped the side of his champagne glass, calling everyone to give him their attention. Like anyone wouldn't give him their full attention. Seriously, the women were already giving him looks, stripping him naked and imagining all kinds of things.

Things I'd already done with him.

I frowned. How the hell was he hotter than I remember? Lean but broad shouldered, dark haired with wickedly soulful eyes, and a mouth that kissed like sin.

He grinned and there it was, the memory of what he'd whispered against my ear flooded back. I closed my eyes, remembering the feel of him behind me, in me.

When the brawl broke out and I'd been hit with a shoe, I never saw him again.

An opportunity lost.

He could not be here.

Holy shit. Would he recognize me? Probably not. He would have seen that night for what it had been. A bit of fun in a darkened nightclub. An opportunity that unfortunately had been cut short due to a brawl.

I downed the last of my champagne, raised my glass and had another promptly delivered.

Had I really nailed him?

No. I never nailed him, but he certainly nailed me.

Over and over again.

It could not be him.

Hell to the no.

CHAPTER
Two

THE SPEECHES WENT FOR HOURS. Every time the best man laughed, smiled at the happy engaged couple, I couldn't help but think how he had been in the nightclub. Was it the same guy? Was I certain that this best man was the dark, dominant, hungry stranger who had led me into the VIP room and fucked me to within an inch of my life? Where I didn't know what or how to survive such an onslaught of sensations he evoked in me?

Sensations that hadn't been matched, not in the two years since that evening.

This guy was too clean shaven, too put together, too suave to be the one I had allowed so many liberties. A stranger. Even now I couldn't believe I fucked him without fear of where I was or what I was doing. I wasn't the type of girl who engaged in one-night stands.

But…maybe I was if he was the one offering them.

A shiver ran through me, and I shifted on my chair, feeling dampness between my legs. He was still so damn hot. The single women in the room watched him with a hunger that matched mine. I couldn't catch my breath knowing what it was like when he was the one ravenous and hell-bent on seeking satisfaction.

"Stop drooling, Maddie. You look like every other unmarried woman in the room who's interested in the best man."

I laughed, sipped my champagne, only to realize it was empty. Lifting the glass I caught the eye of a waitress who filled it up without delay. "Clara, I think I know the best man."

Clara looked at me, puzzled. "What do you mean? We haven't been anywhere for us to meet anyone yet."

"No." I leaned close to my friend. "I think the best man is the guy from the Ibiza nightclub that I fucked." Clara stared at me, her eyes wide and I waited for her to remember, to realize what I was referring to.

"Seriously?" she asked.

I nodded. "Oh yeah, I'm serious."

Finally the speeches ended, and dinner was served. I ate what I could, the little lobster entrée was particularly delicious, along with the tuna main course, but I couldn't concentrate. Had he noticed me? From where I sat, he had a clear view in my direction, but then, it had been two years. And we'd fucked and rarely looked at each other during that crazy time.

No. He wouldn't know who I was.

I was merely one of many women he fucked in darkened nightclubs. No one special.

"You need to act cool. Just go up to him and tell him hi and that you're relieved to see that he survived the brawl. Make a joke of it, lighthearted, you know. You never knew what happened to him and now you do. He's fine."

"You make it sound so easy and casual." I didn't feel cool and collected at all. And something told me the moment I spoke to him I'd fumble and choke on my words. It was different being sober and at an engagement party to being in a nightclub, drunk and carefree.

Still, I had done nothing that I should feel ashamed about. I had enjoyed my vacation with friends and happened to sleep with a guy on my last night abroad. It was good that he was here. At least now I knew I hadn't imagined him in my erotic dreams.

"Because it is, Maddie."

"I'm just inside my own head a little. I didn't expect to see him here or see him ever again."

"He's certainly the type of man who could get a woman into a tizzy, but you've got this, Maddie. Everything will be fine."

I thanked the waitress who cleared the main course, leaving room for dessert.

I sipped the champagne, the bubbles making the room spin a little. I placed it down, reaching for water instead. I needed to pace myself, not drown my nerves in alcohol. The white chocolate mud cake was set before me, with seasonal fruit and cream. I took a couple of bites, needing more food in my churning stomach.

A live band started to play down on the terrace that overlooked the ocean. Dusk kissed the horizon and over the next several minutes, guests made their way down onto the terrace to enjoy the nighttime entertainment.

The band London Revival, an indie up-and-coming band in England played to the gathered guests.

"Clara," a feminine voice screamed from nearby.

Emma, the bride-to-be ran up to Clara and embraced her when we stood to leave the table. I smiled, waited to be introduced and hoping they did not mind I was here as Clara's plus-one when I had never met either of the engaged couple before in my life.

"I'm so happy to see you, Em! Congratulations again. You and Robert look so happy."

"We're so excited for the wedding next week and that you're here to celebrate with us." Emma turned to me, smiling.

"Emma, this is my best friend Maddie Webb. She's my plus-one."

"Welcome, Maddie. Thank you for coming. I hope you're ready to dance the night away?"

"Oh, definitely, and congratulations on your forthcoming marriage."

"Thank you." Emma called out to her fiancé and waved him over to join us. He sauntered toward us, but also, so did his best man. I held my breath, unable to breathe at the thought of seeing and talking to him again.

"Robert, this is Clara's best friend Maddie Webb," she introduced us. "And this is our fabulous best man who's allowed us the use of his hotel tonight. Henry Fairfax," Emma explained, clutching her fiancés arm as if she'd never let him go.

Henry Fairfax…

As in the owner of the Dudley-Fairfax exclusive hotel chain…

Fuckkk…

My one-night stand owned this hotel, among many, many others.

Clara threw me a knowing grin but held her hand out to Henry and shook it.

"Just Henry will be fine, Em." He shook Clara's hand and then it was my turn. I reached out, sure he wouldn't remember me. Our hands locked and our eyes met. His widened, and I would have missed the surprise registering on his face had I not been intently studying him.

And then I saw it.

The moment he remembered where he had seen me before. Like a flick of a switch, his eyes darkened, burned with a memory that would forever be etched in my mind.

"I'm Madeline Webb," I said, although why I didn't say Maddie I'd never know. Maybe I wanted him to know my full name after losing him that night in Ibiza. If we were separated again, maybe this time he would be able to find me. Look me up as I had always wanted to do but never knew where to start.

"Madeline." His voice was deep, and as alluring as I remembered it. I swallowed and bit my lip. Did he know how he made me feel? Like my skin was on fire, prickling with awareness and longing. It was like my body remembered him on a visceral level. I could only hope his did as well.

"I think we've met before..." His lips lifted into a knowing grin.

I could have laughed, and I was certainly not going to say where we had met. Only my two closest friends in the world knew what I had done that night, and never had I done it again. It wasn't a normal occurrence for me, and it had only been with the man before me that I had acted so out of character.

"I think you're right." I sipped my champagne, my mouth dry. Damn, my stomach was in knots and my body ached to feel him again. What was it about this guy that made me crave? Made me want him to do all sorts of delicious, dirty things to me.

Before another word was spoken, a woman joined us and wrapped her arm about Henry's in what only could be termed as possessive. He started at her joining him before he schooled his features, smiling pleasantly. She looked familiar... Where had I seen her before? I didn't want to study her and merely muddled about her identity myself.

Was he seeing her? Was he off the market?

Damn.

"This is Henry's girlfriend Margot Hathaway." Emma did the introductions. All the while I pretended to be pleased to meet her. Margot Hathaway? The realization struck me, and I remembered where I'd heard her name before. She was just one of the most famous European actresses who was taking Hollywood by storm after her latest film that had Oscar murmurs attached to it.

That was Henry's girlfriend?

Of course it was. Who else would dare to hang off the Italian god's arm? No mere mortal like me.

Wholly naïve to think I had a shot with him again. I was a drunken fling. Margot and her type were the ones who gained HEA with men of his ilk.

I excused myself, needing the bathroom, or at least, pretending I did. In truth I just needed to clear my head and think straight. The abundance of champagne I had drunk rushed back to my head and the room swam.

I made the bathroom and locked myself away in the opulent stall, lowering the seat and sitting for several minutes, taking deep, calming breaths. I was just drunk and shocked at seeing Henry again. It would pass and so too would the disappointment that I couldn't have another shot with him.

I was in Sorrento for heaven's sake, on a working vacation, one of the prettiest places on the planet. There was nothing to be downcast about. So what if I never saw Henry again? At least it was story to tell my grandchildren one day that I had a brush with European royalty, not literally, but they would get the point.

With one last deep, calming breath I flushed the toilet even though I didn't use it, exited the stall and washed my hands. With renewed determination to enjoy the night I left the bathroom and skidded to a stop.

"Hello, again." It was Henry.

Fuckkkkk. This was bad.

CHAPTER

Three

"HELLO."

This was not happening. We were not talking to each other again, face to face, and in front of a lady's restroom of all places. Not that he seemed the least concerned that he had followed me here. He leaned against the wall, arms crossed, watching me like a lion looked upon a nice monkey ripe to eat and devour.

A stupid part of me wanted to be eaten, devoured, and gorged upon, if it was by him.

He has a girlfriend. Get a hold of yourself.

"I did not think I'd ever see you again. In fact I had a terrible feeling that you had been injured in Ibiza. I'm very pleased to see that you were not."

I studied him, drank in all the handsomeness and reveled in the thought that he cared, even a little. My memory hadn't done justice to his features. He was so much more gorgeous than I remembered, had conjured in my memory.

"I was injured that night. I got hit in the head by a flying shoe and it knocked me out. It's why I was never able to leave in time to meet you for dinner."

A muscle worked on his chiseled jaw. I couldn't stop looking at him, drinking in his perfect, straight aristocratic nose, almond-shaped brown eyes with the longest black lashes I'd ever seen.

Nerves skittered along every pore of my skin at his inspection of me. It left me warm, achingly aware of the interest that burned in his piercing, dark eyes. But things were different now. He had a girlfriend. One who was here with him.

"You were injured." He stepped close and cupped my cheek, inspecting my face as if I still bore the mark of the Massaro loafer.

I stepped away, not wanting anyone to see the familiarity between us, and certainly not his girlfriend. "It's long healed, Henry. It was two years ago after all." I laughed off his concern, but an anger simmered in his eyes that I couldn't make out. Was he angry at me stepping away or that I'd been injured? "I'm happy to see you were not hurt as well. I was making my way out of the club when the brawl started."

"I was waiting in a car outside when all hell broke loose. I tried to get in to find you, but the police were there in minutes and wouldn't let anyone back inside. I'm sorry that we didn't get our dinner date."

His words were sweet, and nice to hear, still, I shrugged, knowing our time had passed. "Well, it was a long time ago now. It's nice seeing you again. I'm pleased to put a name to the face I've dreamed about quite often."

I paused, gaped, and heat rushed to my face. Had I just said that out loud? Bloody hell, what was wrong with me tonight? He didn't need to know that little secret of mine. Ever.

"You dreamed about me?"

Why had his voice dropped an octave and why was he looking like the cat who found the cream? "I umm… I should probably return to my friends." I slipped past him, wanting away from my self-induced embarrassment. He clasped my arm and pulled me into a small nook separating us from those at the party.

The feel of his hand on me left me reeling, my skin burned where he held me, and the soft swipe of his thumb across my arm left me tottering to succumb to his charm. "After what we had done in the VIP room, I had hoped to haunt your dreams, if only you would try and find me in reality."

I shook my head, unsure of what he was saying. "I did try and find you, but I didn't even know your name."

"I looked for you too." A pained expression crossed his features, before he blinked, and it was gone. "You can probably tell I was as unsuccessful as you were."

"There is little we could do about it. It is what it is. But at least I have learned from my mistake, and I always introduce myself now when meeting new people." I crossed my arms. Our inability to share our names had perhaps robbed us of a great opportunity, and nothing could change the past now.

His face darkened and he frowned. "You've fucked others in VIP rooms since me?"

What the hell? "Ahh, no. I just meant that I introduce myself now and leave nothing to chance."

He seemed to relax in front of me. His shoulders dropped and he let out a relieved breath. Did the idea of me fucking others disturb his peace? He was the one here with a girlfriend, not me.

"It was lovely meeting you officially, Henry. Have a good evening." I left him, could feel his burning gaze singeing my back as I walked away. I fought not to hurry my steps, and thankfully made it back to Clara and Eve without incident.

By the time I stepped onto the terrace, everyone was dancing. I joined in with my friends, both of whom who had found attractive men to dance with. I joined in with them, laughing as another guy joined our group and focused his attention on me.

I rocked to the music, swayed with the beat. The warm, Mediterranean air was like a comforting blanket. The sea stretched out for miles, dusk about to kiss the night hello. A masculine body came up behind me, and I clasped his hands, holding him against my stomach. Why not have a little fun? Enjoy the night, who knew where or what it would bring. It had already brought Henry Fairfax back into my life, the night could only get better from here.

"I'm Merrick," his deep, European baritone whispered against my ear, tickling me.

"Are you single, Merrick?" With the way he was grinding against me I hoped that was the case.

He chuckled, kissed the underside of my ear, sending a shiver over my skin. "I'm very single. Your friend tells me you are as well. Perhaps this engagement party won't be a total bust after all."

"Perhaps not." I turned and looked at the man holding me far too close for someone I'd just met. Then again, he was a guest, friend of the future bride and groom, he couldn't be all bad. Probably another rich boy looking for some fun. Not that I would be that for him tonight, but a dance wouldn't hurt anyone.

"You're very tall."

He grinned and wiggled his brows. "Would you like me to pick you up so we're the same height? I wouldn't mind," he added. "Anything to get me closer to your sweet lips."

I threw back my head and laughed. The guy was laying it on thick. "I'm fine where I am, but thanks for the compliment."

"You're American."

"I am," I said proudly. "And you are?"

"I'm Italian, but I live in London. I went to school with the groom-to-be."

"Not another banker or hotel magnate, I hope." I let the statement hang and he didn't reply right away.

"Most of us, but there are some exceptions."

Merrick's gaze shifted to somewhere over my shoulder, and he frowned. "Friend of the bride?" he asked.

"Sort of. I'm best friends with her cousin and I'm here as a plus-one. I'm on a working vacation here in Sorrento. Eve and Clara are just on vacation."

He mock-gasped and clutched his heart. "Don't tell me you're not cruising around Italy on Mummy and Daddy's money like so many others here this evening?"

I laughed, liking he was able to make a joke and be down to earth. "No, unfortunately. I don't even have a trust fund."

"I can be your sugar daddy if you need one."

"I think that would be impossible since we're around the same age. Aren't you supposed to be older than me to have that title?"

"Good point."

The music changed tempo and we broke apart, but continued to dance. Merrick kept losing his attention on me and glancing across the terrace. He probably was here with someone else, and they had spied him being a flirtatious ass.

I turned through the dance, grabbing Clara and pulling her close for a little spin and that's when I saw what had occupied Merrick's attention.

Henry was leaning against the terrace, his stunning girlfriend beside him in animated conversation with other guests, but he couldn't have looked less interested. His gaze burned a path across the terrace directly to me.

My steps faltered and I caught myself, not wanting

Henry to know I was aware of his interest. Still, even from the distance I could see the strain across his jaw, the lowered brow, the livid expression on his handsome visage.

Not at me, but Merrick.

He was pissed.

Merrick came up behind me and I clasped his arms, grinding against him as I watched Henry from afar. Henry wasn't mine to have, but that didn't mean I couldn't show him what he was missing. What we both were, thanks to fate.

CHAPTER

Four

AS THE NIGHT progressed I lost track of Henry. Not that I was stalking him or anything, merely was aware of where he was at any given moment… But with Henry's attention no longer focused on me, my interest in flirting with Merrick waned. I couldn't lead on an innocent guy who possibly thought the night may end differently than how it would. That wasn't me and I didn't want to go down that road and entangle myself in anything on my first few days on the island.

"I'm going to get a drink and sit for a while. Have fun." Merrick seemed confused before he danced off into the crowd, leaving me alone. It was for the best, as handsome as he was, he wasn't for me. I found the bar, ordered a beer, and sat on a vacant sun lounge.

Eve spied me and danced to where I sat and joined me. "I saw a guy go after you when you excused your-self earlier. Where did you get to?" The interest in Eve's eyes was clear to see.

"I used the restroom, but Eve, that was Henry, the guy I had a one-night stand with in Ibiza two years ago. He's here and with his girlfriend."

"Holy shit, the best man was your one-night stand?" Eve laughed, clapping her hands as if this was the most amusing thing she'd heard in a while. "That is a wild coincidence."

Wasn't it? Utterly bizarre and not what I expected. Nor was seeing him attached, but such was life. You won some and lost others.

"And he followed you to the restroom?"

"Sort of. He was waiting for me when I exited the ladies." I sighed. "Looking as deadly as sin and as handsome as I remember." And utterly unavailable, which sucked.

"And...tell me what you talked about. I need all the details."

"We just spoke about that night in Ibiza and I told him the reason why I never met up with him."

"The shoe?"

I rubbed my forehead, remembering the blunt force of being hit with the loafer. "Yeah, the shoe...and we exchanged names, wanting to make sure we could look each other up if we wanted to next time."

"Really?" Eve looked sly. "So there's possibly a next time." She paused. "I will mention that his girlfriend did not look impressed that he went after you when you excused yourself. She looked downright offended, but he appeared determined."

The idea that he could still be interested in me made

my stomach flutter. In the two years since I'd seen him, there hadn't been a week that I hadn't thought of him. Wondered who he was and chastised myself for not introducing myself at the time. To see him again tonight seemed like a second chance…

No, it wasn't that. He was taken and I needed to respect his choice.

"The way he looked at you, Maddie…I don't think he's finished with you yet. And I doubt his car ride home this evening with his girlfriend will be pleasant."

I cringed, not wanting to cause trouble. I found him attractive, yes, a woman would have to be dead not to, but that didn't mean I'd try anything that was wrong. I'd never been the other woman and I wouldn't start now.

No matter how tempting Henry was.

"I was going to head back to our Airbnb. It looks like the engagement party is dying down anyway and I have work tomorrow." I looked out onto the ocean, the dark, starlit sky having long overtaken the golden hues of dusk.

"Oh no, you can't go yet," Eve protested. "There's still plenty of hours left in the night."

I hugged Eve, but I was determined. I needed to arrive at the café early anyway and meet my new boss to go over what I needed to know before my shift started at nine. "Truly, I have an early start, but you stay and enjoy yourself. I don't want to be hungover for my first shift. I need this job to enjoy my summer here with you and Clara, remember?" I didn't want to put the guilt trip on Eve, but sometimes my friends forgot that I wasn't flush with cash like they were, and a little reality check was needed.

"Fineee," Eve drawled. "Be safe, we'll see you tomorrow."

I bussed her cheeks before heading out of the engagement party. Others heading home gathered in the hotel foyer, waiting for their cars and taxis to pick them up. I walked past everyone, thankful that our rented apartment was only a short walk from the hotel. Even as late as the hour was, the streetlights illuminated the road and there were many tourists and locals still out and about the town, making my short walk safe.

My thoughts drifted to Henry as I walked along the sidewalk. The view, had it been day, would show a cobalt-blue ocean stretching out before Sorrento, the cement balustrade the only thing keeping people from falling over the cliff it ran along.

As if my thoughts of Henry conjured him, my steps faltered at the sight of him leaning over the balustrade, talking on his phone in a thick Italian accent. No longer a guest, a best man, but a high-powered businessman who needed to sort something out that was important.

I couldn't quite reconcile the man I had in the nightclub and the one who stood before me, unaware of my inspection and busy with his business. This man was all work and no play, and yet the guy in the nightclub had given in to desire, to need, and to me.

I wrapped my arms about myself, shivering at the

sea breeze, even though the night was warm. I didn't initiate conversation, he was busy and distracted with something else. Nor did I want to look desperate for his attention and conversation.

"Hey, you leaving?" he called, a few steps after I passed him.

I didn't turn for fear he wasn't talking to me, and my presumption may come across as too forward and full of myself. I kept walking toward our apartment before heavy footsteps sounded behind me.

"Madeline?" He clasped my arm for the second time tonight and my body warmed at his touch. There was something seriously wrong with me that he affected me like no one else had. We fucked once. Why was I reacting to him in this way? Like my body was on fire and only he could douse the flames.

I schooled my features, not wanting him to know the effect he had on me. He didn't need to know how much I wanted another night in his arms. He was taken. Had a girlfriend.

Not single. Not single. Not single.

"Sorry, I was lost in thought." The lie slipped off my tongue with ease and I was pretty proud of myself that it sounded believable. I pulled my arm free of his grip and watched him, drinking in the sight of my Italian god, for what may be the last time I'd ever see him.

"Where are you going? Home?" He checked his watch before looking at me with confusion. "Early, isn't it?"

"Yes. I have an early morning and didn't want to

make it harder than it already will be." I glanced up the street, anywhere but at his dark-brown eyes, which watched me with an intentness that left me discombobulated and nervous.

"Maddie." His deep baritone pulled at a part of me that needed to deny him. I'd heard that tone before, in the nightclub before he took me, and I didn't need the reminder of what I couldn't have. "I wish things could be different, but my life is…difficult at the moment. There are things at play…" He ran a hand through his hair, his attention dipping to my lips. "I'm sorry we never had our dinner date."

I made an odd, mumbling sound of agreement, hating the prickling of tears that blurred my vision. I blinked, not wanting him to see his words hit a part of me that always struggled with rejection. As a child in the foster system, I was used to being unwanted, but still, the notion stung, no matter how old I was.

"Me too, but meeting you tonight, putting a name to a face I'd never forgotten has been a nice closure." Before I could think better, or lose my nerve, I closed the space between us and brushed my lips against his. A kiss goodbye, a final farewell that I'd never have again.

He leaned into the kiss, reaching for me, but no, I didn't want that. I pulled back and started down the street. Thankfully he didn't follow, and I refused to glance behind me. I couldn't trust myself or my actions if I did.

CHAPTER

Five

"MADDIE, come quickly. That Henry guy is on TV."

I popped my head around the corner from my bedroom and watched the entertainment part of the news that was mentioning him. In the five days since I'd seen Henry, I'd settled in well at the local café and got along great with all my fellow workmates. A good thing since I was there for the summer. It was also a short walk from home and getting around Sorrento was easier than I thought it would be.

I slumped onto the lounge and cringed at the scene the news was playing on repeat. That of Margot Hathaway on bended knee before Henry at some fancy restaurant in Paris, clearly proposing to him.

Instead of accepting right away, Henry pulled Margot to sit back on her chair and a heated discussion ensued. His features were hard, hers also, and for several minutes people filmed the conversation, which didn't look at all romantic. And although the video didn't pick up the audio, Henry's gestures were not promising for Margot to get the answer she hoped for.

If I thought the train wreck playing out on the TV before me was over, how wrong I was. Margot picked up her red wine and threw it all over Henry's face. His pristine white shirt turned red, liquid dripping onto his designer suit and the restaurant floor. Henry picked up his napkin and dried his face before Margot wrenched back her chair, smacking into another diner's table before storming from the restaurant.

Wow. That was a lot.

"I guess that means he's single again, Mads." Clara grinned, wiggling her brows.

"Don't be awful. That's the last thing he'd be thinking after just breaking up with his girlfriend." I'm not sure if I was more shocked Henry was in Paris only a few days after being here or from watching the footage, but Clara was right, he was single again. I had hoped I may run into him again on the island, and yet all the time he was in another European city, far, far away.

"Well, I'm sorry for him. That breakup, if it was a breakup—we don't know for sure—looked upsetting. I don't think he'd have me on his mind, and I'm not going to track him down and see if he's up to picking up things where we left them."

"But it does show that he was not inclined to marry her, even if they have been dating for years."

"How do you know they've been dating for so long?" I asked.

"I did a little Googling on him now that we know who he is, and it looked like of all the girls he had short flings with, his relationship with Margot Hathaway stems back to childhood. Families are good friends from what I read."

I wasn't sure how knowing that about Henry made me feel so I went back into my room and finished getting ready for my morning shift at the café. I packed my water bottle and a small snack from the kitchen for my break and, throwing it into my tote, started for the door. "Well, I'm sorry for them both if they did break up. They're never nice. And now I'm off to work. I'll see you guys later tonight."

A horrible, selfish part of me was relieved Henry could be single again. Not that he'd given me any indication of coming to see me or asking me out for dinner. He had my name now, surely a man with his connections could've found my Insta handle and slipped into my DMs.

I would like to think I would never have broken the girl code and messaged him back if he had reached out while having a girlfriend, but was that even a concern now? The footage looked like they'd broken up, so would I DM him back?

I started up the steep incline toward the café, which overlooked the Sorrento harbor. Of course I would reply now if he messaged. How could I not? It wasn't like I'd be doing anything wrong, but he hadn't and I needed to stop thinking about him and all the possibilities that were likely never to eventuate.

The sun warmed my skin, and I breathed deep the fresh, morning sea air. There were few cars in this part of town, mostly tourists walking about, and I said good morning to several people who passed me on the street. I made the café on time, Romero, the sweetheart manager that he was, had a hot, steaming cup of coffee waiting for me to kickstart the day.

There was one other woman working, an older lady named Chiara who was a whiz with the cakes and food that the café served and who worked most days, and a young lad who washed dishes. Already the café was full of customers, and I quickly went out back, dropped my bag, and slipped on my black apron. I served several customers, filled up waters and cleared away their dirty dishes, all the while trying not to get distracted by the amazing view the café had of the harbor below.

Out of my peripheral view, I noticed a group of businessmen enter and Romero sat them out on the balcony. I finished serving a brioche bun stuffed with a couple of scoops of gelato to a young mother and young daughter before heading out to take the new customer's order.

"Welcome to Bar Sorrento, what can I get for you?" I smiled at the gentlemen who were all busy studying the menu, bar one.

The very one who haunted my dreams and my memories.

What the hell was Henry Fairfax doing in Sorrento?

What was he doing here?

I clutched the Apple pen like my life depended on it

and fought to mark on the iPad the orders the men tossed at me.

"I'll just have a black coffee and croissant." Henry's wicked, teasing grin just for me left me unsure on how he made me feel. The man had a charisma about him that drove my libido wild, and I needed to get a hold of it.

"I heard you worked here. Romero is an old friend and I often breakfast here. But what a pleasant surprise running into you again."

"Is it?" Two of the men with Henry threw me curious glances and I fumbled for more words. "I'm working here for the summer. Romero was good enough to give me a job."

Henry watched me with a hunger he did nothing to disguise. There was something about his gaze that said he wasn't here for the croissant or coffee but something else entirely.

Me?

"I'll be seeing you often then. I'm staying in Sorrento for a few days. No doubt we'll cross paths again."

I nodded but didn't respond to his suggestion. "I'll be right back with your order." Like a fleeing thief, I shut myself behind the counter and busied myself with paying customers and cleaning away dirty dishes before Henry's table's order was ready.

"Romero, can you deliver Mr. Fairfax's food for me? I need to use the restroom." A lie, I just couldn't face him again. His eyes on me made me nervous and clumsy, which was so unlike myself. What was he doing back in Sorrento so soon? He couldn't possibly be here because I was. Who did I think I was to dream of such a situation?

"Of course. I'll cover you until you're back."

I disappeared out the back again. Henry was probably here to avoid the paparazzi after Margot's botched proposal and nothing more.

I'd believe that until I knew otherwise.

CHAPTER
Six

I COULDN'T AVOID them anymore. Romero had delivered their orders and I'd not been brave enough to stick around and see Henry's reaction to my nonattendance. But now I needed to clear their plates and see if they wanted anything more, and I really didn't want to.

It was like I was back in high school, crushing on the football quarterback and being the poor foster girl with no chance, but too much hope.

Sad.

I rallied and took a fortifying breath. I was a grown woman. A woman who had a college degree behind her and great friends. I didn't need to feel intimidated and out of my league. Even if I was, they didn't know that.

Or perhaps they did…

"I hope your breakfast was to your liking." I packed up the dishes quickly, smiling at each of the men who agreed the meal was satisfactory. Once I had delivered the dishes to the kitchen, I returned with my iPad. "Was there anything else I can get for you today?"

"A round of coffee, sweetheart." The older gentleman with graying hair passed me his menu, his hand grazing my arm.

I stepped away from the table and input the order. I could feel Henry's gaze on me and damn it all to hell I looked in his direction. Henry stared at my arm where his friend had touched, but before I could say a word to distract him, Henry's attention shifted to his work colleague and if looks could kill, the poor guy would be dead.

"Bring the bill with the coffees." His tone was cold, annoyed.

A muscle worked on Henry's jaw, and scooping up the remainder of the menus all I wanted to do was remove myself from the situation. "Great, your order shouldn't be long."

"Is everything okay?" Romero asked, tidying up behind the counter.

I nodded, ignoring the realization that Henry, as little as he knew me, was acting possessive. Did I like that he was this way around me? Was his being here this morning by chance or by design?

I couldn't help but think the latter.

I cringed as I stood before the servery to the kitchen, blindly wiping it down and sorting the array of menus that came back with the dirty dishes.

"Coffees for the Fairfax table, Maddie," Romero called, placing the last of the two coffees on a serving tray. I didn't want to go back onto the terrace to face them all. This was the last order I needed to deliver them and then they could leave, and I could relax, breathe again. I printed out the bill and quickly delivered the order. Henry continued to discuss his business with the men and ignored my presence, which I was happy about. When he pretended I wasn't there it made my work all the easier. His possessive, hungry looks rattled me, and I didn't need to navigate them at work along with everything else.

Not when a need foisted on me by Henry niggled inside of me and I knew I'd act on those desires if given the chance. That road only led to heartache at the end of what had started as a wonderful summer.

A group of tourists on one of the many bus tours entered and kept me occupied for the next half an hour. A godsend to forget who was sitting but a few feet from where I worked. The sound of chairs scraping on the balcony caught my attention. Henry and his work friends were standing, shaking hands, and preparing to leave. The sight of him smiling at something one of the other men said made my stomach clench. Damn, the man was hot when he wasn't so serious. I wiped a table with more vigor than necessary, trying to ignore his presence that caught everyone's attention in the café.

"A word, Maddie?"

His deep baritone didn't ask but commanded me to do as he said. I stopped what I was doing, crossing my arms, and faced him, not wanting to do what he wanted, but unable to ignore him at the same time. "Is there something else you need, Mr. Fairfax?"

Henry's eyes darkened and his gaze shifted over me like a caress. "A word in private if you can take a break for ten minutes."

I could feel everyone's eyes on me, but when I looked about the café no one's was. "Romero, can I have my break now?"

Romero caught my eye, his attention shifting to Henry before returning to whatever he was doing behind the bar. "Yeah, take my back office, but be back in ten."

I started toward the office, my senses on edge. The man walking behind me made my breath catch and my skin prickle. I opened the office door and walked to the desk before turning to face him. He closed the door and stood there, staring at me in the way that no one ever had before in my life, except him.

Before I could ask him what he wanted, he closed the space between us, cupped my face with his strong hands, and kissed me.

Hard.

I forgot all about him having just broken up with his girlfriend. So much for hoes before bros. I was a terrible human being, but like a woman possessed, desperate…I kissed him back. Molded my body against his like a woman starved, and perhaps I was in a way. I hadn't been satisfied in two years, not since Henry, and I knew what he could give me, how well this interlude could end.

The kiss took on a life of its own. He backed me up until my legs hit the desk. With little effort, he lifted me and set me on top. I was shameless and wrapped my legs about his hips. A wanton who was ready to give myself to him on my boss's desk.

His hands were everywhere, and I cursed my leggings and short skirt that hindered feeling flesh on flesh. His hand kneaded my breast, and I gasped through the kiss. His nimble finger and thumb twisted my sensitive flesh and I moaned.

"Henry…" A plea for more.

"I've wanted you for so long. Do you have any idea how hard it was for me to keep from touching you at the engagement party?"

His words doused me with reality, and I pushed at his hard, chiseled chest. "Wait. Wait a minute." He stepped back, his breathing heavy. I wiggled off the desk, needing to think clearly. "I saw you on the news being proposed to and now you're here, kissing me. Before anything else happens, I think I need to know what's going on with you."

He ran a hand through his hair and the disheveled look he created made my knees wobble. "There is a lot I need to tell you and explain. Not everything is as it seems."

I knew that as well as anyone, but I needed to know what it meant in regard to him. Was he engaged? Single? Complicated? What? "Then perhaps you could explain it, so I understand what I saw. Because to me it looked like your long-term girlfriend proposed, you failed to answer and ended up with wine on your face."

"I dated Margot for years on and off. In fact, our families expect us to marry one day. Two great Roman families joined together in matrimony, but it's all a lie. Margot and I broke up months ago. She begged me not to announce that news while she promoted her latest romantic comedy that released at the beginning of Summer. I agreed, I wasn't seeing anyone anyway, so it didn't matter."

I frowned. What did it matter if Margot was seeing Henry or not to promote a film, but then maybe she just didn't want the hassle of answering questions regarding her broken relationship when trying to promote a romance film. "But why would she ask you to marry her if your relationship was all a front? Unless she grew feelings for you again or they never left in the first place."

Henry stood before me, watching me, his gaze intense. "Oh, believe me, she's incapable of emotion, but her little proposal did catch me off guard. We were supposed to just break up, but she couldn't just do what we planned. The proposal was a way for her to make me look like the villain after doing what she wanted all along. Anything for a headline, which she gained at my expense."

I swallowed. That was a low blow, especially if Henry had played along with her plan to suit her needs and not his. "How long have you been pretending to be a couple?"

"Fourteen months."

"And you've not been with anyone in all that time?"

"No." He stepped close, his hand settling on my hip. "Up until recently I was content to pretend to be unavailable, but that all changed after the engagement party, and I saw you."

"Me?" WTH! I tried not to stare at him like a crazy person, but what did his words mean? Did he want to break up with Margot on my account so he could be here now, kissing me, taunting me with his fucking hotness?

"Yes, you." His gaze dipped to my lips, and he ran his tongue along the underside of his top lip. I bit mine, craving his mouth on me. "I told Margot that it was time to end the charade and as we were both in Paris for work last week we did it publicly at dinner. Her little performance was as shocking to me as it was the press, hence why I suppose it looked so genuine and made headlines."

Well, it would probably make headlines anyway due to who they were, not that I'd mention that now. "What do you want from me, Henry?" I had to ask, as bluntly as I could to save my feelings later.

He pressed me up against the desk and I reached for him, needing to feel his warmth, his strength, and remind myself he was real. "I want to spend as much time together while you're in Sorrento this summer. I just want to get to know you, enjoy our time, and have some fun. I feel like I haven't laughed in years, but seeing you the other evening, a lightness settled on my shoulders, and I needed to see you again. There hasn't been a day since Ibiza that I haven't thought of you, Maddie."

I tried to read his features, but he gave nothing away. Was he being sincere? I didn't know this man, not really. Yes, I knew him intimately, but that was nothing. Could I spend the summer with him? I knew the answer to that better than I knew how he made me feel or why. "You want to spend the summer with me?"

"I do. Every spare moment I have when I'm in Sorrento."

I took a leap of faith and wrapped my arms about his neck. "Okay then, I agree to these terms. What happens in Sorrento stays in Sorrento?"

"Sounds perfect."

CHAPTER
Seven

BEFORE HENRY COULD FINISH his words, his lips were on mine. I kissed him back with everything within me, reveling in the feel of his lips on mine, his tongue sliding deliciously, temptingly alongside mine. I ached everywhere, and need ran rampant through my body. I pulled him close. He understood the assignment and surged against my sex. I moaned at the satisfaction that thrummed through me. I didn't care where we were, or who could walk in at any time. I just needed Henry. Wanted him.

"Fuck me."

His eyes widened before they darkened in determination. He reached under my skirt and pulled my leggings off before stepping between my legs, spreading them so that my skirt slipped about my hips, his eyes on mine, wild and untamed. I shivered as he glided a finger into my aching core. I moaned, closed my eyes and relished the feel of him inside of me, clutched at him, undulated against his hand like a crazy woman in need of release.

And perhaps I was. It had been quite a long time between drinks.

"I'm going to fuck you so hard, Maddie." His voice sent shivers of expectation down my spine. He reached into his pocket, pulling out a condom and tearing it open with his mouth.

The sooner the better. I reached for his trousers, fumbling with the button and zipper. His heavy cock sprung out into my hand. I stroked it, thick and hard, the velvety skin making my mouth water. I wanted to lick every part of this man's body, tease him, please him.

An array of filthy, erotic thoughts bombarded my mind and made me wet.

He moved my hand aside, slid on the condom and set himself at my entrance. I watched, entranced as he slipped into me. His cock stretched my folds, giving way to his sizable girth. Pleasure thrummed through me as he thrust deep into my cunt.

The desk creaked, a pot of pens tipped over, falling to the floor, but we didn't care. Our attention wholly on each other.

We moaned.

"Henry…" I couldn't catch my breath. I leaned back on my arms, more papers slipped to the floor. He was so tall and broad, thrusting into me with unmatched ability. Every nerve in my body prickled and I knew I was close. That he was going to make me come on my boss's desk.

"I've dreamt of fucking you like this again. I didn't think I ever would."

His words were sweet, and only made me like him more. "Right now I'm very glad to have run into you again too."

His mouth twisted into an amused grin and his grip hardened on my legs. "You like me fucking you?" He thrust hard, teasing a part of me that was at the brink of ecstasy.

"Yes." He took me, hard and fast, leaving me breathless, dragging me toward the hasty road to orgasm. My release lurked in the shadows, teasing, taunting me, edging ever closer with each thrust of Henry's hips.

"Come," he demanded, his eyes burning into mine, brooking no argument. More desk items fell to the floor, the wood creaking beneath our enthusiasm.

He was so fucking hot when he commanded me to do as he wanted. I'd never particularly liked overbearing men before, but with Henry it was different. Something told me that I would do whatever he commanded no matter how he asked.

"Come, Madeline," he commanded again.

"Make me," I taunted, even though I was close.

He growled, lifted my ass off the desk, changed his angle, and fucked me with a fury that tipped me over the delicious edge. My orgasm ripped through me with a ferocity that left me breathless. I lost sense of time, of location, and reached for the edges of the desk, needing to hold on to it, to anything before I became ungrounded. He kissed my screams away, silencing me as much as he could as I came.

"I'm coming. Fuck, Madeline."

I clutched at him, my legs wrapped about his back, and he kissed me through our orgasms. How was I to survive a summer in this man's arms? He was so distracting, so deliciously sexy, and could fuck better than anyone I'd ever been with before. I would never survive it.

Or at least, I was scared my heart wouldn't.

We untangled ourselves and fixed our clothing. Before long he was standing before me, all casual elegance. No one would ever imagine he'd just fucked with abandon.

"What time do you get off? I'll come and pick you up."

"Two," I said, pulling my skirt down and stuffing my G-string into my pocket.

"I'll be out front at two." He leaned in, satisfaction and pleasure darkening his stormy, brown eyes. "See you then, New York."

I nodded, fighting to regain my composure before I had to face my boss and the awkward conversation that could ensue if he asked what took so long. Henry's cocky grin was the last thing I saw before he opened the door, leaving me to watch him stroll through the café as if nothing had happened.

My boss looked up from the front counter and smiled. "All okay, Maddie?" he asked.

I nodded. "Yes, everything's fine." I quickly went to the bathroom, fixing my clothing and hair.

Thankfully Romero didn't question me about Henry. I wouldn't know where to start or what to say. Already he had my mind in a whirl and my body in a twist. I wasn't sure what I felt for him, but whatever it was it was different from the other guys I'd ever dated.

"Do you know how much Mr. Fairfax tipped you?"

I shook my head and came to stand behind the counter. "No, how much?"

He handed me the receipt and I did a double take. Five hundred dollars! Holy shit! "I don't deserve all of this. It's too generous. I only took out the orders, I didn't make them. I cannot take all of it. I'll share it with everyone. Can you disperse it evenly?"

"No, the tip is yours, Maddie. You offered good service that he was grateful for."

Heat kissed my cheeks at another service I just provided. Thank God Henry had tipped before coming into the office with me. I wasn't sure how I would have felt about it after the fact. "I insist."

The remainder of my workday passed quickly and without issue. Eve and Clara came in with some of Clara's family from the engagement party for lunch and it was nice to see them again and get to know a few more people who were staying on the island for the duration of summer.

All anyone spoke of was Henry getting proposed to by Margot. I didn't say anything about seeing him this morning. I wanted to keep our rendezvous between us.

The way people gossiped about Henry didn't bode well for me. If I were to start seeing him, the fewer people who knew of that fact the better. I didn't want to be termed the other woman or the reason why one of Europe's most loved actresses had a broken heart.

Not that she did in truth, but her fans weren't to know that…

Seeing Henry Fairfax would be difficult enough. I didn't need to make it even more complicated than it already would be.

I FINISHED my shift at two and stood outside the café's portico and waited for Henry to pick me up. Would he take me out and show me more of Sorrento, or to an early dinner? So far I hadn't seen much of the island, but planned to on my first day off at the café.

A black Porsche Cayenne pulled up before the window rolled down. Henry smiled at me, sunglasses on, polo top and tan shorts, the epitome of vacation casual.

"We meet again, New York."

I chuckled, going around to the passenger side door, and slipping in. I shrugged off the differences between us. Me in my cheap café uniform and Henry in attire that oozed an income far greater than mine. As much as I knew there was a chemistry between us that was off the charts, there were also many other things that were vastly different.

Our lives. Our upbringings. He was from an old

Italian family, practically European royalty. I was from the US foster system and a mother who placed cocaine far above anything else, myself and the nameless man who sired me.

I reached for my belt, snipping it locked before Henry reached for me, taking my lips in a kiss that stole my wits.

Why did I lose all self-control around this man? He drove me to distraction. All afternoon I had done nothing but count down the hours until I saw him again. I was a lost cause.

His hand slipped into my hair, fisting it, and need rocked through me. The drumming of my heart matched that of my overstimulated libido. I ached between my legs, and as his tongue teased mine I moaned, my fingers gripping him, trying to pull him close, even though the car halted such nearness.

He broke the kiss and stared at me with stormy, dark eyes before sitting back in his seat. His hands gripped the steering wheel, his knuckles white before he put the car into drive, and we moved away from the café.

"My place I think?"

I nodded, not about to disagree with him. We drove away from Sorrento and up into the hills, the road winding its way high above the town, giving the most spectacular views I had seen so far.

"Is this where you're staying? I didn't know there was a hotel up here too. I thought you'd stay at your own in town?"

He smiled but kept his eyes on the road. "It's our family's villa. It looks over the ocean and gives spectacular views that you'll soon see."

"You have a villa in Sorrento? I thought you came from Rome?"

"Oh, I do. I live in Rome most of the year, but my family originated from Sorrento and the villa is for any one of us to use whenever we're in town."

I looked out the window at the dry landscape. There were trees of course, but being summer and hot, a lot of the undergrowth was drying off. The ocean was forever in view, a turquoise blue so pretty that one couldn't keep their eyes off it.

I thought over how different Henry's life was to mine. I was on a working vacation and had parttime jobs in New York all through college. Although I hoped to gain employment upon my return to the US, it wasn't guaranteed, and I could struggle for some months if my job prospects didn't pan out.

Henry, on the other hand, seemed to have money to burn. Not a care in the world. How was I even here, sitting beside him, going to his family's villa about to spend time with one of Europe's most sought-after bachelors. Especially now that he was single in the eyes of the paparazzi.

The car turned a sharp corner and the villa's electronic gate, and house, came into view. I tried not to gape, I really did, didn't want to look like the shocked, less-privileged tourist I was, but failed.

Miserably.

"Holy shit, Henry. This is your villa?"

For a start, it wasn't the villa I pictured. Where I had imagined a small, terracotta-roofed building with olive trees and perhaps a water feature or two, this wasn't it.

"Yes, do you like it?"

I nodded, doubted there would be anyone who wouldn't. The villa stood three stories high. The white-washed stone home with a terracotta-tiled roof rose up from the top of the mountain, surrounded by olive trees and an array of native bushland and manicured gardens. We drove up to the gates and Henry typed in a code. The gates slid open automatically and we drove through. I looked into the side mirror, seeing it close behind us, locking us away in this oasis.

We drove up the paved driveway, and Henry waved to several gardeners who worked in the yard. Not that it looked like they needed to do much. The lawns, the hedges, and trees were all pruned and cut into perfect alignment and length.

I took a deep breath, nerves tumbling in my stomach before this kind of lifestyle. I was out of my league and didn't want him to know it. Not that he'd once made me feel unwelcome or below his notice, but before such opulence, it was hard not to be self-conscious of our different lives.

The car jerked to a halt and Henry jumped out, coming over to open my door. He held out his hand and I took it, seeking his strength as I joined him.

I could do this. Not be impressed by how different our lives were.

"Come, I'll introduce you to Beatrice. She's our housekeeper and her husband is our head gardener, along with his two sons. They live here year-round and are like family."

"I look forward to it." We entered the foyer, the temperature dropping by several degrees. I glanced up, the ceiling opening to the full three stories of the villa. Ahead of us was a wall of bifold doors that were open, the infinity pool that looked connected to the ocean that stretched out before this million-dollar view.

I didn't know where to look or how to react. How could this be his life? His home away from home?

The air was fresh, mixed with pine and salt. I moved into the lounge that overlooked the pool and stood, staring at the view. "Can you get to the ocean from here?"

"Yes, there are stairs, but we also put in a lift for grandmother when she was alive as she struggled in her later years."

I bit my lip and relaxed somewhat when Henry's arms went about my stomach, his head resting on my shoulder, looking at the view that I couldn't tear myself from.

"My grandfather proposed to my grandmother here many years ago on the anniversary of him opening his first hotel in Rome. They built the villa soon after and it's been here for the family to use ever since." Henry kissed my neck and I shivered, linking my hands with his.

"I don't think there is a childhood summer vacation that I don't remember with fondness in this villa."

"It's an amazing place, Henry."

Just then an older, gray-haired woman entered the foyer, a white apron tied about her ample waist. "Henry dear. Welcome home."

Henry went to her, pulling her into his arms and hugging her soundly. I smiled at the sweet homecoming. "Beatrice, it is good to see you. I hope you're well?" he asked.

Beatrice nodded but glanced in my direction. "I'm very well, thank you, Henry. Now, enough of me, introduce me to your friend," she asked, moving toward me.

"This is Madeline Webb. She's my guest if you're able to cater for one more for me."

Beatrice waved Henry's request aside. "More the merrier, Henry dear. Always, anything for you." She came over and patted my cheek, looking me up and down. "You're lovely, Miss Webb, and most welcome here."

I glanced at Henry and smiled. "Thank you for the warm welcome. It's lovely meeting you."

Henry took my hand and squeezed it. "I'm going to show Maddie around, but can we have lunch on the terrace in half an hour?"

"It'll be ready for you, enjoy your tour, Miss Webb."

"Please, call me Maddie," I said, before Henry pulled me away toward the stairs. "Where are you taking me?" We made our way to the second floor, the continued opulence that this house possessed beyond striking.

"We have a little time before lunch, but I thought a light snack may be necessary."

"A snack?" Was there another kitchen on this floor?

Henry pulled me into his arms, his lips devouring mine in a kiss. "I'm going to snack on you, New York."

I couldn't form words, merely melted into a puddle of need. He pulled me down the hall, no argument from me. I was more than happy to be snacked on if it was Henry who was eating me.

CHAPTER
Nine

HENRY WALKED about the room and took off his suit jacket, hanging it over a valet stand before he stood before a cheval mirror undoing the buttons on his crisp, white shirt. His eyes met mine in the reflection and a wave of longing, of need, ran through me.

"Am I staying here with you tonight?" I wasn't rostered back on at the café for two days, so if he wanted me to...

"If you like. I know I'd like it very much."

His words, low and compelling, had a power over me that I'd never experienced before, and in all honesty, did not know how to handle. He was so alluring, hot, made my skin prickle with awareness, my body ache in all the sweet places. I went to him and hugged him from behind, wanting to drink in the feel of him in my arms, of having him close.

He grinned, that sexy, dark smirk that made me not

myself. I drew his shirt off his shoulders, ran my hands down his chiseled arms before throwing it aside.

"Am I to gather that you want me, New York?"

"Hmm, you can." I brushed my lips across his back and he started beneath my touch. "Do you like me kissing you here?" I continued across his shoulder blades, my hands dipping to the button on his pants.

I heard him swallow, his body taut with expectation.

I moved to stand before him, bending to kneel and finished undoing his pants. I slipped them down his legs, exposing his cock, heavy and hard to bulge before me. I took him in hand, stroked him, worked him with my fingers. He sucked in a startled breath when I licked the tip of his cock, tasting him.

He was delicious, just as I imagined.

I sucked his cock, taking him deep, wanting to push him toward release. Tease him as torturously as he had teased me. His cock grew harder, wider in my mouth, but I didn't relent. I wanted him at his brink, to have the tantalising taste of release without actually jumping over that cliff.

"Hmm, I love your cock." He groaned and moisture pooled between my legs. I wanted him, wanted him to fuck me with this magnificent cock.

"Maddie, Jesus, your mouth is fucking magic."

I took him deep, sucked him hard and he groaned my name. Pre-come filled my mouth and he pulled back, wrenching me to my feet. Henry clasped my face and kissed me.

Hard.

I gave myself up to our hunger. I wanted him just as much, there was no denying that. Our tongues tangled, taunted, and teased. He nipped my lip playfully before licking the bite better. My wits spiraled, but I wanted more. So much more.

He walked me backward as he kissed me until my legs hit the bed and we tumbled onto the soft, blue linens. I reached for my leggings, but Henry was there already, pulling them down before discarding me of my skirt. He threw them aside, and I heard them land somewhere on the floor nearby. He kneeled before me, a mouth-watering god, no shirt, his muscular chest and abs all for me to admire.

I reached for him, needing to feel his corded muscles, the warmth of his skin beneath my palms. His breathing ragged, he watched me as I touched him, his eyes glistening with determination and need as he popped his pant button open and lowered his zipper.

I bit my lip and swallowed as his hard cock slipped into his hand.

He reached over to a bedside cabinet and grabbed a condom, sliding it on. Warmth pooled between my legs, and I wiggled on the bed, trying to soothe myself. I wanted him inside me. Filling me. Fucking me.

I slipped my leg about his hip, pulling him close, no longer willing to wait.

He came over me and thrust into me with purpose. I gasped, wrapped my legs about his back, and moaned with each plunge. His kiss was deep and devastating, my senses on overdrive.

"Fuck, Maddie. You're so fucking hot." He thrust again, my orgasm achingly close.

I moaned, drew him close, and held on as he pushed me toward release. I fought to catch my breath, to keep up with my body's reaction to his touch, but it was no use. He played me like a musical instrument, knew which strings to tap and tease to make me sing.

"I'm coming." The delicious telltale signs spiraled, convulsed through me.

He moaned, grabbing my thighs, and lifted my ass off the bed. The position deepened his thrusts and hurled me into a second orgasm. "Henry," I screamed, clinging to him as he fucked me through my release.

"Maddie." Henry's orgasm followed mine and he pumped into me, kissing me as his release mingled with mine. "I think I'll have to steal you for more than one night."

I chuckled, sated and satisfied, unable to move and not in any particular hurry to do so. Henry lay beside me, his arm lazily over my stomach as we tried to catch our breaths.

"When do you have to return to work at the café?"

"I don't have to be back for two days. Why do you ask?" Of course, I hoped that he wanted me to stay with him in truth. He'd said as much earlier, but it would be good to hear that absolute.

"I want you to stay here for the next couple of days, that's why. I'll drop you back at the café when you work next so we can spend as much time together before I go back to Rome."

"You'll be in Sorrento for the next couple of days? Are you sure? I know you're busy most of the time." I met his eyes, unable to believe this beautiful, sweet man, my one-night stand wanted to see me, wanted me to be here with him and nowhere else.

"I have an office here and can run Rome for a few days with no issues. And I'm the boss. I want to be here with you." He leaned over me, kissing me with such tenderness my heart jumped. "I didn't think I'd ever see you again. If you think I'm going to let you disappear so easily again you're mistaken, New York."

I chuckled, feeling absurdly giddy. "I didn't bring any clothes with me. I can't wear my café uniform for the next two days."

"I don't know. I kind of like your uniform and ripping it off you." Henry grinned and jumped from the bed before going into the bathroom. I heard the shower run, before he was out again, strolling into the room as naked as the day he was born. He pulled on a white linen shirt and black cargo shorts. "Come, shower and I'll find you some of my sister's clothes. She won't mind sharing."

"You have a sister?"

"I do. She's in Rome now, hopefully keeping a close watch on Mother who's been a little down as this year marks the five-year anniversary of my father's death."

"I'm so sorry for your loss, Henry." Sensing he didn't want to speak about it, I did as he asked, enjoying the rejuvenating shower, which was bigger than my whole room at the Airbnb. For a home that his grandparents had built, the opulence of the whole villa seemed very new and modern and utterly decadent. Maybe they had remodeled recently…

Henry came into the bathroom, watching me as I soaped my skin. "My father died of cancer. It was found late and very little could be done but to keep him comfortable."

"I'm so sorry." I rinsed my hair, turning off the water when I was done. "If you're needed in Rome I'm not going anywhere and I'm more than happy to wait until you're back visiting again."

Henry busied himself at the basin, slipping on a watch. I could see he was lost in his thoughts, maybe thinking upon my words, but either way, I didn't want to intrude. I wrapped a towel around me, and another about my hair.

With no clothes to get dressed into, I stood on the bathmat, unsure what to do. Henry's gaze locked with mine in the mirror before he turned and pulled me into his arms. "I don't want to be anywhere else. Believe me when I say that. If I did, I wouldn't be here now."

I wanted to pinch myself to prove that this was real. "You're a real charmer, aren't you?"

He nodded. "Mmhmm, only when I want something."

He let me go and slapped my ass and I squealed, before he went back into the bedroom, coming back in with a woman's set of shorts and a shirt.

"These should fit. You're a similar height as my sister."

I took the clothes, ignoring the fact that they were designer and of high quality. Clothing that a mere mortal such as I could never afford. "Thank you. These will do splendidly."

"I'll wait for you in the bedroom." With one last kiss he left me to dress. I turned to the mirror and stared at the wide-eyed, rosy-cheeked woman looking back at me. I didn't recognize her. How could I be here with this guy, one who appeared too perfect to be true? Would this last or would the summer end in heartbreak?

I quickly shot off a text to my friends, telling them where I was and how long I may be away.

Either way, no matter what happened between us I was determined to enjoy Sorrento and Henry for as long as I was here. A lifetime of memories of my summer in Henry's arms was worth any pain that could follow.

You only live once, and this summer I intended to live life to the fullest.

CHAPTER
Ten

WHILE MADDIE DRESSED I slipped into the office beside my bedroom and opened my laptop, looking at whatever had come in that may be urgent or need my attention. My inbox was flooded with messages from more news outlets and paparazzi sites wanting to interview me on Margot's absurd proposal.

What had she been thinking? By the time I got back to the hotel that night to confront her she had checked out and the last I heard she was in London partying it up with her friends there. Not that I cared. I hadn't cared for some time, but I did want to confront her about her bullshit move that put me in a bad light.

The only good thing to come out of our breakup was Maddie. I still couldn't believe she was in my life, that I had found her. The moment I had seen her at the engagement party I had almost swallowed my own tongue. She was a beautiful woman and the entire night

I had to stand back and watch her be flirted and danced with, gifted drinks and whispers on the dance floor.

I had wanted to kill every one of those men for daring to speak to my girl.

But she was here now, with me and mine.

I frowned down at my desk at my thoughts. Mine? Seriously? I doubted she would appreciate being seen as someone else's chattel, but by God, I wouldn't share her, not now or ever if I could help it.

Not that we'd promised anything but a fun summer, but the idea of her leaving for New York left a hollowness in my chest.

"Henry?"

"In here," I called, relishing the sight of her out of her café uniform. Not that she didn't look particularly delicious in whatever she wore.

Maddie came into my office and walked about the floor-to-ceiling shelving that had hundreds of books, some first editions in the collections. "What a wonderful room. If this was mine I'm sure I'd never wish to leave."

"It was my father's favorite part of the house, and I haven't changed it since his death. I'm glad you like it." I leaned back in the leather chair, watching her sweet ass and pretty features read the names of the novels, pulling several out to read the first few pages.

God, what was wrong with me that I couldn't stop looking at her? Wanting her?

We'd already fucked twice. I couldn't fall on her

again like some crazed bastard who needed to get off every five minutes.

I heard her gasp and saw that she was now staring out the windows. This room sat near the edge of the cliff the villa was built on and gave a view of the dock below.

"There's a huge yacht down there, Henry." Her mouth gaped and I smiled. I tried to put myself in her shoes, to see everything with new eyes and not a lifetime of privilege. I suppose seeing the views and the yacht that were common household items for me would be new and unexpected for anyone else.

"Do you know who owns it? Are they your neighbors?"

I debated telling her the yacht belonged to someone else. It seemed extravagant to boast more of what I had. Wrong somehow...

"Do you have any idea how your blue eyes sparkle when you're in awe of something?" I went to her, needing to hold her. I wrapped my arms about her stomach from behind and kissed her shoulder. "I can take you on a tour of the villa if you like. There are more spectacular views from other parts of the home. There's also a small deck on the roof for stargazing, if you're interested."

She turned to face me, slipping her arms over my shoulders. "I've never been stargazing before. I'd love that."

She'd never been stargazing. "How could you not

have done so before? Hasn't everyone looked up to the heavens at some point in their life?"

Her smile slipped and she moved out of my arms, commencing her inspection of the room. "You can't see the stars in New York, and I've never lived where one could see them before now."

"I apologize, Maddie. I forget that the big cities deny such views." I sat back at my desk and quickly finished reading my emails and sending off replies to the London office, which ran the London hotel. "You haven't spoken much of your childhood. It was in New York?"

"Yes, it was. But I only met Eve and Clara in college. Up until then, I didn't really have many friends."

"You didn't?" An uncomfortable knot formed in my gut at the thought of her not having friends. Why would she not have? I already hated everyone who ever denied her companionship.

"I moved around a lot. By the time I got to know anyone I was shifted off elsewhere. My childhood kind of sucked." She slumped into my lap, and I laughed, scooping her close. "But yours seems much more interesting than mine. Tell me of yours and what you got up to. Let me live vicariously through you for five minutes."

I raised my brow, having never been asked before. "Well, I suppose it was an easy childhood. I had a loving family and good education, travel, and I never had to worry about anything. I sound like a smug ass don't I?"

She cupped my jaw, angling my face to look at her. Her eyes were a perfect almond shape, and regarded me with such intentness that I was sure she could read my mind.

"I think if any child could choose a childhood yours would be preferable to many others. Do you have any other siblings other than your sister?"

"No, just Sophia. She's two years younger than me and unmarried."

"And where did you go to school? You don't have a thick Italian accent most of the time."

"Most?"

"Well, I heard you on the phone the other day and it was thick when you were speaking in Italian, but your English is quite different."

"Ah, well I went to boarding school in London. So my accent fluctuates."

"I like how you sound when speaking in Italian."

"Do you?" I liked how she was looking at me. I wanted her again, and thoughts of slipping her onto the desk, pulling the shorts down her long legs, and kissing my way back up bombarded my mind. "I like everything about you, so I suppose we're even."

Her cheeks blossomed a pretty rose, and I pulled her close, kissing her. The woman undid me in every way, and I wasn't sure what to do with myself.

A new affliction I wasn't used to feeling but could get used to.

CHAPTER
Eleven

LUNCH WAS SERVED on the outside terrace. A bamboo-type structure ran the length of the courtyard, shading the space from the hot Mediterranean sun. Climbing grapevines grew up trellises on two walls, cooling the space. Staff came and went, topping up our wine and water and delivering a delicious three-course meal.

"Would you like to go for a swim after lunch?" Henry lounged back in his chair, watching me, and I fought the butterflies that his interest always rose within me. To distract myself I glanced at the pool and sipped the Dom Pérignon that I'd never had before, but decided was one of the most delicious wines on the planet.

"Well?" He wiggled his brows and I laughed, wondering what else he had in store for us for the two days we'd be hidden away here at his magnificent villa.

"Can I tell you something?" I had to explain as

much as I could about my life and the differences between us. Ones that I hoped wouldn't pull us apart, but ones he needed to be aware of.

"Of course." He placed down his wine and gave me his full attention.

I stared at the ocean view past the pool and gathered my thoughts. "You know that I didn't come from this kind of opulent lifestyle, don't you? I mean…" I clarified when he frowned at my confession, "I want to be brutally honest with you, Henry and state that I have more in common with your staff here than you."

He stared at me, and I was unsure if he was shocked or just taking in my truth.

"I don't care what kind of upbringing you had, Maddie. I like you, and I'm certain you like me. Does it matter what kind of life we lived up to now?"

"No, it doesn't matter, but…" I sighed, knowing he imagined I had a family, some friends, perhaps a dog or a cat as a child, but if only my life had been so perfect. "I feel out of place and unsure in this world. I don't have the material things you do that make you suit this environment."

Henry glanced down at my clothes, and I knew he was thinking of my café uniform I came here in, and the designer attire I was now wearing. "You look perfectly acceptable to me."

"Because I'm wearing your sister's clothes. I don't have anything like this in my wardrobe." Shamefully I didn't have a lot of clothes at all. Any money I earned went to keeping me in college and I wanted to try to give some to Eve when we moved in together in New York, no matter what her father stated. I didn't want to be a charity case forever.

"Would you like me to buy you some clothes? I'm more than happy…"

"No. No, that's not what I want you to do." I sighed and thought about how to explain. But how did one explain they were poor to a man who couldn't understand that concept? "I don't want you to be embarrassed by me if I say or do the wrong thing. If I use the wrong cutlery or wine glass at dinner. I'm trying to tell you that I grew up poor and I had to save and work hard to even come on this trip with my friends. It's easier for them, they had a similar upbringing to yours, and it was only through their generosity that I was able to go at all. I'm not paying for accommodations you see…"

Shame washed through me, and I hated myself for it. It wasn't my fault I had been born into the life I endured. But I had worked hard to move forward, to make my future so much better than what I was dealt and that was worth something.

Henry reached across the table and clasped my hand. "Your financial position doesn't change how I feel about you, Maddie. It doesn't change the chemistry I feel whenever I'm around you. The moment I saw you in that nightclub, fuck, Maddie, I've never wanted anyone as much as I wanted you that night. Even now, knowing you're across the table from me, a woman I didn't think I'd ever see again, I cannot wait to touch you again, be with you, kiss and hold you. I thank God for providence that we found each other again.

Some of my reservations dissipated at his words and I smiled, relieved he knew a little more about me and my life. "We certainly had a good time in Ibiza, didn't we? I still can't believe we did what we did, to be honest. I've never had a one-night stand before you."

"Ever?"

"No, never. I've always dated a few weeks before going to bed with anyone."

Henry's gaze darkened and a muscle worked in his jaw. "I don't like hearing of you with other men." He placed down his wine and watched me.

"I didn't like seeing you with Margot and when I saw her kneel down to propose I thought any chance I may have had was gone."

His eyes narrowed. "I would have seen you even if I pretended to still be with Margot just to please the gossip columns. There was no way I could have kept away from you. I knew that the moment I saw you at the engagement that we'd end up here."

"Really?" I never wanted to be the other woman, but technically I wouldn't have been. Henry explained why he'd been playing Margot's game to keep the paparazzi at bay, and so technically I wouldn't have been doing anything wrong. No doubt Margot was seeing other people quietly, why not Henry too? "You think quite highly of your charm."

He chuckled, leaning back in his chair. "You know what I'm talking about. Even now all I can think about is touching you, kissing you, and other dirty acts I won't mention at lunch," he whispered.

I grinned. The man was a flirt. "True. I know what you mean. I feel it too." I finished my glass of Dom, watching him. "There's supposed to be a beach disco this weekend in Sorrento. Do you think you'll be able to come with me?"

"This weekend?"

I nodded. "This Saturday. It's supposed to be a safe one to swim at and there will be a bar and live music. Eve and Clara will be there and you're more than welcome to invite any friends and family if they're not already attending."

"I'm not sure if I'll be in Sorrento this weekend. I have a previous engagement in Milan Saturday that's been in my diary for months."

I forced a smile, but the thought of Henry not being here, enjoying live music, sand and sun in my arms was disappointing. I had to remind myself he owned one of the most beautiful hotel chains in the world. Of course, his time wasn't always his own and I needed to remember that before I became disillusioned this summer.

"It was just an idea." A maid placed a bowl of gelato before me with seasonal fruit, and I thanked her, before picking up my spoon. Silence settled between us, and I ignored the awkwardness, concentrating instead on my delicious dessert.

"I would cancel if I could, Maddie. I hope you know that I would prefer to be here with you than anywhere else."

I met his eyes and could see he was sincere, and I chastised myself for being butt hurt over an obligation he had months before I came into his life. I didn't want to be the jealous, clingy girlfriend. That wasn't who I was, and I wouldn't start now.

I rallied my thoughts and stopped my nonsense. "I'll miss you. We could have had a lot of fun."

"You'll not get too drunk I hope."

I shrugged. "I can't promise you that. But if I do, I can promise I won't swim at the same time and drown myself by accident. Would that suffice?"

"Hmm."

I wasn't sure what he meant by that response, but instead of worrying about it, I scooped another spoonful of gelato into my mouth and finished my dessert.

I could feel Henry watching me and I couldn't help but wonder if he was a little annoyed I would go without him. Was he jealous, worried I might meet another handsome billionaire and fall for him instead?

The thought made me inwardly laugh. That was highly unlikely, especially since there was only one guy who occupied my mind day and night and he was sitting across from me, brooding.

But I was determined to make my summer here fun and memorable. He'd already helped with that, and raves on the beach, dancing under the Mediterranean moon was a must for anyone. If he wanted to be part of the fun, he'd attend and make sure I didn't get too drunk. If not, so be it.

Henry stood and came around the table next to me. The scent of vanilla with hints of orange and honey teased my senses before he held out his hand. Hell, he smelled good. Good enough to eat.

"How about that swim now?"

I placed my hand in his. "That sounds perfect," I replied, joining him, and stealing a kiss.

CHAPTER
Twelve

THE TWO DAYS at the villa were flying by all too fast. How was work tomorrow already, meaning Henry would leave. Another several days before I could see him again.

We swam in the pool, walked the manicured grounds, I met Beatrice's husband Nico and their two sons. We enjoyed each other's company and there was an ease between us that I'd never had with anyone else. In truth, I didn't have anything in common with Henry. Our lives and upbringing were so polar opposite that our time together shouldn't be easy, but it was. And as for the sex… Well, that was off the charts.

I stood in the shower, rinsing my hair, daydreaming of what we were going to do on our final day. Henry had organized a cruise around the island, and we were being picked up from the villa's dock. Thankfully Henry had arranged for a bag of my clothes to be delivered from our Airbnb and I didn't have to wear his sister's anymore. I got out of the shower, dried myself quickly, and slipped on a comfortable pair of shorts, a singlet tee, and a white shirt that I left open but tied at my waist. It was a cute, summery outfit which my flip-flops finished off.

"Henry! Are you in here?"

I paused mid-brush-stroke through my hair and listened. Was that a woman's voice in our bedroom? There was no door to the bathroom, merely a little corridor that you walked through into the room.

"Henry! We've arrived."

The woman's voice was louder now, too close for comfort and definitely in the bedroom beyond. I finished brushing my hair and checked that I was decent just as Margot Hathaway, his ex, strolled into the bathroom as if she owned the place.

She paused, her mouth twisting into a displeased line when she saw me. The feeling that I was not expected to be here and that I was also not welcome to stay ran over me and I turned to stare at her, raising my chin.

I had nothing to be ashamed of. Their relationship had been a farce, their breakup a staged show for the paparazzi. I had every right to be here with Henry. The bigger question should be what the hell did she think she was doing here.

"What are you doing in Henry's bathroom?" She stepped around me, looking me up and down, her gaze unimpressed. "Are you not the little fawning American at the engagement party I was introduced to?"

At least we were of similar height, and I didn't have to look up at her. "I'm brushing my hair and getting ready for the day. What are you doing here? Do you always walk into people's bathrooms not knowing who's using them?"

She laughed, a high-pitched sound that was more degrading than happy. "You poor little Yank. I had my suspicions Henry had a new interest here in Sorrento," she scoffed. "You're not the first woman he's brought here to impress, and believe me, you will not be the last. I'll be that woman just so you know."

Wow. That was a lot to take in and consider. Not that Henry had promised anything to me beyond the summer and I was happy with that. All of this was new, and I didn't expect him to fall helplessly in love with me. No matter how well we got along, I wasn't picking out my bridal dress just yet, no matter what this woman implied.

"I think you should be having this conversation with Henry and air your frustrations with him."

She didn't move an inch, tried, and failed to tower over me. I raised my brow, staring her in the eye. I wasn't going to bow down to anyone, and certainly not a rich, European snob.

"Oh, I will find Henry, do not concern yourself about that."

As if conjuring him, Henry strode into the bathroom. The moment he saw Margot his face hardened. He clasped Margot's arm, clearly angry, and pulled her out of the bathroom. I bit my lip, hearing Margot coo greetings to him as they made their way through the bedroom. I took my time finishing my hair and makeup, not wanting to intrude on two people who clearly had a lot of baggage and history together.

I left the bathroom and started to gather my things that I would need to take back to my Airbnb. All the while my mind whirred about Henry and Margot. Why was she here at all? Even with their history, they had broken up. She agreed to that, or so Henry had said. It made little sense that she was here and being all butt hurt that I was sleeping with him.

A decanter of water sat on a sideboard, and I poured myself a glass, trying to remove the nerves that tumbled in my belly. I liked Henry and our summer had only just commenced. I didn't want to cause trouble for him or have Margot all up in my business at every turn. That wouldn't make for a good time, not for anyone.

"I'm sorry, Maddie." Henry strode into the bedroom, shutting and locking the door.

I slumped on the side of the bed and sipped my water. "I think I should leave, and we should postpone our day on the yacht. Margot is clearly upset, and I think you need to speak to her about what you had already decided together. Perhaps put in place some boundaries between you both if I'm to be with you this summer."

A pained expression crossed his handsome face. I wanted to reach for him, comfort him for the mess he found himself in, but didn't.

"My sister Sophia is here too. She brought Margot. They're close friends you see, but I'll be speaking to her when she decides to show her face, but she's gone horse riding." Henry paused. "No doubt by design."

"Your sister is here?" And close friends with Margot. That didn't bode well for us becoming friends.

"I'm sorry for what Margot just did. I never wish to make you uncomfortable."

I shrugged, hating that Henry's ex made me feel awkward and horribly out of place. "You clearly need to have a word with both Margot and Sophia, and I don't want to make trouble. That was never my intention when we met again. I return to work tomorrow anyway and I think it's best we postpone our cruise for another time."

Henry ran a hand through his hair, leaving it on end. He was so damn hot, and I wanted to say screw Margot and Sophia and throw myself into his arms, make him kiss me, and make love all afternoon.

"I'll drive you back now if you wish."

Wow, I had hoped he wouldn't agree, and certainly not that quickly. With my bag already packed, I grabbed my phone off the charger beside the bed. "I'm ready when you are."

We walked downstairs and made it to the foyer just as a petite brunette was handing a riding hat and whip to a waiting servant. This had to be Sophia, Henry's sister, the similarities too striking. She wore a white shirt and jodhpurs, polished riding boots that looked far too clean for someone who had been on a horse.

"Henry, my darling brother. You didn't tell me we had company?" Henry's sister looked me up and down and her eyes narrowed. "Nor did you tell me we've turned into a charity. Beatrice told me you allowed your girlfriend to wear my clothes now. Not very sporting of you."

The tone was soft and said with an air of mirth, but Sophia did not mean the words in a playful way. She was pissed and pinned her brother with a hard stare.

"Watch your tone, Sophia." Henry didn't miss the undertones of her words. "This is Madeline Webb."

Clearly Sophia had picked whose side she would be on, and it wasn't to be her brother's or mine. Disappointment ran through me. I had hoped we could be friends, polite at least, but that didn't seem possible now.

"I apologize for wearing the clothing. I believe Beatrice has already laundered it and returned it to your room," was all I could think to say as I moved toward the door. The idea that Beatrice too had outed me wearing Sophia's clothing hurt more than I wanted to admit. But then, they worked for the Fairfax family and had possibly seen the children grow up since childhood. Of course, their loyalties lie with them.

"I don't want them back now." Sophia's tone was disgusted. "You have a lot of explaining to do, brother. I look forward to our chat when you get back."

Mortification swamped me and I quickened my pace toward his car in the driveway. Thankfully the doors were unlocked, and I slipped into the passenger seat and took deep, calming breaths. My emotions threatened to get the better of me and I could feel myself on the verge of tears. I had wanted to be friends with Henry's sister, maybe even meet his mother... That wasn't going to be happening by the looks of it.

I scrolled on my phone until Henry slipped into the driver's seat. The silence that settled between us was deafening, and I refused to be the first one to speak. This wasn't my war to be engaged in and I wouldn't give an opinion on what I thought Henry should say or do to defend me.

"I apologize, Maddie." Henry sighed, staring over the steering wheel before he pressed the ignition button and started the car. "Sophia shouldn't have spoken to you like that, and she will apologize. As for Margot, I don't even know what she's doing here."

I clutched at my phone in my lap like a lifeline, wishing I were back at my Airbnb and away from this villa. "It's not your fault, but you do need to speak to them. I never intended to cause so much trouble..."

"You didn't though." He reached for my hand, squeezing it. "No matter what we're doing now, know that I don't want you to go." He paused. "I'm no longer with Margot and my sister knows the details of our agreement. I don't understand the game they're playing, coming here."

I nodded in agreement, but inside I was dying. I liked Henry and would love to get to know him better, spend more time in his company, but I also didn't want to be treated like shit just because I dared to see him now that he was single.

"I think no matter what Margot wanted to keep the paparazzi happy, she certainly doesn't want to see you move on with anyone else now that it's over between you. I'm a threat, even if we're not exclusive or that we agreed to have some fun over the summer, she doesn't know that, and she certainly doesn't like it."

He pulled the car out of the driveway and onto the road. For several minutes he didn't speak, merely concentrated on the winding road that weaved its way down to Sorrento.

"We're not exclusive?" A muscle worked in his jaw. "Does that mean you'll fuck other men if the opportunity presents itself?"

I looked out the window, thinking if I wanted to implant myself into this messy situation. If I didn't, now was the chance to lie to him and tell him I would. That I would think he could too if the opportunity presented itself. The idea made me want to throw up, but I also didn't know what we were. Were we boyfriend and girlfriend? Fuck buddies? A one-night stand that would last the summer. What?

I watched him and hated the hurt I delivered to his handsome features. I glanced out the window, knowing I couldn't lie to him. He was a good guy and didn't need me playing mind games with him too.

"No. I won't be doing that," I answered finally.

He didn't reply, and all too soon we were pulling up

before my Airbnb. I reached for my bag, unsure what today and everything that had happened meant for us.

"Have fun at the rave and be careful."

I glanced at him before opening the door and getting out. I hoped he would stop me, reach and pull me in for a kiss but he didn't. "Bye, Henry." I closed the door and didn't wait for his reply.

The car zoomed off and I fought not to stop and watch him leave. The day had turned to shit, and we were both upset. Maybe he needed time to sort out his past with Margot and the issues with his meddling sister. Sometimes people jumped into relationships too fast and perhaps this was one of those times.

Maybe it just wasn't our time…

Thirteen

I WIPED the counter and then took a payment for a baguette. My feet were crazy sore and the day had been uncommonly busy, but then with the rave on the beach this evening, it was no wonder it was so busy. I glanced at the clock. Almost time for me to knock off and it couldn't come soon enough. As much as I tried to look forward to the rave tonight, I couldn't help but think of Henry and the fact he wouldn't be there.

Not that I knew what the hell was going on. After dropping me off earlier in the week I'd not heard from him at all. A social media post had popped up on Instagram of him out for dinner with his mother in Rome, but otherwise nothing but silence.

"Laura's just arrived, Maddie. You can knock off now," Romero called from his office.

I glanced out the front and watched Laura, an Aussie on a working vacation wave goodbye to her boyfriend on the sidewalk. I didn't envy her working this evening. If the day was any indication, tonight would be worse.

Not wanting to be here another minute, I pulled off my apron and collected my bag, more than ready to go home. "Good luck tonight, Laura. See you Monday, Romero."

"Bye, Maddie! Have fun tonight! Super jelly."

I laughed and waved goodbye over my head and started toward my Airbnb. I pretended that I wasn't looking for Henry and hoping that he would be here after all, surprise me and go to the rave with me.

How sad and dependent I was acting, and I shouldn't be. His silence spoke volumes, and no matter him acting all jealous and not liking the idea of us being nonexclusive, it didn't change the fact that he'd practically ghosted me all week.

It took me minutes only to arrive home and I walked into our apartment to find Clara cooking some pasta meal that looked more burned than al dente. Eve chilled on the lounge, scrolling through her phone, her legs up over the back of the chair, and as red as a beetroot.

"You've had a bit too much sun today, Eve." I pressed on her leg, and the little white dot my finger created took ages to disappear. "Doesn't it hurt?"

Eve slapped my hand away. "Ouch, Maddie, you pressing on me hurts and yes, I'm currently regretting my life choices if you must know. Thank God the rave is at night. I can't risk getting burned again."

"Probably a good idea." I moved toward the kitchen. "And speaking of burning, do you need any help, Clara?" I investigated the pot of boiling penne pasta and saw that there was almost no water. I picked up the saucepan and moved it over to the sink and filled it before returning it to the heat. "Pasta needs water to soften," I suggested.

Clara looked up from her phone, the color draining from her face. I reached for her, concerned she was about to faint. "What's wrong? You look like you've seen a ghost."

"I think you need to see this."

The somber tone of her voice had Eve joining us and together we looked at Clara's phone. A headline was splashed in red across the top of the Google news page, but it was the images that took my breath away.

"Holy shit." Eve scrolled through the post, and the many, many pictures it possessed.

Images of Henry and Margot on a yacht scrolled before me. Of them sunbathing, looking into each other's eyes like no one else in the world existed, swimming off the back, enjoying the many water toys the yacht possessed.

Was this the yacht he was supposed to take me on? Had he taken her out onto the water instead? I picked an image that was taken on the water and zoomed in.

"That's Henry's villa in the background."

Eve scrolled to the end of the post, landing on the date. "It's dated the day he dropped you off. Do you suppose he's back with his ex then?"

"Fucking bastard." Clara slipped her arm around me.

I swallowed the lump that wedged in my throat and fought not to burst into tears. What was wrong with me? We'd fucked a couple of times. He'd been nice and charming.

A fucking lying charming bastard if truth be told.

A picture told a thousand words and the story these told of Henry and Margot was that she was right, and I was a fucking idiot.

"It wasn't anything serious and these images prove it. I suppose I can't get too angry about it." But I was hurt also. I thought we had enjoyed our time together, and the chemistry had been off the charts. Maybe my attraction to him had been more than his and I merely deluded myself. "There's a lot of history between them. They've dated for years. I suppose their on-and-off-again relationship is back on." I shook my head, closing Eve's phone, not wanting to look at the images a moment longer. "I wish I hadn't placed myself between them. I don't appreciate being the third wheel or possibly being used for the other's manipulation."

"I'd be fucking livid, Maddie. For real, he was all over you just a few days ago and now he's on a fucking yacht with his ex. He's an idiot if he goes back to a relationship that's clearly toxic and doesn't work. He doesn't deserve to have our beautiful friend on his arm. He's clearly thick."

I smiled and hugged Eve when she pulled me into her arms. "You guys are the best, but I never expected anything major. But I certainly didn't think he'd treat me with so little respect. A summer fling we may have agreed to, but I won't be used."

"Make sure you tell him that the next time you see him," Clara said.

"I will, don't worry about that." *If* I saw him again, which I doubted I would. Why would he seek me out? I clearly meant nothing to him, and that was fine. At least we both knew where we stood.

———

I attended the rave but after an hour of the beach party atmosphere, I realized I didn't want to celebrate tonight. I bid Eve and Clara goodnight and told them to party hard before we agreed to have a day at the beach tomorrow, just the three of us.

Thankfully Eve and Clara weren't too hungover the following morning and after lunch we packed up our beach gear, caught the bus to the swimming spot and walked down to the shoreline, determined to relax and enjoy our Sunday.

Eve, conscious of how burned she already was, purchased one of the biggest umbrellas in Sorrento. Just watching her carry it down to the beach was hilarious and a lot of wrangling so she didn't hit anyone in the head with the long pole.

The beach was packed by the time we were walking along the sand. We chose a spot near a cliff face, where there would be ample shade when the sun moved over in the afternoon. Families and young tourists packed the beach, many of them swimming or content to sunbake on the warm sand.

I set down the basket of food, kept cold by chilled ice blocks from our freezer, near the cliff and out of anyone's way playing games around us. We laid down our towels, set up the enormous umbrella that covered all three of us, sat and people-watched for several minutes. Eve slathered copious amounts of sunburn cream on her skin, and I reached into my bag for my hat. Clara was content to lie on her stomach and scroll her phone.

"I'm going to go for a swim. Do any of you want to come?" I asked.

Eve shook her head, slathering more cream on her legs. "No, I'm going to stay here."

"I'm just sending an email home. My father is questioning when I'll be home." Clara sighed and shook her head. "I told him I would be home to start at his law firm in the fall. I wish he would listen."

I nodded but didn't answer. It was only a short walk to the beach, and if I had any concern that the water would be cold, I shouldn't have. The turquoise ocean lathed at the golden sand, inviting and calm.

I waded out, taking my time, gliding my hands over the water's surface. I reached for my head, pulling off my cap before I dived under when it was deep enough. I came up and floated on my back, staring up at the sky, which was cloudless and in contention to be the same color as the water. What an amazing place. So different to the waters at Coney Island.

"Hey, dance partner," a deep voice said beside me. "Maddie, isn't it?"

I flayed to my feet and stood, throwing on my hat. "Merrick isn't it?" I reached out and absurdly in the middle of the ocean we shook hands. His were large and warm, and a little crinkly from swimming.

"I thought it was you. How have you been?" he asked.

"Great." Which wasn't a lie. I was having a wonderful time here, even if I did have a little romantic blip early in my trip. "I'm working at the Bar Sorrento and enjoying my summer. How about you? I haven't seen you since the engagement."

He pushed back his damp hair, showcasing his muscular, tanned arms. They reminded me of Henry's, and I fought to push him out of my mind.

"Well, I've been back to London since then, but wanted to attend the rave last night so I flew down for the weekend." His lips twisted into a flirtatious smile. "A shame I didn't see you there."

"Ah, yeah." I ran my hands over the top of the water again, unsure how I felt about Merrick and his hungry gaze that bored into me. "I went for about an hour and then went home. I had worked yesterday and just wasn't up for a late night."

He reached out and slipped a strand of my hair behind my ear, his finger sliding down my cheek before he dropped his arm at his side. "My loss."

I swallowed. If I hoped to have the same reaction to Merrick's touch as I did to Henry's I was mistaken.

Instead, his attention made me feel as if I were doing something wrong, even though I knew I wasn't. Henry had done that, not me. I could do what I liked and with whomever I chose, and no one could chastise me for it. Least of all Henry.

"I'm sure you weren't so bereft," I teased, before glancing toward the beach. I expected to see Clara and Eve watching me, knowing smirks on their pretty faces, except both were lying down, sleeping probably after their late-night partying.

But there was one person watching, standing near the steps leading onto the beach, staring at me with a look of astonishment.

Henry…

He stood alone, shading his face from the sun, watching me. His features hardened and he turned, heading back up the stairs.

Was he leaving?

Of course he was, but the question remained. Why was he here in the first place?

CHAPTER

Fourteen

I COULDN'T MOVE, unsure what to do. I pushed down the annoyance I felt at Henry appearing after days of silence only to look at me, seemingly pissed off catching me talking to Merrick. He was the man who had sailed around the Mediterranean with his ex and allowed those images to splash over the glossy magazines and online gossip posts. What did he expect me to do? Wait for him? Pine?

I wouldn't do either, but if he was here already, he could have at least explained himself. Been a man and told me our summer plans were off and that he was giving his ex a second chance or third, or however many chances they'd given each other.

"This is kind of bold of me, and I know we don't know each other well, but would you like to have dinner sometime? I'm back in Sorrento next weekend if you're free."

I started, having completely forgotten about Merrick

at my side. "Ahh…" I hesitated, unsure if I wanted to pursue anything so soon after being with Henry. Even if we hadn't been dating, I was hurt and not looking for a relationship with the next guy who came along. But then, Merrick was more of an amusing friend, and dinner was innocent enough. "I'd like that, but as friends, nothing more."

"I can agree to those terms." He smiled and I was reminded of how good-looking the man was. As tall as Henry, tanned but with longer hair. Water dripped off his long lashes and I smiled. He would be a catch for someone. Just not me.

"Anywhere in particular you'd like to dine? There are several good restaurants here."

"Well, since you're practically a local I'll leave that up to you to decide."

"So, Saturday suits you? I can pick you up from wherever you're staying."

I nodded. "I have next Saturday off, so that works perfectly." I started to wade back toward the shore. "I'm going to go back to my towel for a bit."

"I'll come with you and get your number."

We joined Clara and Eve, and I ignored their knowing smirks and inspection of Merrick as I found my phone in my bag. I faced Merrick and handed it to him. He took it, adding his details before passing it back.

"Nice seeing you again, Eve, Clara. Have you been enjoying your vacation?"

"It's been great," Eve said.

Clara nodded in agreement.

I glanced toward the stairs leading onto the beach, not really listening to their conversation. There was no sign of Henry anymore and I couldn't help but wonder why he was here. He had to have wanted to see and speak to me. Maybe he had been trying to do the right thing and let me down, apologize for what had happened between us.

Not that I wanted him to apologize for anything. I certainly didn't regret my time with him. But I had hoped he would've been more honest with himself and not drag me into his messy relationship problems with his ex.

My phone dinged and I glanced down at the message.

I look forward to dining with you, Maddie. See you Saturday.

I laughed, meeting Merrick's eyes, knowing he must have messaged himself to ensure he had my contact details too.

"Enjoy the rest of the day." He leaned over and kissed my cheek. "See you Saturday."

I watched him leave, noting the women on the beach who were aware of his every move. The man did pull the eye, mine included. I wasn't blind.

I sat on my towel and sighed.

"None of that, not after that hunk just got your number and confirmed a date."

I reached for the sunburn cream, knowing I would have to explain to my friends. "He's hot, and we did have fun at the engagement party dancing, but that's not what's troubling me."

"What is then?" Clara asked, rolling onto her stomach, staring at me.

"Henry was here. I saw him when speaking to Merrick in the water. He was standing at the bottom of the steps to the beach. He looked pissed when he saw who I was talking to."

"Good, I hope he's as jealous as fuck after what he's been up to. Asshole," Eve said without remorse.

They weren't wrong, but I cringed, hating Henry being spoken of in such a way even after what he'd done to me. But what were friends for if they weren't there to keep us honest and stop a person from making mistakes repeatedly? I loved my best friends and would never wish them not to be blunt and to the point.

"I think he was here to explain the photos and tell me that he's back with Margot." Which he could have done by text or a phone call, I reminded myself. How hard was it for men to be honest and not fuck women around?

"Henry is a rich guy, privileged, and used to getting his own way. These men think they're better than everyone, untouchable, and they forget that people have feelings that can be hurt when they're ready to move on."

I looked at Eve, who, like Clara, were both daughters to Wall Street bankers and with trust funds that would rival many of the types of people Henry socialized with. She spoke as if she was speaking from experience, and I wondered at it. Eve and Clara had spent many summers in Europe, so it was a possibility Eve had her heart broken abroad.

"Well, at least I know I'll have a good time next weekend." I looked to where Merrick was now playing volleyball with several friends. His athletic build was something to admire as he spiked and dived for the white ball. I let my eyes devour him, imagine him in different, more private situations, and yet, the spark, the longing that ought to accompany such imaginings didn't come.

Urgh, Henry better not have broken me for anyone else.

"You should also get under him, that would make your weekend even better." Eve chuckled, wiggling her brows.

I laughed, feeling lighter for the first time in days. My European vacation had just started and I'd be damned if I wallowed in a depressed state just because of some intoxicating Roman god I fucked.

"What are you going to do if Henry calls in at the café? You going to talk to him?"

"I suppose I will, but what can he say? Pictures don't lie." I pulled up Instagram, torturing myself by looking at the news article that was still trending on the social pages. "I shouldn't be hurt. I hardly knew him, and we never promised each other anything but a bit of fun, but still, if he had feelings for his ex, he should have told me. I wouldn't have agreed to see him. I would've stayed the hell away."

"Just makes me sick." Clara slipped her sunglasses on and laid back down. "You do what you think is right with Henry, but I think he deserves a good mouthful however that conversation goes."

Oh, he would be getting one of those, that I could promise my friends.

A pang of regret ran through me, and I looked out to where Merrick still played volleyball, requiring a distraction. I needed to get over Henry. Maybe my friends were right. Getting under someone else to move on was just what the vacation ordered.

CHAPTER
Fifteen

THE SOUND of Merrick's voice made my eye twitch and all thoughts of how I could knock the bastard on his ass floated through my mind. Once, he had been my best friend, childhoods interwoven like fabric threads, and yet now… Now I just wanted to lay the bastard flat on his ass for daring to speak to Maddie.

The image of them at the beach, her amusement at whatever fucked-up thing Merrick was saying… I fisted my hands, took a deep breath, knowing that the last thing my housekeeper needed to clean up was blood or broken furniture.

The board meeting was at an end, and I was glad of it. The less I had to interact with Merrick Dudley, a member of the board and second-largest shareholder in the company behind myself, the better.

"She's lovely, Soph and we're going out for dinner Saturday."

Merrick's words snapped the last of my patience. I met Merrick's eye, wishing my view of him would kill him stone dead. "What I want to know is how you came to even know of Miss Webb? Care to enlighten us?"

Merrick smirked, rocking back in his chair, clearly enjoying what he was up to. Pissing me off.

"Margot suggested her at the engagement party. We danced and got along exceptionally well. When I saw her at the beach, I reintroduced myself and we got talking." Merrick paused, raising his brow. "Are you jealous, Fairfax?"

"Ah, so Margot is behind this. I should have known…"

"You cannot blame Margot for this, brother. She is not the evil witch you've painted her these past months."

I glared at my sister. "Really?" I took a deep breath, not wanting to lose my patience with my sibling, but both she and Margot were pushing my last nerve. "Explain then, how images of me and Margot were leaked into the paparazzi from last summer and date stamped on the days I was supposed to take Maddie out on my boat. Do you think it's a coincidence?"

I watched Sophia's complexion pale at my words. I hoped she didn't have anything to do with this farce that led Maddie to think the worst of me. I should have waded out into the ocean on Sunday, demanded Maddie listen to my truth, and know of Margot's deceiving manipulations.

"I'm certain Margot wouldn't stoop so low."

My sister, although prickly at times, was a good person at heart and thought the best of her friends. But sometimes this also made her blatantly blind to what was happening before her, like right now. Which I had little doubt included Merrick Dudley.

That man wasn't interested in Maddie. What he was interested in was trying to get the best of me at any time he could.

"History would state otherwise," I returned.

"I don't know why you're so put out, Fairfax. Maddie never mentioned you, not even when I saw you looking out at us, pitifully I might add. Maybe this chit doesn't like being played, as rich as you are that usually keeps these types of girls hanging around. And whether the images of you and Margot are recent or not, they certainly don't put you in a good light. I think you best move on and let me have a go, yeah?"

"Perhaps you ought to get the hell out of my boardroom and stay the hell away from her."

"How about no."

"You're not going to see her again. Do I make myself clear?" The idea of Merrick, an ex-friend who'd already fucked me over once in my life doing it again wasn't happening. I wouldn't idly sit by this time. I would fight for what I wanted and right now, what I wanted most was Maddie.

"If she agrees to see me, you can do nothing. We're business partners, you're not my boss."

"As majority shareholder you will toe the line. Stay

away from her. You'll not be asked again." I packed up my paperwork, ending the discussion. "See yourself out."

Merrick stood and saluted, an utter arrogant prick to the very end, before walking from the room.

I turned to my sister who remained. "Did you have anything to do with the images being leaked to the press?" She didn't reply and my disappointment took hold. I could stomach her being a little icy toward Maddie upon meeting her for the first time. It was never easy meeting another woman who was replacing a best friend's position in her brother's life, but it was also not my fault that I was in this position in the first place. I hadn't been the unfaithful one.

"I suspected Margot was up to something, but she didn't say what, and maybe it was wrong of me, but I didn't press her to explain. I'm sorry that she may have messed things up for you and Miss Webb."

"Are you though?" I shook my head, longing for my apartment, the day already far too long, even for a workaholic like myself. "I expect you to make Maddie feel more welcome the next time you meet."

"Will there be a next time? It sounds like Merrick is interested, and forgive me, brother, but you know he's like a dog with a bone. Once he has someone in his sights he doesn't like to lose. Not even if he's going up against you."

I knew that better than anyone, but there was no way I'd let Maddie be used by him. It wasn't happening under my watch, even if she never believed my explanation on the whole Margot thing.

"I like Maddie, more than I thought I would, and I will not let her be used. She's not from our world, she doesn't know how vampirish everyone can be when they smell blood. I'll not have her injured by you or anyone. Do I make myself clear?"

"Very." Sophia collected her belongings and strode from the room, leaving me thankfully alone.

We need to talk, alone and without interruption. When can we meet?

I watched my phone, the dreaded three little dots that blinked that said Maddie was online, reading the text and typing a reply. I rolled my shoulders, trying to ease the tension that I was holding on to while I waited for a reply. Surely I deserved a chance to explain, to tell her what she believed to be true was not, merely another game my ex wanted to play.

The three dots stopped blinking and no text came through. "Fuck." I tossed my phone onto the boardroom table, looking at it with disgust. I should go to her. I should have stayed in Sorrento this week and sought her out at her work. Instead, I had put the board meeting penned in ahead of her, a mistake I now regretted.

I could always dial in, the company was growing, plunging ahead well, there was no urgency or issue that couldn't be solved immediately by my competent staff. But Maddie...well, that was a delicate problem that only I could sort and right at this moment I didn't know if I could.

I swiped the phone off the table, determined to get through to her.

I'm in Rome but will be back in Sorrento tomorrow night. We need to talk. I need to explain. Please see me.

I sent the text, not caring that I was borderline begging. But there was something about Maddie that was genuine, made me want to be a better man. I couldn't allow her to think I'd fucked her over when I hadn't.

My eye twitched at the sight of the three little dots again, held my breath...

I think the pictures explained everything I needed to know.

More dots. Unease tumbled through me, unsettling, a foreign emotion I wasn't used to enduring, and nor did I particularly like.

> Our summer fling was short, and that's okay. I wish you well with Miss Hathaway.

I didn't want a future of any kind with Margot. That ship had sailed a long time ago. Did Maddie not know that? I ran a hand through my hair. Of course, she didn't. As far as she knew I'd fucked my ex on a cruise that had been meant for her.

> Let me explain and then you can choose, but give me a chance. It's not what you think. I promise.

> Fine …. You can explain. I have a shift tomorrow and finish at nine pm.

> I'll be there.

I slumped into my chair, turned, and looked out over Rome by night. The city, alive and bustling even at the late hour, the ancient metropolis mixed with modern regimes. I would bring Maddie here, show her my life, my home if she gave me a second chance.

I didn't want to lose her.

Especially over a situation that I had no play in. I wouldn't let us both suffer due to other manipulations. Not ever again would I play that game.

CHAPTER
Sixteen

FOR THE HUNDREDTH time I checked my phone to see if Henry was late. Would he stand me up? I pushed down the disappointment those thoughts stirred in me and reminded myself he was the one who wanted to talk. Had asked to meet up, not the other way around.

What was I doing here anyway? Giving a guy I hardly knew another chance, an opportunity to explain how he was all over his ex in paparazzi images only days ago. What the fuck was wrong with me?

Grow some lady parts, Maddie and tell him to take a long hike off a short pier.

A black Cadillac pulled up and I took a deep breath. I would hear him out, but by God, he would need quite the story for me to give him another chance. If he even wanted a second chance. Maybe he just didn't want us to end on a sour note…

Tonight could be utterly shit, but at least I'd know

the truth and could move on and enjoy the rest of my summer.

Henry got out of the car and like a woman starved I ogled his tall, athletic build, which sent a shiver down my spine and longing to rip through me like a knife. Still, I couldn't let him know how he affected me. That he'd hurt me, even if our fling was short-lived.

I moved my face away when he went to kiss my cheek in welcome.

"Hey." Sheepishly he opened the door and gestured for me to get into the car. "It's good to see you. Thanks for letting me explain."

I gave a small smile. I didn't want to appear hurt to anyone, least of all him. Years of living in foster care ensured that I put up barriers to protect myself. People often took advantage of the weak and I'd never be that again if I could help it. If I was to walk away from this meeting with my heart intact and my emotions under control I needed to appear as if his fucking around was his issue, not mine. That I didn't care our summer fling hadn't led to more.

Like the hopeless romantic I was, I had hoped it would…

I had trusted in what he'd been saying, how he'd been touching, looking at me. I still couldn't believe it was all false. How could anyone be so callous and deceptive?

I pulled my seatbelt on and settled into the seat. Henry pressed a button on his door and a partition separated us from the driver.

"Can your driver hear or see us?" I'd never seen such a feature on a car, well perhaps in a movie, but never in real life.

"No, he cannot. Most of the company vehicles have them. It ensures privacy when we're working and traveling at the same time."

I nodded and faced Henry, not wanting any more chat, just answers. "Are you going to explain to me why you were with your supposed ex on the yacht and how it was plastered all over the internet? How a date that was supposed to be mine ended up being your ex-girlfriend's instead? That's why we're here, isn't it?"

"It is." He frowned and looked out the window. Was he thinking of a way to tell me that he was back with Margot? Was he trying to make up some excuse I would buy? Some shit about true love and soul mates?

I clamped my mouth shut, the thought firing my temper.

"Are you back with her? You seem to be having a hard time forming words." I shook my head. What was I even doing here? We weren't exclusive, and in truth, he didn't owe me shit just like I didn't in return.

"Henry," I said, my tone less accusing. "I've not known you for long. I won't be heartbroken if that's the truth of it. I will survive, you know. You're not the only man in the world."

His dark, hooded eyes met mine and I could see he was shocked by my words. But what did he expect? For me to beg him to give Margot up? To continue the wonderful summer we'd planned. I wouldn't solicit any man to stay with me. My pride didn't stoop that low, not even for Henry Fairfax.

"I'm not with Margot and never was. She sold images to the paparazzi from last summer and paid them to date stamp them the day we were supposed to go on the yacht, making it look like I'd played you. I never did, Maddie. I couldn't."

Henry reached out and clasped my hand. His thumb made soothing, circular motions on the top of my hand while my mind scrambled to comprehend what he'd said. The images were from last year. They weren't current.

WTF!

"I'm sorry you were led to believe the images were true. It's taken me days and threatening a lawsuit for the images to be pulled from the internet. On top of work and meetings, I haven't had time to reach out and fix what I knew you would be thinking, and you didn't deserve that. I should have reached out immediately, even by text."

I stared at our hands and his attempt to placate me. "A redacted statement will be published tomorrow telling of the online magazine's mistake and as for Margot, she's more than aware we're over."

I released a breath that I didn't know I'd been holding. The images were from last year. Sweet relief swamped me, but with it a little caution of the world I was stepping into. I didn't know how these games were played, and certainly Henry's ex was more than willing to lower herself just to get at me.

If what Henry was saying was true, which it certainly seemed the case, I would forgive him, but I also would guard myself, try to not get too swept up in his life and how he was making me feel. Not until I was able to trust in us more.

And without thinking I unbuckled my belt and straddled his lap. Henry pulled me against him, holding me close. His soft lips brushed my shoulder, my neck, his breath tickling my skin.

"I missed you. I thought I'd lost you, that you thought me such a bastard." Henry pulled back and cupped my face in his hands. "But as factual as I am sitting here, I promise nothing happened. I woke to my phone blowing up and saw the article just like you did and almost choked on my own tongue."

I ran my hands over his jaw, relishing the feel of his one-day-old stubble. Damn, he looked and smelled so good, always vanilla and honey, good enough to eat. "From my interactions with Margot I get the sense she doesn't like me, so hearing she forwarded the images to the paparazzi doesn't surprise me. I don't think she wants what you had to be over, or at least, doesn't want you not to be ready to take her back when she wishes to give you guys another go."

Henry nodded slowly, agreeing to my words and I debated whether I should say more about what was bothering me. "Margot and your sister don't like me, Henry. I hoped I could be friends with Sophia, but she's good friends with Margot and that's to her credit, but I think if we're to spend more time together, then it's probably best it's just you and me. I don't want to cause any more complications for you. Especially when this is just a summer fling, right?"

There, I had given him the opportunity to disagree with my words. Would he though? Did he want what we'd started to be more than a summer romance?

"I'm sorry about my sister. She's been warned over her actions toward you." He leaned forward, his lips brushing mine in the softest kiss that made my stomach flutter. The man was far too intoxicating for his own good and he knew it. "I want you and no one else. I'm not going to let anything ruin our summer. Bar the few times I will leave for work, I'm all yours."

"I'm glad to hear it." I leaned forward and kissed him. After the last week of thinking the worst, I needed to feel his lips on mine. His eyes darkened in hunger, and heat licked along my skin. The visceral reaction to Henry was unlike anything I'd ever known. My body became a stranger and did things that were out of character.

"Where are we going?" I asked.

"To my villa." The car started toward his home, winding through the hills. "Speaking of plans, I have a surprise for you."

"You do?" Excitement thrummed through me, and I smiled, happy for the first time in days. "What is it?"

"Well, I asked your boss when you were rostered on again, and it's not for a couple of days so I thought why don't we go on the yacht like we planned. It's fully staffed and at my disposal. Would you like a couple of trips around the island before I return you home later this week?"

"I would love that."

Henry tipped up my face, his thumb running over my bottom lip. My breath hitched and fire coursed through me. "I would love that, too."

He kissed me then, and I lost myself all over again. The kiss was achingly sweet, not frenzied with need, but a slow, intoxicating glide of seduction that made me more achingly aware of him than ever before.

The man was hallucinogenic, and I was certainly under his spell.

CHAPTER
Seventeen

LATER THAT NIGHT we stood on the pier, Henry's arm about my waist as we waited for the tender that slowly approached from the yacht. This evening, the ocean was calm, lapping softly against the wooden pylons, and millions of stars shone brightly in the endless sky above us. A young man in a dark-blue top and white shorts docked the small boat, tying it to the pier before greeting us.

"Good evening, Mr. Fairfax, Miss Webb. If you would climb onboard, we'll get on our way."

"Thank you, Owen," Henry said, assisting me onto the tender.

I settled onto the seat at the back of the small vessel and within minutes we were at the yacht. Two new deckhands greeted us and assisted me out of the tender. I took Henry's hand, and he led me up one of the two sweeping staircases that led to the sundeck above. Jet skis and other water sports equipment were neatly stowed near the railings and an array of deckchairs and tables sat in the space between.

"I like to breakfast here. You get a lovely view of the coast without being windswept, which can happen when on the front deck."

I turned and looked back toward the villa, the few lights high on the cliff marking where we'd come from.

"The front bathing deck is viewable from the captain's cockpit, so just remember that if you like to sunbathe topless."

I laughed. Was Henry serious? His amused grin told me he was. "I will not be doing that, not unless it's just you and me."

Henry pulled me against him, his hand clasping my ass. Warmth pooled between my legs. I ached with want for him. Had it been only a few days since we'd been with each other? It felt like a month. He left me all at sea, which I suppose I now was. A perfect place to be considering the situation I was in.

"Good, because I don't want anyone seeing what is mine."

I laughed off his words, not willing to read into them any more than face value. Henry led me through the yacht, it was far larger than I thought it would be.

"This is the interior lounge and bar. We have a full team working on the boat, so if you're hungry or want a special cocktail, water, or coffee, just let one of the crew know and they'll get it for you right away."

"How many crew work on the yacht? Is it staffed all the time?"

"Yes, they're twenty full-time crew members. The yacht does move around the Mediterranean, but is always docked near Sorrento during the summer months. I often come out and stay on it, but it's available for the family always. No point having a yacht if it's not used."

I lost count of the many rooms on Henry's tour. I wasn't sure what I expected to see from a mega yacht, but the dark, wooden floorboards, rich curtains, opulent lounges, and sweet-smelling flowers that gave the boat a homey feel weren't it. The yacht was of a mostly neutral color palate with few decorations, but family pictures littered the sideboards and walls, even the grand piano wasn't immune to memories.

"The yacht has several floors and there is a lift if you don't feel like walking the many stairs. On the floor beneath this one is the gym and movie theater, I'll show you those later, along with a beauty salon and sauna if you want to be pampered."

"You have a beautician working here?" My steps faltered at Henry's words.

"Yes, of course. I have a sister, remember?"

The rooms and levels blurred as the tour continued before we came before two large double doors that were open to yet another lounge with plush cushions, which threatened to swallow anyone who sat on it. A large television hung on the wall and colorful artwork.

Henry shut the double doors and before I could say anything about this magnificent vessel, he scooped me up in his arms and carried me into the room beyond. I squealed in surprise before grinning, wondering what else he had in store for me.

"This is where I wanted us to be before everything blew up in our faces last week. I'm sorry you were dragged into a situation that has nothing to do with you."

"It doesn't matter," I answered, reaching for him. He kissed me and took my lips in a kiss that left me breathless, my body simmering with need.

Henry set me down, his dark, hooded gaze watching me with a heat that seared my skin. "Undress."

I swallowed at his order and watched, enthralled, as he pulled at his tie, throwing it aside before starting on the buttons of his shirt.

Jesus, he was hot.

Still wearing my uniform, I unzipped my shorts, slowly pushing them off my hips to pool at my feet. I reached for the hem of my work shirt, pulling it over my head.

Henry was on me before my shirt hit the floor. He unhooked my bra, wrenching it off. His mouth was on my breast, teasing my nipple. His tongue flicked the pebbled flesh before suckling hard.

I moaned, bit my lip, and fought not to come from his ministrations.

I clasped his hair and held him against me, my body afire with need. My other nipple was not to be denied. Henry kneaded my breast, his thumb and forefinger squeezing my peak.

"Henry," I gasped when he teasingly bit me.

He stooped lower, going to his knees. His eyes rose and met mine, his wicked intent clear on his face before he slipped my panties off, leaving me exposed.

I bent down and pushed at his shoulder. "Before we do anything I need to shower. I've been at work all day."

"I don't care."

Heat spread across my skin. "We haven't showered together yet, Henry. It could be fun," I suggested.

He stood and led me toward the bathroom. The room was floor-to-ceiling marble, chrome fixtures, with a double shower. I stood, staring at it, stunned at its beauty before Henry turned on the shower, setting it to an agreeable heat.

He turned and stared at me, his eyes heavy with intent and appreciation. "You're so fucking beautiful. I knew the moment we met I'd never be the same. I still cannot believe I found you again."

"Well, actually," I said, sauntering up to him naked. "I decided to be Clara's plus one at the engagement party, so technically I found you, because had I not gone that day, we would never have crossed paths again."

"I would like to think that at some point in our lives, we would have found each other." He untied his belt and buttons before slipping his pants to the floor.

His sweet words made my knees weak. "Are you going to shower with your socks on?" I teased, stepping into the water. I ran my hair under the spray and washed it as he quickly discarded the remainder of his clothes.

"Absolutely not."

Henry stepped under the water with me, and turned me about. "Let me wash your hair."

I grinned, having never had a man wash my hair before. I heard him reach for the shampoo and soon his fingers slid into my hair, kneading my skull, washing me with great care. His touch was divine and I closed my eyes, more than willing to lose myself in this little pampering session.

"You can rinse it now."

I ran my hair under the water. Henry reached for the loofah and poured body wash on it. I finished rinsing my hair and wondered what he had in for me next.

"Now I'm going to wash you, New York."

He spun me about yet again, his hard body against my back, his hand clasped my hip while his other soaped my skin. Starting near my arms and working his way across my chest. Soap sliced between my legs, the water making us both slippery. He washed my breasts, taking time to softly roll the loofah over my pebbled nipples, sending delicious spikes of desire to my core.

"Your breasts needed particular care." His deep chuckle against my ear made me shiver.

"Where else needs special attention?" I ached for him to touch me between my legs. I was wet, even under the water I could feel my need for him.

The loofah slipped to my stomach before he slid it over my sex, between my legs, rolling it against my clit.

I moaned, clasped his arms for support, closed my eyes as pleasure taunted me. "Henry, you make me want you so much."

"You make me want you as well. So fucking much." He wrenched me around, and our mouths fused, teased, our tongues entangling with thirst. Water sluiced over us, making us slippery. He wrenched from my hold, strode dripping wet to the basin and grabbed protection.

He was back to me in a heartbeat, guiding the condom in place. He clasped my ass, lifted me as if I weighed nothing at all. His cock pressed between my folds. His eyes burned with determination, and I shivered in expectation.

He thrust into me with such force I gasped, his savagery a promise, a declaration. The beautiful, delicious feel of him deep within me.

I wrapped my legs about his back, hooking my ankles under his ass as he fucked me against the shower wall. He was so large, so hard, so consuming. My body ached, burned, strove for release, for the pleasure he could give me.

"Yes, Henry."

He was relentless, his kiss devouring, his body demanding a response, commanding me to his will. I willingly let go, let him taunt, lead me to a release that I craved.

I came, hard and far quicker than I ever had before.

His kiss turned savage, and I reveled in it. I wanted

him, this raw, uncensored side of Henry, where he was wild and untamed, opposite to his everyday character.

"Fuck, Maddie. You make me come so hard."

His words spiked another release, and I screamed his name, riding every delicious tremor he bestowed as his flowed through him. Euphoria swamped me being back in his arms, knowing the truth and the lies that had tried to separate us. But there was something simmering between me and Henry, and although I didn't know what that was right now, it was growing, blooming, and heating up.

Just like the summer in the Mediterranean.

CHAPTER
Eighteen

I STARED at the ceiling of my stateroom, Maddie asleep at my side, my mind unable to rest, to comprehend what was happening between us. She made me feel so damn much that I ought to run for the hills, ignore the emotions that warred inside me with each breath. Feelings that were new and unexplored.

There was something different to how I was with Maddie to any of my past relationships. Somehow this seemed genuine, easy, a breath of fresh air that I didn't know I needed. After seeing her again at the engagement party I had wanted her, even then I knew we'd end up here, her in my bed and my possessive side raising its ugly head, not wanting to have her out of my sight.

Maddie snuggled into my side, and I kissed the top of her head, breathing in the sweet scent of her hair. She occupied my thoughts far more than a man of my commitments should allow. I had a multibillion-dollar business to run, I shouldn't want to put it aside for weeks on end so I could spend it with the woman asleep at my side. The notion of having a vacation and not being at the Dudley-Fairfax beck and call was unheard of, out of character.

But I also couldn't deny that I enjoyed letting business take care of itself so I could be here with her.

Maddie.

Damn.

I like her.

A lot.

I rolled her onto her back and kissed her neck. Jasmine teased my senses, and I ran my hand over her stomach, down over her sex to tease her. Already she was wet, ready, as needy it would seem for me as I was for her.

She mewled awake, her eyes heavy with sleep and expectation. "This is a nice way to be woken up."

"You like that?" I knew she did, I certainly didn't need her answer. I slipped between her folds, running a finger into her aching heat and fucked her with my hand.

Her eyes glazed over with pleasure. "Yes, don't stop."

I didn't intend to. I needed to make her shatter in my arms, have my fill of her in every way before I had to leave again for work.

"Henry," she gasped, biting her perfect, plump lip.

I kissed her, hard, tangled my tongue with hers and

drank from her mouth. She tasted of sin and sweetness combined. I moaned, my cock rock hard.

"Fuck me, Henry. Please."

Her hand reached for my dick, and she worked me, teased me as we both pleasured the other. Her hands were magic, the perfect tension that had I been standing would've brought me to my knees. "Maddie, I'll come if you keep doing that."

She let go and before I could protest, straddled my legs. She reached for my cock, guiding me into her.

"Protection," I gasped, the feel of her without the latex layer beyond my endurance. She left me bereft for a moment, reaching over to the bedside cabinet to pull out a condom. With an expertise I didn't want to think about or how she became so proficient, she slipped the condom onto my cock.

We moaned as she lowered herself on me to the hilt. I clasped her hips, found a rhythm that satisfied us both. Her breasts rocked, her hair falling over her shoulders, framing her pretty face.

I didn't know what to do or where to look. She consumed me in every way.

I was in so much trouble.

"Henry…" She rolled her hips, taking me deep. I ground my teeth, prayed for perseverance. I wasn't a green, virginal lad who came at the first stroke, and yet, she pushed me to my limit with each rock of her body.

"Fuck me, please."

I rolled her onto her back. She slipped her legs about my waist, and I reached up, pinning her arms above her head. I thrust into her, taking her, fucking her as she wanted. Forced myself deep into her weeping heat. She moaned, pinned me against her with her feet, urging me on.

So fucking hot. I longed to come. In fact, I wanted to do a lot of things to her. A kaleidoscope of dirty thoughts tumbled through my mind and there never seemed to be enough time.

I was lost in my focus to pleasure her, to make her happy. She moaned my name, her fingers curling about mine where I held her. The first contractions of her intense orgasm convulsed around my cock, and I couldn't hold on any longer.

"Henry, fuck yes, fuck me. Oh God, yes. Don't stop."

I fucked her as she begged and rode out every delicious tremor that tightened about my cock and sparked my own orgasm.

I came.

Hard.

I slumped beside her, our bodies slick with sweat and sated pleasure. For several minutes we lay there, our heartbeats slowing returning to normal.

"You look like the cat who got the cream."

"Oh, I definitely got the cream." She laughed, her cheeks red, her hair mussed.

I rolled to face her, wanting to remember how she looked forever. She was so beautiful all of the time, but after the throes of lovemaking, she was breathtaking.

"You hungry? I promise I didn't steal you away to

our room to make love to you and not feed you. We can have a late dinner if you like."

Maddie looked at me sheepishly. "Actually I'd love that. I'm starving and haven't eaten since lunch."

"Oh no. I'm so sorry." I kissed her quickly and got out of bed, pulling on slacks and a shirt. "I feel terrible. I'll order something from the chef now." I went to the phone and rang through to the galley, ordering a light meal to get us through to breakfast.

Maddie climbed out of bed. I devoured the sight of her nakedness, her small waist and womanly hips, her abundant breasts that were utterly perfect, not to mention her ass… I could feel myself getting hard and I took a deep breath and helped her locate a robe. She didn't need me to molest her again. Jesus, I needed to get a hold of myself.

"I haven't got anything to wear." She put her hands on her hips, clearly troubled by that fact. "I can't spend the rest of my time here wearing a robe or my work clothes."

I chuckled. "I have a confession to make."

"You do? What is it?"

"I visited your Airbnb before picking you up at work. Eve and Clara packed a bag for you once I explained the truth of the photos." I smiled at the memory of their grilling, their unending suspicion of me that was to their credit. They were good friends to Maddie and no matter how long it took me to convince them, I was glad Maddie had such loyal people in her life. "I hope you don't mind I took the liberty."

Her smile warmed my heart and put my fears to rest. "That is amazing, thank you. I had visions of having to wear a robe for the next few days." She chuckled. "I'm glad Eve and Clara forgave you. They were pretty mad the other day."

"I did have to bribe them a little." I grinned.

"Really? With what?"

"I bribed them with a day of pampering and unending champagne on the yacht tomorrow with you. I hope you don't mind."

"I don't mind at all." Maddie flung herself into my arms and I held her, pulling her close. She fit me like a glove, a perfect fit. I stole a kiss, needing to taste her, remind myself that she was mine. "I'd love to have them here."

"Good, because what makes you happy makes me so." The delight etched on her pretty face made me drunk with happiness. What was this madness that had overcome me? I liked it, it was addictive and didn't want it to end.

Maybe our summer fun could extend into fall…

Always worth a thought.

CHAPTER
Nineteen

"THIS IS UNBELIEVABLE. How good is this pampering?" Eve groaned.

"It's amazing," I mumbled into the massage table, staring down at the floor as Lena the masseuse and her staff all worked out the knots they had found in our backs and shoulders. Apparently Eve had several knots and needed to relax more.

"I don't think we'll leave tonight. We're going to move in here instead."

I chuckled, closing my eyes, and reveling in the pampering. Oh, it was heavenly, just like my entire time on the yacht had been since arriving last night.

Henry had gone above and beyond in making sure every want and need of mine was met. Breakfast had been out on the rear deck, overlooking the coastline of Italy. The smoked salmon and eggs benedict was delicious, the best I ever had. And as for the coffee, well, far superior to what I got in the US.

We had spent a couple of hours enjoying the sight of the Bay of Naples in the distance and Vesuvius towering over it all with its grandeur.

And now my friends had been delivered to enjoy the day with me while we cruised along the coastline.

"Tell us, how was the make-up sex? We've been dying to know."

My face heated and I felt my masseuse pause mid knead. "Change the subject, Clara," I warned.

Eve laughed and I heard her thank her masseuse before sitting up. I did the same, stretching as Lena packed up and left us alone in the room to talk. "Now that they're gone, you have to tell us. Henry explained about the photos and we believe him. What about you? We can only assume since you're on his mega yacht that you believed him too?"

"I do believe him, and it's been wonderful so far." I pursed my lips, wondering how much I should actually tell my friends. Could I admit aloud to what I was feeling, how Henry made my blood quicken, my breath catch? How his lovemaking was overwhelming and utterly addictive. That the way he looks at me makes my heart stop. "I think I really like this guy."

"Well, it's pretty obvious he likes you too. Have you seen how he watches you?"

"No." A delicious shiver ran down my spine at Clara's words and a hope that I shouldn't give way to sparked to life within me. "How does he look at me?"

"He's obsessed. When you're in the room, no one else exists. That's how intense he looks," Clara clarified.

Eve nodded. "Are you sure this is only going to be a summer fling? It seems very intense just to be fleeting. I'm getting long-term vibes from both of you."

I scoffed, but I was getting the same vibes from Henry. When I thought about returning to the US at the end of the summer I also wondered why we couldn't give it a go long distance. The world was smaller now, there were planes and FaceTime. It wasn't an impossible possibility. But would he be interested?

I know after the past few days I would be.

"We haven't really talked about what happens after summer, but I think I'd be open to continuing if that was something that he would consider. I certainly don't have any inclination to date other men or even seek out new dates in New York. I couldn't think of anything worse, to be honest."

"Well, why would you when you have a man like Henry pining for you? I know which I'd choose," Eve said, waggling her brows.

Clara and I laughed before I slipped off the massage table and reached for my dressing gown. "Shall we go sit in the sauna?"

"Oh yes, let's do that," Clara agreed.

We settled into the sauna and poured a little water on the coals. The room steamed up, hot but not to an uncomfortable level. "Can you believe people live like this?" Eve said.

"You do live like this," I reminded her.

"My parents have money, yes, but this is a whole other level of wealth."

"It is a lot. What do you think about it, Maddie?" Clara asked.

"To be honest I'm a little nervous by it. You know my past, and while I've told Henry snippets, he doesn't know everything. If he did want something long term I'm not sure I'd be the right woman for the job. I'm educated, yes, but I'm not in his league. Even I'll admit that."

"You are in his league and he'd be lucky to have you," Eve protested.

"You know what I mean. He's from a successful, old Italian family. They're close, they're wealthy, and have connections that are probably beyond our comprehension. What will his family and friends say when they find out I'm an American, raised in foster care and had an addict as a mother who dumped me a couple of months after I was born?"

"They should only show compassion not contempt, and if they do anything different then they're not worth your time."

I reached across the wooden seat and squeezed Eve's hand, happy to have such loyal friends. "His sister doesn't like me, which could be a problem. She's close friends with his ex and I think she's already picked which side she'll be on. A shame because I didn't have anything to do with Henry and Margot's relationship breakdown."

"She'll come around, especially if you and Henry decide to take this summer fling further. She'll have no choice if he wants you in his life."

A comforting thought. Henry would have my back and had done so already when it came to Margot. Surely his sister couldn't hate me forever. "Well, I suppose only time will tell what will happen between us. I would consider seeing him past summer. Do you really think he may as well?"

"I think he definitely would put a title on your relationship and ask for exclusivity. He'd be mad if he let you go," Clara said, pouring more water on the coals.

"You're biased, but thank you." We sat in silence a while, sweating our assess off and each of us lost in our own thoughts. While I didn't know how we would make it work long distance, it was certainly a possibility that we needed to talk about.

The feelings he evoked in me were unlike anything I'd ever known. Never had I wanted to be exclusive with anyone before meeting Henry, and the thought of him moving on with someone else left a hollowness inside me.

Did that mean I was falling for him?

The realization struck me in the face like a slap. I suppose it did.

I was falling for Henry Fairfax.

Billionaire.

One of the most eligible bachelors in Europe.

How the hell was I supposed to navigate that and remain sane? Impossible.

Twenty

LATE THE FOLLOWING afternoon I lazed in the spa on the top deck. I leaned on the edge, watching as the yacht sat anchored off the town of Sorrento. Henry had given me a pair of binoculars and I spied on the people on the beach, watching as they set up a stage. Was there going to be some sort of concert there tonight? The many people arriving certainly made it appear to be the case.

I put the binoculars down and leaned on my hands, watching Henry as he spoke on his cell, his computer open before him. He spoke in Italian, and I had no idea what he was saying, but whatever it was seemed important if his hasty and firm tone was any indication. I ogled him, the man whom I was seeing, sleeping with, falling for, not that I would tell him that just yet, but it was the truth. He was so sweet, handsome, and sexually charged that he stole my breath.

Today he was dressed in casual linen shorts and

shirt, his feet bare, and yet I could tell by the slight frown between his eyes he was in management mode. What was it like for him to run such a successful family business? The Dudley-Fairfax hotels were all over Europe in the most beautiful and exquisite locations, being the boss of all that would be a mammoth task for anyone. Keeping shareholders happy, his family, his staff…

Henry hung up the phone and leaned back in his chair, running a hand through his dark locks, clearly distracted.

"Is everything okay?" I asked.

He smiled, but I could see that he was dealing with something that was causing him unease. "A little problem I've now taken care of. Nothing to worry about or ruin our day." He stood and pulled off his tee and climbed into the spa, not caring about his shorts. "Nothing that holding you in my arms won't fix."

There was nothing more I'd like to do. I moved over to him, straddling him. He clasped my ass, pulling me against his hardening sex. I slipped my arms about his neck, leaned down and kissed him. The kiss was slow and sweet, and I lost myself in his touch. The last two days had been the best I'd had since arriving in Italy and I never wanted to leave. If only we could forever cocoon ourselves here.

"You drive me to distraction."

Henry's whispered words evoked a need within me that wouldn't be tamed. He nipped my bottom lip, teasing me, before I felt his thumb slip under the little ties of my bathing suit bottoms, pressing downward.

I pushed off his lap, wagging my finger at him for being naughty. "What are you up to? We're in the spa. Any one of your staff could walk in and see us." Not that his touch didn't conjure a need within me that only he seemed to be able to sate. A fire burned between us, simmering, that at any moment could be lit to a flaming inferno.

He pressed a button on the side of the spa and it started to bubble, the heat of the water creating a mist of steam about us. I shivered as his dark eyes burned with need, with determination. His gaze moved over my body like a physical touch, and I swallowed, knowing where this was going and where it would end.

"Are you going to stay over there?" he asked, not moving.

"Are you going to take your shorts off?" I returned.

His raised his brows before he reached under the water and worked his shorts off, throwing them over the edge of the spa when he was done. "Your turn, Maddie."

I fought not to giggle. Was I really going to fuck him here in a spa on the top deck of his boat where we could be come upon at any moment? He ran a hand through his hair, a wayward curl falling over his brow. Jesus, the man made me wet without even trying. His tanned skin, dark hair and eyes were so captivating I could not look away.

"Okay then." I did as he asked, slipping my bikini

bottoms off and throwing them over the side of the spa just like he had.

He watched them land near his shorts and a wicked grin lifted his lips.

"Now what?" I asked.

"Now you get your pretty fucking self over here."

He didn't need to ask twice. I slipped into his arms, and he kissed me. Hard. His tongue, his mouth, his everything overwhelming me. I ached for him, undulated against him and teased myself against his rigid yet velvety cock. His dick slipped between my folds, teasing my clit and I pressed harder, wanting to come, needing release.

His muscular arms strained as he guided me against him, and we were soon breathing hard, at our delicious limits. "We don't have protection here. Let me make you come like this."

"Just fuck me." I was on birth control, and Henry wasn't the type of man who would put himself at risk. But nor could I wait for him to get protection. I needed him.

Now.

"We shouldn't," he stated, yet his kiss turned molten, melting away any residual reservations I may have held.

"I'm on the pill. Please, Henry. I need you inside of me."

He groaned and clasped my hips, thrusting into me with perfect precision. We moaned, his hands like a vise against my hips, working me on him like a master.

Fuck he felt so good. With each thrust he hit my sweet spot inside, his thick cock filling me, satisfying my every want. I held on to the spa and worked myself on him, lost to my desire and the pleasure that he built within me.

"You're fucking magnificent."

He kissed his way down my neck, licked my collarbone, and kneaded my breast, his thumb and forefinger teasing my pebbled nipple.

I shivered, pre-orgasmic spasms wracking my body. "Fuck yes, Henry."

We forgot where we were, the crew a factor neither of us cared about. If they did see us, observed what we were doing, we never noticed, so lost in each other's arms.

His ferocity of pace increased as he took me. I tittered on the edge of release, so deliciously close, teasingly near to bliss. "Yes, Henry," I moaned as the first spasms of release quivered through me. "I'm coming."

"Fuck yes you are and so am I."

Our eyes met and I watched as his orgasm ripped through him too. His dark-brown eyes sparked with ecstasy and another emotion I'd not seen before, nor could discern. I clasped his jaw, kissing him as every tremble of release thrummed through our bodies.

"No one has ever made me feel like you do," I whispered, unashamed to let him know, no matter how fleeting our liaison would be, what he did to me.

His face sobered, his grip tightened. "You're not

what I expected either. We're both on untutored ground here, Maddie."

I ran my fingers through his hair, wanting to bathe in his handsomeness. So many thoughts ran through my mind. How could I walk away from this intoxicating man at the end of summer? Ending what could be the foundation of something great.

"Tell me again why we can't see each other after summer? I'm starting to think our summer timeline was a bad idea."

"And why is that?" His tone was teasing and yet unease ran through me when he didn't just agree with me.

"I um…well…I like you, and we get along well, in all ways," I teased, winking at him.

He grinned back. "I like you too."

"Maybe we could say that our summer fling could also be a fall and winter one too. A summer that never ends."

"All things end, Maddie."

His rejection stung. I nodded at his no-nonsense tone and moved off his lap. His answer doused any hope I had in thinking the relationship could be of longer duration.

"Of course," I said, feeling foolish for allowing him to know I wanted more from him. I reached for a towel, fighting to ignore the feelings that rose within me of having never been loved, never good enough, not even for my own parents.

Not good enough for Henry Fairfax either, not long term anyway.

I climbed out of the spa and picked up my bathing suit bottoms, reminding myself that we only agreed on casual, on a summer romance. I shouldn't be butt hurt over him reminding me of our terms, even if he'd not come straight out and said it. As I dried myself I could feel Henry's gaze on me. I ignored it, not wanting him to know how hurt I was.

"I'm going to shower. I'll be back in a minute." I bit my lip, fighting tears that wouldn't help anyone. I shouldn't feel ashamed of how Henry made me feel, nor could I help that he didn't feel the same way.

Not everyone got what they wanted. I knew that better than most.

I showered and dressed in a pink linen floral dress and flats before heading up on deck. The crew had laid out a platter of sushi, vegetable appetizers, and fruit. Henry was already seated at table, and I joined him without words.

I picked up a sushi roll and slipped it into my mouth, hating that it had become awkward between us. I shouldn't have said anything. I should have just ignored what he was making me feel and simply enjoyed the summer like we'd planned.

"You're upset with me. I can tell." Henry reached across the table and slid his hand down my arm in an attempt to catch my notice. An impossibility because the man, no matter what we were doing, always had my attention.

I shouldn't be ashamed for allowing myself to be vulnerable. I ought to own what he made me feel and not be ashamed just because he didn't feel that way in return. I'd like our time to be longer than a short summer. I wanted to see if what we enjoyed could be given the time to grow, to blossom into something great.

A shame he didn't.

"Maddie, you know I've not long come out of a relationship that wasn't healthy, nor satisfying in any way. It was more like a contracted position than anything else. I don't want to hurt you. I just can't jump into another relationship so soon. Please tell me you understand my position."

"I understand, of course." And I did. His relationship with Margot sounded like a business deal that went sour. She wanted Henry, but also didn't want to stay exclusive to him. "But I do like you, more than I thought I would, considering how we started." Remembering our one-night stand. "I'm going to own those feelings. I think you're lovely and I would've loved to see you for longer than just a summer." I paused, meeting his gaze. "I do hope you're treated better in your next relationship, whenever that happens."

"The summer has only just started. We have so much time ahead of us. Let's not talk about the end when this is just our beginning."

I nodded, sipping my white wine, and forcing it past the damned lump in my throat. Why did I have to catch feelings, damn it. Why couldn't I just enjoy the summer and have great sex? Fuck him to my heart's content and then leave like a normal person.

"I understand, of course, no hard feelings." I reached for another sushi roll and some salad. "There seems to be a beach concert setting up for tonight in Sorrento. We should go. It looks like fun."

"If you like."

I smiled at Henry, hoping he believed the visage I was portraying as an indifferent woman who hadn't just been shot down after trying to own what I felt. The small frown and worry across Henry's brow told me he didn't believe me at all and knew exactly how I felt.

Like shit.

CHAPTER

Twenty~One

MY STOMACH CHURNED and I reached for a glass of water. For the first time ever on a boat, nausea threatened. Maddie sat before me, eating a pre-dinner meal. She was so beautiful, a dark-haired beauty with the bluest eyes I'd ever seen. Eyes that had been shadowed with hurt after my denial of her.

I looked toward Sorrento, needing time to gather my thoughts. I hadn't handled the conversation well. Nor did my words sit well with me. It left a sour taste in my mouth and my mind scrambling to make sense of my words.

It wasn't like I hadn't thought about seeing her past summer. I had debated that idea myself, so why, when she mentioned it, would I panic and flee to the hills? Tell her no. That I wasn't ready. That I didn't want to commit.

Maybe because you don't want to at present.

"Mr. Fairfax, the tender is ready if you wish to go ashore."

"Thank you, Owen. We'll depart in five." I finished my wine, hoping to calm my stomach. It didn't help, if anything, it only made it worse.

"So we're going to the beach party?" For the first time since our awkward conversation Maddie appeared happy.

I nodded and stood. Hating myself even more. "Yes, and if you would like we can have dinner at the restaurant that overlooks the harbor. But only if you're hungry and wish to. We've just eaten, after all."

"Oh no, both ideas sound wonderful. I'll just go grab my bag."

I kicked my heels on the top deck, watching the evening descend over the Med and Sorrento start to light up the shore with its many twinkling lights.

Maddie joined me and I took her hand, needing to touch her as we made our way to the tender. She started at my touch, surprise registering on her pretty face. Did she think I didn't want her at all now? That I didn't think about her every waking hour and sleeping one's too?

She was all I fucking thought about.

The tender ride into shore was quiet and I wracked my brain trying to think how to fix things between us. Make her feel wanted, even if I couldn't promise the world right now. It took a torturous half hour before we were seated in the restaurant beside a window that gave a view of the ocean beyond. Maddie placed her napkin on her lap, quiet and reflective as she looked out over the amazing view.

"You're very beautiful this evening." If only I could remove the sadness that clouded her eyes, make them sparkle again with expectation and hope.

"You don't think what I have on is too casual? I feel a little underdressed after coming in here."

"No, you look perfect." I reached out, wanting to hold her hand. She placed it on her lap instead and grinned.

A waitress came up to us to take our order. "Good evening, Mr. Fairfax. What can I get you and your guest this evening? Would you care for water to start, and wine?"

"Yes, thank you." I picked up the menu and looked at the wine selection. "We'll have a bottle of Dom Pérignon to start."

"Of course. I'll be back shortly with the drinks and then take your order."

"Thank you."

Maddie turned back to the view. People started crowding onto the beach and the band started to play, the music echoing through the glass. She was pissed at me and clearly I'd fucked up how I'd responded to her asking for more time, to giving what was happening between us a name.

But how to fix it without looking more like a dick?

"You're angry with me." I wanted us to go back to

how we were before our conversation. Forget that I'd practically told her I only wanted to fuck her for the summer and then she could be on her way. That I was now a commitment-phobe, which of course I wasn't, I was sure.

"I'm not angry, just disappointed I suppose. I would like us to see each other longer. You don't. I'll get over it, but I do think we've missed a trick here." She paused, pointing toward the beach party. "It looks like the party is getting started down there."

The drinks were delivered to our table, and I downed a glass of Dom, hoping to calm the nerves in my stomach. I disliked feeling unsettled, especially regarding Maddie. I could feel that she was pulling away, taking a step back, putting her guard up, and I only had myself to blame.

Dinner was not what I hoped. The silence was deafening between courses and no matter what I tried, nothing fixed the void I'd placed between us. We soon left the restaurant and headed down to the beach and the party that was in full swing by the time we arrived.

I ordered two beers from the bar, moving over to a standing table where I had seen Maddie last. I looked around, searching for her and spied her with her two friends Clara and Eve, who were already dancing.

I sipped my beer, thankful she was laughing again, even if others had brought her happiness and not me. Would she forgive me? Give me time to sort my head out?

A hand clapped me on the shoulder, and I turned to see Merrick, all smiles and carelessness, which he embodied most of the time. He picked up Maddie's beer and drank from it. I'm sure just because he knew it would piss me off.

"Put that down. It's not yours," I warned.

He chuckled, set it down and nodded toward Maddie. I ground my teeth, knowing the bastard was only interested in her because I was. He liked nothing more than chasing what was mine.

"She's a doll, isn't she? Pity you stopped my little date with her. I actually intended to invite her here, but it looks like you've weaseled your way back into her bed."

"I didn't weasel my way into anywhere, unlike you, who can't seem to find his own fucking bed to stay in."

"Why would I do that when the opposite is so much more enjoyable?" Merrick laughed at his own joke and the idea of making his nose bleed with my fist was almost impossible to deny. "I don't know what you're doing with her anyway. You always run back to Margot no matter who you play with while she's off making movies. We all know you'll not give her what she wants. You're destined to marry Margot Hathaway just as your and her parents ordained from birth. It would be a kindness if you let me have a go with Maddie. She may be even good enough to keep me from straying."

"You're a vile piece of shit." I sipped my beer, trying to ignore Merrick as Maddie and her friends started toward us.

Before I could request we leave, Merrick swooped Maddie into his arms and carried her out into the bustle of dancers.

"You might want to watch that one," Eve said, joining me at the table and gesturing to Merrick.

"Yeah." Didn't I know it.

CHAPTER
Twenty~Two

I FORCED myself into enjoying the night and forgetting what had happened between me and Henry. I danced under the twinkling Mediterranean starlit sky, enjoyed the warm sand beneath my feet, celebrating being young and carefree. I forced my troubling thoughts aside, of what could be, but wouldn't in the end.

Life wasn't always fair or easy. I knew that better than most.

Merrick clasped me about the waist and spun me about. I laughed, he was a nice guy and had spoken to Henry before pulling me out to dance. I could only assume he'd asked if it was okay beforehand.

"I was disappointed to receive your text the other day canceling our date. I didn't know you were so serious with anyone, least of all Henry Fairfax."

His question gave me pause. "Do you know

Henry?" I asked, shouting over the music so he could hear. I suppose Henry was often in the papers and news, probably a lot of people knew of him, but not necessarily knew the man himself.

"I do actually. We're old school friends and our families have known each other for years."

"Really?" I continued to dance, but my mind whirled. Henry certainly didn't seem overly friendly toward Merrick. Especially the first time I'd met Merrick at the beach, Henry had looked pissed. Maybe seeing me with Merrick, not merely some other random guy, had been what sparked his annoyance.

"We're no longer close." A mischievous light entered Merrick's eyes and before I could stop him, he wrenched me into his arms and kissed me.

Hard.

I stilled, unsure what was happening or how it had occurred. But no sooner were Merrick's lips on mine, he was jerked away.

I watched as Henry's fist slammed into Merrick's nose in two quick successions. Merrick reeled back and landed hard on his ass, people who had been dancing, going to him to help, others merely gawked like myself, trying to figure out what had happened.

"Leave her the hell alone, Merrick. Take that hit as a warning shot."

I looked between them, knowing that there was far more between these two guys than myself. They had a history, and not a good one.

"Henry?" I wasn't sure what I was going to ask, only that I needed to understand the situation.

The music started again, and Merrick climbed to his feet, brushing the sand off his shorts, an amused, cocky grin on his face. "Sorry, mate. I got carried away." Merrick winked at me, and I took a step back. I didn't like being played, nor being a ploy in a game that I was unaware of taking place.

Clara and Eve came to stand at my side as Henry joined me. "Can we talk?"

I nodded, swiped my bag off the table we'd procured upon arrival and started toward the dock.

Henry kept pace with me, quiet and self-reflective. "I know Merrick asked you out on a date and you agreed. Did you know that he would be here tonight?"

"What?" I rounded on him, annoyed he'd dare ask such a question. "No I didn't know he would be here, but what would it matter if I did? I don't control his every move. I met him at the beach, and he invited me for dinner. That doesn't mean I'd fuck him, even though I gave myself up to you on the first night."

He flinched as if I'd slapped him. "You have no idea who he is, do you?"

"What?" I asked. "No, I don't. Does it matter?"

"He's Merrick Dudley. Second-largest shareholder in the Dudley-Fairfax Hotels and my ex best friend for reasons I don't need to go into."

My mind raced. "So you're saying he's only shown interest in me because you did?" I tried not to let that thought deflate my self-esteem, but it did.

"It wouldn't be the first time he's done so, yes."

"Wow, what a way to make a girl feel worthy." I shook my head, walking toward the dock, needing to clear my head.

"You're worthy, but he's not. Don't fall for his false charms, Maddie."

"I wasn't going to. I didn't kiss him, he kissed me, remember?"

"Do you like him?"

"What?" I shook my head, staring at this handsome, jealous man who didn't want anything beyond summer and yet was butt hurt when someone else showed an interest. Or perhaps not. Maybe Merrick was using me to piss Henry off, who knew.

"Why do you care so much? We're only a summer fling. What does it matter when we're not going anywhere?"

Henry's eyes widened and I wanted to rip the words back. Shock ricocheted across his handsome features as if I'd slapped him. "I just don't want to rush anything, that's all. I have a lot on in my life, it's messy and stressful and not healthy for a new relationship at present. I don't want to fuck up what we have going, but I also can't be distracted with personal complications right now. I'd prefer to step back and part as friends if that's the case."

"So you don't want to see me at all now?" I clasped my stomach, hoping to halt the nerves that tumbled within me.

"I think it's best. I'll have your belongings returned to your Airbnb. I'm sorry, Maddie."

"I think you're scared. You know damn well what you want but just won't admit to it."

He ran a hand across his jaw, his eyes pained, but they couldn't hide the truth, not from me. I hadn't been imagining how well we got along these past days, how much he made me feel whenever we were alone or intimate. He could deny, make excuses all he liked, but that didn't mean I had to believe them.

"Why don't you admit that meeting me has put a spanner in your perfectly planned life. That you want me as much as I want you and it has you running scared. Merrick kissing me was just an excuse for you to run, but I in turn can't be with someone who won't fight for me. Who is ashamed of me in some way or thinks I'm not good enough."

He stood before me, tall and strong and stubbornly handsome in his refusal to say or do anything.

"I'm sorry."

I couldn't catch my breath and like a train wreck was unable to pull my attention from him as he returned to the tender, unaffected and uncaring.

Asshole!

"I may be not from your world, Henry. I may not know the dynamics that are at play between everyone in your life, but I know I want you and no one else. Can you say the same?"

Henry turned and looked at me. He was so unreadable, not giving away anything he was thinking. He didn't respond, just climbed on board the small boat, ordered Owen to go. The whir of the engine disappearing into the night and dark ocean beyond was as if he never was, and maybe in my delusions he wasn't.

CHAPTER
Twenty-Three

EVE AND CLARA JOINED ME, their shocked attention on the dock and the fact that Henry had up and left me here. How the hell had the night gone so wrong? I knew it was partly my fault. I had been disappointed that he'd been spooked I wanted to see him beyond summer. There was nothing wrong with wanting to prolong a relationship if that union was passionate, fun, and relaxed. But did I really want to give my time and effort toward a man who wouldn't give me a chance long term?

I think not. I had too much self-respect to beg him to forget what I said and continue as we were. It only hammered home that Henry needed to find a woman who suited his lifestyle and upbringing. That would never be me. I wasn't sophisticated enough. I could fake it for a while, but it was only a matter of time before his friends and family found out about my upbringing and sneered at me over it.

Not that it mattered now. It was so fucking over.

"Mads are you okay? What happened?" Clara asked.

"We broke up. If one can break up with someone that you're not really seeing." I tried to interject nonchalance into my tone, but failed miserably. "Let's go home. There are too many people watching."

Eve put her arm around my shoulder, comforting me. "I'm so sorry, babe. Maybe the time just isn't right?"

That was the understatement of the century. We started for the stairs and headed back up toward the town. Clara ordered an Uber to take us back to the Airbnb and my friends' silence spoke volumes. They didn't know what to say or do. I could relate. I didn't know what to say or how to react either.

We only had to wait a few minutes before our small car arrived, the cool evening breeze helping to keep my tears at bay. I took deep, calming breaths, not wanting to cry in front of my friends for a man I hardly knew. I made the mistake of looking out over the bay and spied Henry's yacht alight on the water beyond. He would be back on deck by now. Would he head back to his villa or order a helicopter to pick him up and take him to the airport to return to Rome?

Would I ever see him again?

"I didn't even know Henry knew Merrick. Apparently Merrick holds shares in the Dudley-Fairfax hotel chain but they're not friends. But I never agreed to the kiss with Merrick. One minute we were dancing and the next he was kissing me. I never wanted that."

"I know." Eve paused. "There must be bad blood between them that you're not aware of for Henry to be so incensed over a kiss that was clearly to get under his skin. Do you think that's why he broke up with you?"

"I think it's definitely played a part, but I don't think that's the only reason."

"What was the other reason?" Clara asked, waving as our Uber turned onto the beachfront road to pick us up. "I told Henry this afternoon that I would like to see him beyond summer. That perhaps we could try long distance."

Eve frowned. "Well, what the hell is wrong with that?"

"Nothing," I returned. "But it seemed to trouble Henry and then with Merrick kissing me, I suppose he didn't want to bother with the hassle of what happened. He clearly hates Merrick and maybe he thinks I'm untrustworthy? I have no idea and quite frankly, I don't want to waste my summer trying to figure the man out."

"Henry's jealous. The rage on his face when he saw Merrick kiss you… Wow, I've never seen a guy so furious. Maybe he's so pissed off that he found it easier to walk away than to fight for something that's making him feel more than he's used to. I think you've scared him and he's running from what you're making him feel."

"Well, I'm not going to chase him if he's not willing to in return. I don't know what conclusions he's jumping to or why he'd prefer to push me aside instead of talking to me, but I'm not playing those games."

The Uber pulled up beside us and Clara confirmed the details before we jumped in.

"I think I should return to New York. I have some work I could get ahead on before I start my internship."

"No, you can't leave. I won't let you be run off by some rich, European asshole."

I smiled, but I didn't feel like making light of the situation just yet. How had everything gone so wrong when our two days together had been so wonderful?

"I'll think about staying, but I don't know. The summer isn't turning out like I hoped it would." I'd come to the Mediterranean to enjoy the sun, the hot climate and fresh air. Maybe a summer fling or two, but running into Henry had thrown my life into chaos.

A lovely, exciting kind of madness, but still chaos.

We made it back to the Airbnb and after wishing my friends goodnight I went to bed. I stared at the ceiling from my bed, watched the fan go around and around, giving little relief in the hot room. Sleep eluded me.

Morning came all too soon and instead of moping around the accommodation on my final day off, I grabbed my beach bag, umbrella, and towel and headed for the swimming beach up the road. Several families were already there, enjoying the morning water and beating the heat. I laid down my towel and set up my umbrella away from everyone, wanting peace and quiet.

I applied sun cream and laid on my stomach, pulled

out my much-neglected Kindle and settled in to read, forcing my mind from wandering to the man who occupied far too much of my thoughts already.

But it was no use. After reading the same page three times I put it aside and stared out over the beach. I had a choice to make. Stay in Sorrento or go home. Fight or flee. Not that I was staying to fight for Henry, but I was fighting to enjoy my vacation.

I reached into my bag for my phone. A little downtime on TikTok always perked up my mood, but the 1,062 notifications on my Instagram caught my attention. The notification jumped by ten. Okay, make that 1072.

WTF!

I opened the app and scrambled to sit up. I saw series of images of Henry and Merrick during their altercation on the beach. Of us arguing on the dock and then us leaving separately. I scrolled, unable to pull my eyes away from the captions, the laughing emojis, the slurs against me, the insinuations, and tags. So many tags.

Fuuuucccccckkkk.

I read the few articles that were already up on the paparazzi sites. All of them incorrect and assuming shit that hadn't happened. Articles of who I was and what I was doing in Sorrento. How I had come to know Henry.

I scoffed at that article. What they wouldn't give to know he was a one-night stand from two years ago.

"Shit." They had tagged the café I worked at in

Sorrento and had reached out to where I would intern next year in New York. Did Henry know of these articles? Were his socials blowing up as well?

A new notification popped up and I opened it. It was a picture of me now, sitting on the beach, under my umbrella, in my bathing suit staring at my phone in horror.

I fought to school my features and put my phone away, not wanting to give anyone who was lurking on the beach any more ammunition than they already had. I packed up my gear, needing to get out of here before anything else was published of me.

How the hell would I fix this mess? Maybe I should message Henry and ask him to sort this all out. He'd been the one to punch Merrick, after all, and caught everyone's attention while doing so.

I quickly grabbed my stuff, wrapped my sarong about my waist and started toward the stairs leading up to the car park. I had to pass the photographer who shamefully continued taking photos, as if invading people's private spaces was irrelevant to a good shot. I bit my tongue, stopping myself from calling him a fucking jerk-off, but didn't.

Instead, I ignored him and hoped he'd lose interest. I could hear the camera shutter continue to go off as I headed up the stairs. The thought of my ass ending up on some social media site was mortifying and I hurried my steps, wanting out of this situation.

I got to the parking lot and waited at the bus stop.

The photographer joined me and snapped another ten images. Jesus, the guy was relentless.

"A bit of a downgrade from the mega yacht you were on yesterday. Do you have any comment as to your relationship with Mr. Henry Fairfax of the Dudley-Fairfax Hotels? Or that of his shareholder Mr. Merrick Dudley?"

I ignored him and looked up the road, praying the bus would be here soon.

"Are you still in a relationship with the billionaire playboy? The actions of last night would state that you are not. A shame, for a woman of your ilk—a waitress aren't you—could use a man who has money to burn."

I shouldn't have, but I looked at him at that question. Was that all these men thought? That women only dated rich guys because they had money? I didn't know who Henry was when I first met him, and the attraction was there long before I found out.

Not that I'd tell this leach anything, but still, his words were insulting.

I spied him holding his cell phone as if he was filming me. "Are you livestreaming these questions?"

Never in my life had I ever been treated with such disrespect. What was wrong with people that I of all individuals in the world would be news to them? Did Henry have to put up with kind of treatment all the time? Any wonder people like him protected themselves as much as they did.

"Of course. Henry Fairfax is one of the world's most

eligible bachelors. Everyone wants to know what's happening in his private life and it's not often his ex gives us such easy access to them." He paused. "Are you his ex? Can you confirm or deny the statement?"

The bus pulled up at the stop and I couldn't get on the vehicle quickly enough. The bus driver's gaze moved to the photographer, noted him filming me and the camera about his neck and stood. "Not you," he said. "Off."

The photographer stumbled back off the bus, almost falling on his ass. "Hey, I have a right to public transport just like everyone else."

"You can grab the next bus. You're not following a woman while filming." The bus driver closed the door and thankfully we moved off and the vile piece of flesh was left behind.

"Thank you, sir," I said, settling back in the seat, grateful that there were at least some kind people left in the world.

"You're welcome, love."

The bus dropped me not far from our Airbnb. My morning swim was ruined, and now I didn't know if I could ever go to the beach again. What did the café think? I hope they weren't being harassed also. As for my internship in New York. Jesus, what if they changed their mind about taking me on? My future could be put in jeopardy over this.

Maybe I should move to a different town along the coast and finish my summer alone. Where no one knew me. Where I couldn't cause any more trouble for anyone.

Or maybe I should do what I'd been debating since last night.

Go home.

CHAPTER
Twenty~Four

RELUCTANTLY I RETURNED to Sorrento a fortnight later. I told myself my return to my family's ancestral town was because of my mother's annual fundraising event at the hotel, held yearly for underprivileged children in third world locations, but it wasn't. I'd be lying if I hadn't looked for Maddie when my vehicle had driven through the town heading for the villa. I'd even debated grabbing a coffee at her café, if only to check in, see if she was okay after the shitstorm my fisticuffs on the beach with Merrick had caused.

For two weeks I'd gone about my business on automaton, working off caffeine and aggravation. Not at Maddie or even Merrick, but at myself for walking away, leaving her on the dock like the bastard I was. How had I left her there, fodder for the wolves who had over the past weeks certainly had their fill of her character? They had been relentless in chasing Maddie all over Sorrento, even going so far as to try to ask questions when she'd been at work.

I checked my phone, noted no new messages from her, but what did I expect? I would turn back the clock if I could, change how I'd reacted to Merrick and escorted her back onto the yacht as I should have. The headlines now read that I'd parted from Maddie after a heated and quick affair. The articles placed Margot in a far better light than Maddie, saying I'd run back to her after losing my way in the American's arms.

Nothing could be further from the truth.

Fuck.

And now tonight I had to attend the charity gala and pretend nothing was awry, that everything was as it should be. All fucking bullshit.

I tightened my tie and checked over my suit one last time in the mirror, before heading downstairs to catch the limousine with my mother, who was ready and waiting in the foyer. Thankfully my mother hadn't said a word regarding the scandalous articles in the papers of late, but she was aware of them and curious as to who the Madeline Webb was who had captured my attention. Not that she would question my personal life. She was too well-bred for that.

We rode down to Sorrento with idle talk of the company and the opening of the Capri hotel in the coming months. The limo pulled up before our hotel, red carpet lined our way indoors and I stepped out, reaching back into the car to assist my mother to join me.

We smiled at the photographers. I ignored their questions regarding Maddie and Margot and the love triangle that had ensued this summer. If only they knew my relationship with Margot had been over for months and that my remaining with her was to save face while she promoted her latest movie. Her attempt at hurting Maddie had been spiteful and unnecessary since we were over.

"Well, I think we need to have a chat tomorrow regarding this Madeline woman everyone's talking of," my mother suggested, breaching our agreement that my personal life was off limits and not for discussion. "It seems that's all everyone is interested in and not our charity this evening."

I could hear the annoyance in my mother's tone, and I had to agree. Tonight was for a good benefit, and it was disappointing that the paparazzi were only inter-ested in my love life. "There is nothing to speak about. I was seeing a woman in Sorrento and now I'm not. That's all they need to know, or anyone else for that matter."

"I can see by your taut jawline that I've hit a nerve. You sure this little scandalous summer romance is over? We have work to do this evening and I don't need you distracted."

I took a deep breath, ignoring my mother's chastise-ment and escorted her into the ballroom and our table where she was soon distracted by her many rich friends and her schmoozing, which she hoped would end with a sizable donation.

I patted my pocket, checking for the umpteenth time I had my annual speech that I hoped would garner sizable donations to our not-for-profit charity.

A waitress carrying a tray of champagne circled our table. I took a glass, thanking her before doing the dutiful rounds as host. I spoke to as many people as I could, listened to their gripes, all trivial to the troubles other people faced in the world. Their boasting of property purchases and vehicles, horses, and private jets, and jested that I hoped they had enough money left for this evening's charity auction.

The conversations left me feeling like a fraud. Not only because I too partook in such a lifestyle, but because I didn't want to be here boasting about it. Did not want to pretend to enjoy myself in these people's company.

I only wanted the company of one and I had fucked that royally up.

The lights flickered, indicating for everyone to take their seats. I made my way up onto the stage, pulling out my speech and setting it before me. "Thank you everyone for attending this evening. It's one of the highlights of the Dudley-Fairfax families that we're able to host and fundraise for Fairfax Homeless Children's charity for the twenty-fifth year."

Applause sounded and I smiled, continuing to play

the part of host in this superficial world. I stared at the speech and rallied to continue with the false encomiums that always made these types of people think they were an asset to the wider population instead of one most people loathed.

I concluded my speech as I always did, thanking everyone for attending and to remember that their charity would change the world. I almost choked on my own lie. Although we did help many children, there was always more that could be done. I stepped off the stage, and made my way back to my table.

The first course of dinner was served by the time I took my seat and servers started pouring out of the kitchens, all of them assigned to different tables. I patiently waited, placed my napkin on my lap and discreetly watched, making sure everything ran smoothly.

The sight of someone familiar made me take a second look and my blood ran cold. The sight of Maddie running back and forth from the kitchen to the tables serving was not what I expected. Nor was the reaction that rioted inside of me seeing her serve people who ignored her as if she did not exist. The bastards weren't good enough to wipe her boots, how dare they not even thank her when she placed down their meals?

Why the fuck was she working?

Here?

Like a trainwreck, I couldn't pull my gaze from her. She shouldn't be here. No one, not even me, deserved to even look at her pretty face and sweet nature. She was too good for them all, myself included.

How had I not known she was on the list of servers this evening?

Without thinking I stood and started for the kitchens. I went into the little alcove where the servers lined up taking up their plates before moving into the ballroom. Maddie stood in line with everyone, looking determined to get through the night, her features unreadable.

"May I have a word?" I said, pulling her from the line.

I felt the eyes of the other servers watching us, but ignored them. They knew who I was and wouldn't argue with the boss if he wanted to speak to one of the waitresses.

Maddie's eyes widened in shock before she nodded and followed me into the ballroom. I walked us to the back of the room, wanting privacy and some answers. But in truth, I just wanted to speak to her. Hear her voice.

"What are you doing working here?" The words came out harsher than I wanted, but the sight of her as a maid, serving my ilk didn't sit right with me. She wasn't a waitress, she was Maddie, not some fucking servant for the rich.

"Good evening, Mr. Fairfax. I'm a waitress here this evening. Is there a problem with my service?"

I drank in the sight of her. Her long, brown hair was tied back into a bun at the base of her neck. She had little makeup on, highlighting her natural beauty, which overshadowed most of the diamond-encrusted cronies about us.

Her formal response made my eye twitch. "Yes there is something fucking wrong," I whispered. "You shouldn't be working here."

"I have to work, Henry," she said, slipping out of formalities. A good thing because I wasn't sure I could survive her talking to me like she didn't know me intimately as she did. "This is a working vacation for me, remember?"

"Where the hell are Eve and Clara? They need to come and pick you up straightaway."

"They can't. They're in Capri for the week."

I shook my head, growing more furious by the second. "Well, why the hell aren't you with them?"

She paused, and her eyes narrowed on me. "Because I wouldn't let them pay for yet another ticket for me. I do have a little pride you know."

Her words caught me off guard and I looked around, glad no one was watching our conversation. "You have a job at the café."

"I *did* have a job there. I lost it after…well after what happened between us on the dock. The paparazzi wouldn't leave me or the customers alone and I was let go. I have to work to stay here for the summer, but I can leave if it's a problem."

"You were fired from the café?" I would slay Romero by the end of tomorrow if this were true. I fisted my hands at my sides, fighting the urge to pull

Maddie into my arms and hold her, promise that I'd make everything right after fucking everything up for her summer.

"If you're going to let me continue, I need to get back to work, Henry."

I nodded and Maddie left me looking after her. She appeared so different to the woman who had been on my yacht, carefree and enjoying her summer. Now she looked broken, a little downtrodden by her financial woes. How bad had the press been here for her, really? Outside earlier they had certainly been in a frenzy that I was back in Sorrento and may run into Maddie. I should have checked, put in place some security to keep her from harm after I'd certainly caused it.

I returned to my seat, ignored my mother who watched me with consideration I didn't want to debate. But something told me she had caught my conversation with Maddie and her interest was piqued.

"I hope that waitress isn't causing trouble," she whispered, ensuring none of her friends heard our conversation.

"That was Madeline Webb, the woman I'd been seeing. I was surprised to see her here, that is all." I ground my teeth, picked up my wine and downed it, still not comfortable with that fact.

My mother's eyes flew wide. "She's a waitress? Remember, my dear, we don't date the help, Henry."

I gave my mother a warning glance. Jesus, of all people I didn't need to get involved in my personal life was my mother. "She's not the help, but even if she were and I wanted to date her, not even your overstim-ulated opinions of yourself or your rich friends would stop me."

My mother glared and I matched her energy. She turned to her table guest and thankfully left me alone. I spied Maddie bringing out a jug of water and refilling glasses in-between courses. Even in her black pants and standard white shirt uniform she was the prettiest woman here. How the hell would I keep away from her? Why were we not giving us another chance? I needed her to forgive me, give me a second chance.

"Sorry I'm late."

I stilled at the sound of Margot's obnoxious voice before she sat beside me, reaching to clasp my mother's hand.

"Margot dear, I'm so pleased you came. Your contri-bution is most welcome."

"Oh, anything for the children," Margot said, her words as fabricated as her nose.

Instinctively I looked across the room and met Maddie's eyes. She'd stopped pouring water, was watching, judging…

The hurt in her dark-blue eyes tore me in two.

"Still pining for the American. Do get a grip, Henry. You'll embarrass the family." Margot's words sliced open the last of my patience and left it spilling out of me.

"No one wants you here, Margot. You should leave before you embarrass yourself."

She laughed, but I could see my words stung.

"Do be a sport and get your favorite waitress to bring me a glass of champagne. I'm parched."

"How about you get one yourself?" I stood, moving toward the kitchens where Maddie had fled, determined to make my wrong right before I couldn't, and it was too late.

CHAPTER
Twenty~Five

I **FLED** to the staff room and changed out of my uniform. I didn't need the job so bad that I would stay and suffer what was playing out before me. To see Henry and Margot together again, the distaste in his mother's eyes directed at me, was all I needed to know that there was definitely no future with Henry.

I slipped on my floral dress and flip-flops and tossed my bag over my shoulder, needing away from here now.

"Maddie, where are you going?" I turned and faced my young boss for the night, the annoyance on his face just another one to join the list of people who disliked me here.

"I'm quitting. You have enough staff to work the dinner."

"You'll not get paid for the last hour of work."

"I don't care." I pushed the door open that led to the side of the hotel and climbed down several fire escape stairs and onto the street. It was only a short walk to the Airbnb, and I couldn't get home soon enough. I stupidly talked myself into believing Henry wouldn't be here this evening, even with his family on every advertisement around Sorrento.

I stood in the doorway of my empty Sorrento accommodations, Clara and Eve gone for the week, their exuberant and friendly smiles not here to greet me, make me feel better. What to do? Stay? Or join them in Capri, put the ferry fare on my credit card and fuck the repayment that I couldn't afford.

But the possibility of running into Henry was all the incentive needed to make the decision.

I slammed the door and went to my room, throwing clothes into a small backpack. I grabbed my purse and passport and was back out the door before I could talk myself out of it.

Capri it was.

———

After a hasty race to the Sorrento port I arrived in Capri in the early hours of the next morning. I scored a room at the same hotel that Clara and Eve were staying at, even though I was yet to tell them I would join them.

I'm in Capri. Let's meet up later.

Yes, best news! We're in room 402, fourth floor. Just getting ready to go to the beach for the day. Come with.

I lobbed my backpack on the small desk and slumped on the bed. My eyes itched after the little amount of sleep I'd gained last night and a day at the beach just didn't feel like the thing right now.

Will sleep first. But up for catching up tonight. Any plans?

Damn, we'll miss you. 🙁 But we're clubbing tonight. What room are you. We'll pick you up at eight and we'll go together. Let's have some fun, girl!!

Sounds great. See you then.

I showered and changed into my pyjamas. Upped the central air to cold and slumped on the bed, climbing under the covers. The cool room was a nice change to the Airbnb flat, which could often get a little hot and humid with only fans.

I lay there, stared at the ceiling and thought about what I'd done in the past twelve hours. The past few weeks for that matter. I'd allowed myself to grow feelings for a guy I shouldn't have. We were so different, our lives and upbringing were so vast that I should have known it was a mistake to want him as I had. I was here in the Med for a vacation, for fun, to party and have a great time with my friends. I was probably being a huge drag for them.

A tear slipped down my cheek and I swiped it angrily away. Crying over Henry Fairfax. What the fuck was wrong with me?

At some point I fell asleep and woke up several hours later, feeling much better and more clear thinking. I sat up and clutched my knees in my arms. I would enjoy tonight, party hard, and then tomorrow tell Clara and Eve that I was going home to New York. With no job or prospect of one, not after all the paparazzi harassment, returning to the US seemed the best way to remove myself from this circus. I needed to make up to my work in the states anyway, especially after the press had reached out to them for comment on my love life here in Europe.

How the fuck had everything gone so wrong and twisted?

I showered, washed my hair, and dressed in soft, white linen full-length pants and a black singlet top and flat shoes, great for dancing. Sore feet after a night out was the worst, and I didn't need to feel any more wretched than I already did.

I spied Clara and Eve in the lobby and laughed when they both squealed in excitement and pulled me into a group hug.

"You're here. Are you ready to party, girls!" Eve shouted, not caring how loud she was in the hotel.

Clara raised her arm and squealed in response. "We sure are! Let's go!!"

The taxi ride was quick, and I forced myself not to allow myself to think too much. Just enjoy where I was, who I was with and that I was alive. All great things that so many people took for granted.

The line up to the club was long and it took us two hours before we were allowed in.

"My feet will be sore before we even start dancing," Clara complained as we entered. We walked along a dark corridor with blue floor lights lighting our way. The passage opened onto the ground floor. I glanced up, in awe of the three floors above us that were full of revelers, flashing lights, and people enjoying life.

I let the music flow over me, ordered a wine from the bar and moved out onto the dancefloor with my girls. We danced, laughed, twirled and enjoyed ourselves far more than we had in ages. Being away from Sorrento was just what we needed.

"I'm so sorry, guys for being down lately," I yelled over the music.

"Oh no, we understand, babes. You have nothing to be sorry for," Eve said. Clara nodding in agreement.

The tone of the dance changed to a slow, seductive melody, and we started toward the bar to get another drink. Arms wrapped about my waist and pulled me against a very masculine body. I turned, open to anything tonight. Needing to escape my own torturous mind.

A man, tall and muscular, his skin kissed by the sun, his dark-brown eyes and long eye lashes were just what the doctor ordered for my broken heart. I gave myself up to allowing him to try to seduce me. I wrapped my arms about his neck and moved with him, brushed against him, teased him…

"I've been watching you. You're not from here are you?" he asked, his Spanish accent thick but cultured.

"No, I'm from New York. You?" I asked, moving with the dance beats.

"Barcelona."

"A beautiful city."

"It is." His grin was mischievous, and I threw myself into the dance and the possibility of losing myself in this guy's arms for a dance or two. His hands moved over me, turning me with the music. I laughed for the first time in weeks.

Again the melody of the dance changed to fast pace and Clara and Eve joined us, shots in hands. We all drank them down, the room flashing with lights and laughter. The Spanish god moved over to me, clasped my face and kissed me, a brush of lips that I didn't want to end. I wanted him to fix my heart, make me forget the man who haunted my mind, but he couldn't. I smiled, pushed him playfully away, wagging my finger at him, warning him to behave.

He smiled, took the hint and just enjoyed his time with us. Others joined us and we ended back at the bar, doing more shots and talking of our travels and where we were all from.

"What brings you from New York all the way here?"

"A working vacation for me," I explained, but I'm going home the day after tomorrow."

"You are not!" Eve protested, having been listening.

"I am," I replied. "I need to sort out where I'm going to work this year, and I don't want to be a drag."

"You are not a drag," Clara joined me, and turned my stool so I faced her. "You're not going anywhere, Mads. You're staying with us and that's it, end of story."

"Where are you having your vacation?" the Spanish god asked.

"We're staying in Sorrento."

"Nice place. A shame you're not staying here so I could try and convince you to prolong your vacation."

I laughed off his comment but could tell that he meant every word. At one time or another I would have allowed him to try, been up for whatever fun he could give me, but not now.

Fuck, I was a drag and all because of my stupid feelings toward a man who couldn't commit or give me a chance, thought myself too low for his elevated blood.

CHAPTER
Twenty-Six

WE STUMBLED out of the club just as dawn kissed the sky good morning. "Holy shit, it's the morning." I pointed toward the light like a drunk idiot who didn't think everyone could see what I was.

Eve gasped and pointed too, far more smashed than I was, not that the guy holding her upright cared. He was smitten already and had only met her two hours before.

My Spanish god grabbed my hands and held them, facing me as we waited for an Uber. "So I suppose this is goodbye for us. It was nice knowing you, Maddie from New York."

"It was nice knowing you for the last few hours too, Barcelona." A nickname I had made up for him after I forgot what he had said his real name was. "Thanks for giving me a great night. I needed it far more than you know."

"Anything to make a lady pleased."

I leaned up and kissed his cheek before hugging him. "Bye, Barcelona." The Uber pulled up and Clara, Eve, and her guy and I jumped in. I waved goodbye to my god, and sat back in the car, relief pouring through me and a weight lifting from my shoulders. I so needed to get away from Sorrento and what happened there. Tonight was fun and proved to me that I could enjoy myself, maybe even flirt and who knew what... Maybe sleep with another man without always thinking of Henry Fairfax.

The Uber pulled up in the valet area of the hotel and we stumbled out. My foot got caught between Eve and her lover's when they started to get too hot and heavy in the car and I stumbled out onto the driveway, landing on my ass.

I lay there a moment, Clara coming over me, laughing and reaching for my hand. "Here, let me help you up, you drunk fool."

I reached for my friend's hand, and she helped me stand. We wobbled our ways into the hotel foyer. This early in the morning, only the hotel staff was there to see our intoxicated laughing messes.

All but one.

Standing in the same suit he wore to the fundraising dinner in Sorrento was Henry. He looked as sleep deprived and shambolic as we did after a night of clubbing.

"Holy shit," I heard Eve mumble, her guy friend asking what was wrong.

I glanced over at my friends, silently asking them to

leave. They took the hint, moving toward the lifts and leaving me with Henry. I walked up to him, lifted my chin, and attempted to stare him down. "What are you doing here?"

"I thought you'd left Europe. It took me fucking hours to find out where you went after the fundraiser."

I shrugged and started toward the lifts. "It was best that I leave that event. I was making everyone uncomfortable, me especially. I left and flew here to party with my friends. Not that I owe you an explanation. My life is my own."

"You don't think I know that?" His tone was low, tortured and I fought not to react to the longing in his words.

The lift door opened, and we stepped inside. I should have told him to get out and go home. That we were ovvveeerrr, but I didn't. Stupid idiot that I was. An occupational hazard I suffered from whenever I was around Henry.

"Why are you here, Henry?" The door to the lift closed and started to move up to the third floor that I was on. He didn't answer, merely stared at me through the reflective lift doors before they opened again.

We moved into the hallway, and I pulled out my room key from my bra, opening the door. The room was very much not to his standard, but it was to mine. I placed the key onto the desk and kicked off my shoes. I slumped onto one of the lounge chairs placed near a window, which overlooked an interior courtyard.

"Well, are you going to answer why you followed

me here? We're not together, nor do either of us want us to be." The lie slipped off my tongue, but I couldn't regret it. He flinched at my words, but I couldn't allow myself to care. He'd pushed me away. Left me for dead in front of all of Sorrento after being kissed at no fault of my own. I wanted to rail at him, throw angry, hurtful words at his handsome face, but I couldn't let him get under my skin any more than he already was.

"I can't seem to stay away from you. The last few weeks have been the worst I can remember. I think of nothing but you, what you're doing, who you're with. I torture myself with the idea of you with anyone who isn't me."

"Well, good thing you weren't at the club tonight because there was a particularly hot Spanish guy that gave me a good time."

Henry's gaze narrowed and he took a menacing step toward me. "You fucked someone?"

I shivered and crossed my arms. "I should've." I glared at him as he digested my words. But I wasn't done with him, or what had been festering in my mind these past two days. "How was your dinner with Margot?"

"I never invited Margot. My mother did and placed her at our table without my knowledge. My family is complicated and wants things that will no longer take place. No matter how much they manipulate situations to get their way."

He hadn't invited her. Was that true? Even if it was, that didn't mean there was any future for us. In the end he wouldn't disappoint his family, the people he loved. "You should go home. There is nothing here for you anymore."

I pushed up from my chair and went into the bathroom, searching for my pyjamas. My eyes itched from lack of sleep and the room sporadically spun. I slipped off my pants and singlet top and pulled on my pyjamas. The bed called my name, and I ignored Henry, who stood silently watching me.

"You're going to ignore me and go to sleep, is that it?" He watched me, the shock at my slight a satisfying sight.

"You know where the door is. Use it." He debated my words for a heartbeat or two. My stomach twisted at the thought of him leaving, even though I'd baited him to do so. He took a step toward the door, calling my bluff, but stopped.

"You don't mean that. I can see it in your eyes you don't."

"You don't know what I want."

"I know what I want."

I looked at him and fought not to hope for things that hadn't worked out so far. We were too opposite, too different. He was rich. I was certainly poor. He had breeding, a good family. Mine abandoned me and were dead due to the drugs that ruled their lives.

"And what is that, Henry? Because you abandoning me on the dock was a pretty clear indication of what you didn't want. So please, enlighten me."

He stood beside the bed, looming over me. Like a

moth to a flame I took in his every nuance. His ruffled suit and bedraggled hair, the five o'clock shadow on his chiseled jaw. Desire and heat sliced over my skin. Thoughts of what I wanted with him, mad or not, tumbled through my mind.

Now it was his turn to explain himself.

CHAPTER
Twenty~Seven

"COME AWAY with me for a few weeks and let's start again. There have been so many distractions in Sorrento, with your work and mine interrupting us all the time. I want to take us both away from it all." I sat on the bed and caught Maddie's eyes, wanted her to know that I meant every word. Like a man starved, I was desperate to make her hear me, see sense, forgive, and give me a second chance. Fix my fuckup. "Say you'll come with me, please."

"What about Margot? What will your family say? It's clear from the charity dinner the other evening your mother along with your sister don't want me in your life."

I cringed, knowing that was true. But I also didn't care what they thought or wanted. I wanted Maddie, to pull the woman before me into my arms, kiss her sweet, pouty lips and make everything as it was. I missed her and wanted her back.

So goddamn much.

"I choose you, I don't let others choose for me. And no matter what my mother believes, what was between Margot and myself is over. Long over. Don't fall for what others portray as true."

She studied me. What was she thinking? Did she believe me or was she merely trying to find the words to end it for good?

"I want more than a summer fling. I want you beyond this season. Losing you these past weeks have forced me to look at what I really want in my life and without you in it, well…it's been empty, unexciting, boring, lonely…" I could have said more, but didn't want to look as desperate as she made me feel. I was so different around her, and I liked that I was. She made me closer to how I once was, carefree, willing to enjoy the moment, take time for myself and not always put my family first or work.

"As much as I want you, have missed you, I don't fit into your world, Henry. I grew up so very different to you. There are things in my past…"

"You do fit into my world. I want you in my life. If you're not beside me then I don't want the life I've had up to this moment."

Maddie sighed, the sound unconvinced and fear ran through me that I had lost her for good. That there was no coming back from what happened between us.

"Don't say that."

"But it's true. All of what I said. I want you back and if that means I'll have to grovel at your door for weeks until you believe my apology then I will." I reached for her hands, needing to feel her, hold her in any small way I could.

Maddie threw me a small smile, the first in weeks, and relief poured through me.

"I want to take you to London, my favorite city in the world. I want it to be just us. No distractions, just time to be together where we can see if what's happening between us is what I hope it is." I took a chance and leaned in to kiss her. Thank heavens she didn't pull away. If she had I wasn't sure I'd survive the rejection. Her lips yielded and I clasped her nape, deepening the kiss. She tasted of beer and spirits and was as addictive as I remembered.

"Are you sure this is what you want?"

"My jet's on standby at my private airport here, all you have to do is pack your suitcase and come with me." I caught sight of her backpack and grinned. "Or your backpack in this case."

Maddie chuckled and I basked in the sound of her happiness. Never with anyone had I fought so hard to win them back. I was a lost cause when it came to her. All Maddie needed to do is say jump and I'd ask how high.

"I was in a rush, and I was only going to Capri a couple of days. I didn't think I needed much."

"So you shouldn't take long to pack?" I stood, waited for her to decide. Would she give me another chance? Nerves twisted in my gut as she thought over the proposition.

Maddie threw off the blankets and scooped up her bag, going into the bathroom. I heard the shower run. I wanted to go in there, join her in the shower and satisfy my craving for her that was long overdue, but decided against it. She needed time to think, to clear her head, and if she decided yes, there would be plenty of time for that. I didn't want to push my luck too soon before she gave me an answer.

I stood before the window, looking out over the small courtyard. No one sat in the paved space bar one fellow guest who was asleep on a wooden bench, one arm laying across his eyes to shield his face from the rising sun.

"Okay, fine, I'll give you another chance, but if this doesn't work and something else comes between us, that's it, Henry. We need to admit that this isn't going to work, and we aren't compatible. Do you agree to those terms?"

"I agree." Not that I had any intention or would allow such an outcome. Time away in London, where no one would meddle or cause trouble was just what was needed. I wanted her to myself, to show her how it could be if only we gave it another go. I wouldn't fuck it up again.

Maddie slipped on her black flats she wore the night before, denim three-quarter slacks and a white T-shirt. She appeared smart but casual as she hoisted her backpack over her shoulder. She picked up her phone and quickly typed up a message. I assumed to her friends to let them know where she was going. "Right then, let's go."

I chuckled, reaching for her hand, and pulling her toward the door. "I'm ready if you are." Silence fell between us as we rode the elevator down to the foyer. Maddie dropped the key off at the desk and I escorted her to my car, which waited in the valet area.

My driver opened the door, and I assisted Maddie in before I slid in next to her. The drive to the airport didn't take long and we soon pulled up beside my jet for our flight to London.

"Is this your plane?" Maddie leaned across my lap and gaped, taking in the sleek, modern design of the jet. "I mean, when you said you had your jet waiting for you, I kind of thought you were joking, and we'd be flying commercial."

"I rarely fly commercial."

I climbed out, reached for Maddie's hand and helped her from the car. "I travel quite a lot around Europe with all the hotels. It's necessary that I'm not waiting in airports for flights to depart on time." I took a chance and pulled her against me. She fit me like a glove. I wanted to kiss her, taste her sweetness. "Do you have your passport on hand?"

"I do." She reached into her backpack and handed it to me.

I handed the passport to the airport official waiting at the jet's steps.

"Good morning, Mr. Fairfax. You're off to London today?"

"We are," I answered, biding my time until all the travel documents were approved and sorted. The airport official handed me back the passports and signed off some paperwork. "Have a safe flight."

"Thank you." I led Maddie up the stairs and greeted the pilot and first officer, both good friends of mine, and Suzanna, our attendant who had been working for the Dudley-Fairfax chain for as long as I could remember.

"Good morning, Mr. Fairfax. Miss Webb. Please take a seat and I'll serve you breakfast as soon as we're at cruising altitude."

"Thank you, Suzanna."

"Umm. Wow." Maddie's mumble made me smile as I led her down the aisle to where two seats faced each other with a small table between us. She sat, and pulled her seatbelt over her shoulder and buckled in. "I've never been on a private jet before. This is pretty amazing, Henry."

I looked about, trying to place myself in her shoes. She'd had such a different upbringing to mine, or so she said, so flying privately would be a new experience. "I want to spoil you, make it up to you after acting like a dick. I'm sorry, Maddie."

She shook her head, her blue eyes piercing my soul. I hated that I hurt her, and for no good reason. Being pissed at Merrick wasn't a good enough reason to do what I did.

"It was my fault too. But I can't help but wonder if I'm honest with you again, tell you how you make me feel and my hope for us, will you flee again? You know I can't help how I feel about you."

"I'm not going to run this time." I reached for her hand. She took pity on me and placed hers in mine. "Seeing Merrick kiss you…well, I wanted to kill the bastard for daring to try something like that in front of me. When you told me you'd like to continue seeing me past summer, a part of me panicked. I'll admit it, what I did was a coward's move. But Maddie," I said, meeting her eyes. "You make me crazy. Even now, I feel like you're too far away. I've never felt like that with anyone before."

"I'm right here, Henry, and I'm not going anywhere. Not now."

CHAPTER
Twenty~Eight

THE JET TAXIED onto the runway. To say I was excited was an understatement. A private jet! I checked my phone was on flight mode and smiled when Henry came and sat on the spare seat next to me.

Our backs were to the front of the plane, giving us privacy. It had been weeks since I'd seen him, touched and been intimate. I missed him, more than I would admit this early into our relationship, but after our little chat, perhaps there was a chance for a future together.

I leaned into him, and he turned his handsome face, our lips but a breath apart. I could almost taste the longing that radiated from him. He intoxicated my soul, made me want things, want to do things to him I'd never done before. In a way, he made me lose myself in his eyes, but in a good way, not bad.

Not bad at all.

I lay my hand on his chest, enjoying the feel of his perfect abdomen beneath his soft shirt. His chest rose and fell beneath my fingers, the hardened muscles all mine to enjoy. His eyes darkened with need. "I missed you."

I touched his belt buckle, slipping my hand lower and over the growing bulge in his pants. "Hmm, I missed you too."

He shifted on his seat. "What are you doing, Maddie?" His whispered words called to a mischievous part of me I only wanted to explore with him.

"Nothing." I ran my finger along his waistband. He swallowed, the sound almost audible before touching lower. "So hard, Henry. You have missed me?"

He sucked in a startled breath and cleared his throat. "You know I fucking have."

I shivered at the deep, gravely tone of his voice. Damn, the man was hot. I wanted to drive him wild. I wanted him, here and now. I pressed my legs together, trying to soothe the ache that pulsated between my thighs.

Not satisfied with touching him through material, I slowly unzipped his pants and touched him. Stroked his hard, thick cock and watched, transfixed, into his eyes.

"No boxers? You're a naughty boy."

He smirked and raised one knowing brow. "Are you going to be a naughty girl?"

Oh yes, I was. I clasped his cock with renewed vigor and stroked him with unapologetic verve. He swore under his breath, and I kissed his neck, biting the lobe of his ear, reveling in his cologne.

"I'm going to make you almost come."

"Almost? Why not the culmination?" He pressed into my hand, working himself as well as me.

"Call it delayed gratification."

He growled, clasped my face, and kissed me.

Hard.

His tongue swept against mine, making me drunk on his touch. I continued to work him with my hand, but it wasn't enough. I wanted to drive him as crazy as he drove me. These past weeks had been torture not having him in my bed, waking up beside him and enjoying endless happy days in his presence.

I pulled from the kiss and, checking the whereabouts of the flight attendant, bent over his lap. I took him into my mouth, teasing the tip of his cock, running my tongue over the engorged head before taking him deep. He swore, his fingers ran into my hair, fisting it as I blew him. His breathing hitched, his body tensed and I knew he was close.

I ran my tongue along the underside of his cock, following the engorged vein from base to tip and met his eyes. He looked like a wild beast above me, barely holding on to his control and I wanted to snap it. Break it so badly that it could never be fixed.

"Fuck...Maddie."

"You like it?" I took him deep again and he pumped into my mouth like a man starved. I rolled his balls in my hand, swallowing the pre-come that released just as the engines roared and propelled us along the runway for take-off.

The nose of the plane lifted, and Henry's hand fisted my hair. "Fuck yes, suck hard."

He didn't have to ask. The plane left the tarmac and as we climbed high in the sky his orgasm ripped through him. He moaned my name, jerked into my mouth, all the while trying to be quiet. I swallowed, not wanting to waste anything before sitting up and reaching for my glass of wine.

I downed it, picked up a napkin and ensured I didn't have anything on my mouth. He fixed up his pants, his breathing ragged as he tried to collect his thoughts.

I looked out the window. We were already high in the sky and on our way to London. I'd never been to the city before and it was surreal that we were going there now.

Together.

"Are you going to look at me?"

I turned and met his eyes. I bit my lip, unable to hide my self-satisfied grin. He'd come so hard, and fast for that matter. Maybe he'd been celibate too during our time apart. I hoped he had been. The thought of him with anyone else made my heart jump into my throat.

"I don't think I've ever come so hard in my life." He reached for me, pulling me in for a kiss. I didn't deny him. I didn't want to. I wanted him. I ached for him to fuck me. Getting him off had made me as horny as fuck and as soon as we could I was going to see if this fancy jet had a bed so I could get what I wanted.

Him.

"I'm glad you enjoyed it." I wanted to please him, in all ways. If he felt half of how he made me feel, want and need, then life would be perfect.

"I want you so bad," he admitted.

"Hmm." I ran my finger along his bottom lip. "I'd like your mouth on me. Maybe after breakfast?"

His eyes darkened, and a muscle worked on his jaw. I'd never seen him look so wild and untamed. I liked this side of Henry. No longer so pristine and cultured, manicured, but dirty, wild, and disheveled.

"Or I could have you for breakfast?"

I squeezed my legs together, liking that idea even more. "That could work too."

Twenty~Nine

WHEN THE PLANE was at a cruising altitude, breakfast was served, and our plans were put on hold for a time. Croissants, jam, honey, hot pot of English tea and salmon and eggs benedict were served with a steaming pot of fresh coffee.

Maddie had a good appetite. I smiled, knowing she probably hadn't had a lot in her stomach after a night of clubbing. "Did you have fun in Capri? You all looked like you had a great night when you stumbled into the hotel this morning."

"We did, we danced and drank far too much." She popped a little bit of croissant into her mouth, and I ached, having a whole new appreciation for her pretty mouth. A devil of a thought, but there it was…

"Do I have any reason to be jealous of this Spanish god who looked after you?" My tone was light, unaffected, but it was all a front. I hated the idea of Maddie being with anyone else. These past weeks, watching her social media, dreading seeing her partying, dancing, growing close with other men had almost brought me to insanity a few times.

Not the best response to a woman who was free to do what she liked. It was my fault she had fallen through my fingers, a decision I regretted the instant I climbed onto the tender without her.

"You ought to be scared. He was very handsome and even kissed me twice."

I stilled, finished my sip of coffee, and set it down. "He kissed you? I thought you were merely joking back at the hotel."

"No, I wasn't. I was being honest." She looked at me, raising her brow in a challenging way that I'd never seen before from her. Was she testing me? Well, I wouldn't fail a second time. I could be jealous as fuck and I was, but I couldn't say shit. We weren't together as of last night and I needed to remember that.

I stood and reached for her hand. "Come."

"Where are we going?" she asked, doing what I said anyway.

"Suzanna, we're not to be disturbed."

"Of course, Mr. Fairfax."

Maddie's cheeks pinkened as I pulled her through a door that led into the bedroom. I locked it behind us, leaning against it as I watched Maddie take in the space. A king-size bed, silk bedding with an abundance of pillows greeted us.

"He kissed you twice?" I stalked my way over to her. She backed up, a sensible reaction to the fire that was building within me. Her knees hit the bed and she stumbled onto it.

"You know that's what happens when people aren't exclusive. We do things with other people."

I clamped my jaw shut, forcing myself to calm the fuck down. She was teasing, testing me. I wouldn't react, but I would lay claim. "Lie down, Maddie."

She shuffled up on the bed and leaned back on her elbows, a cocky little grin on her lips that only spiked my determination to have her screaming my name and no one else's.

"What are you going to do to me? Are you jealous, Mr. Fairfax?"

"Fuck yes I am." I kneeled on the bed and clasped her legs, ripping her toward me. She squealed, laughed, and fell onto her back. I reached for her pants, undoing the little buttons that separated me from what I wanted. I ripped them off, taking her panties with them before throwing them on the floor.

"Now, it's my turn." I spread her legs, her glistening cunt made my cock hard and my mouth water. I dipped my head, running my tongue along the inside of her leg. She tasted so sweet, like wine. Mine and not some motherfucking Spanish bastard.

I spread her sweet lips and dipped my tongue against her clit, teasing her. She mewled beneath me, and I held her still, holding her legs apart as I ate her with a fervor that left her squirming. The tangy flavor of her burst onto my tongue. I moaned, having not known how starved of her I had been. I needed to hear her call my name, come on my face, and beg me for more.

"You're so fucking sweet." I dipped a finger, then two, into her, fucking her as I lathed her sex with my mouth. She wrapped her legs about me, grinding against my face. I suckled her and she gasped, lifting off the bed in surprise. "Like that, did you, New York?"

"Yes," she gasped.

I flicked my tongue across her swollen button, catching her gaze and watching her as I ate her out. Her eyes were wild with need, her bottom lip clamped tight between her teeth. I wanted to please her, so damn much that she'd never look to anyone else but me ever again. I relished her cunt, worked her to a frenzy, made love to her with my mouth until the first pulsations rocked through her and she came apart in my arms.

"Henry," she screamed as she shattered.

I kneeled and ripped my pants off and flipped her onto her front. I entered her from behind, sheathed my hard cock into her glistening, sweet heat. We moaned. I held her hips, rocked into her, watched my cock spread her pretty pink flesh and made her mine.

Her second orgasm came hard and strong. Her pleasure pulsated around me, wrenching me to join her. I thrust into her with a savagery I'd never known.

"Fuck, Maddie. I can't get enough of you."

"Then don't," she replied.

Her words solidified something in me, a truth, a determination not to lose her again. I slipped out and tumbled onto the bed next to her. For several minutes we lay motionless, catching our breaths. After a time we climbed under the bedding, and I pulled her into my arms.

"I have to ask, and you can tell me to fuck the hell off, but it's killing me not knowing."

She looked up at me, her head resting on my arm. I pushed a strand of her dark hair off her face and marveled at how she made me feel. I was possessive of this woman and that alone should frighten me. It was a new emotion and one I wasn't used to having with anyone. I was jealous of situations that I didn't even know were true, of situations that hadn't even occurred yet.

What the fuck was wrong with me?

"He meant nothing to me, Henry. And he was the only man I have hung with these past weeks, if that's what you were going to ask. The kiss was fleeting and nothing worth your worry."

"How the hell did you know what I was going to ask?"

She laughed and relief replaced the unease running through me. I adored her happiness, that she enjoyed her time with me. I had missed her.

"You were acting a little jealous. Your face was as easy to read as a book and when I mentioned the Spanish god, your face was worth a thousand words." She clasped my cheek, ran her hand over my jaw. "For a businessman you're not very good at hiding your emotions. I thought you'd have a much better poker face than that."

"I normally do. But with you I can't seem to control anything."

"Really?" she asked, slipping her leg over mine and tangling our limbs together.

I reached for her, wanting her close, if nothing else. "Really." I paused. "What is the saying from Jane Austen? *You have bewitched me, body and soul.*"

"You're not so bad either," she responded. "I could get used to salmon benedict for breakfast on future plane rides."

"Whatever you want and it's yours. You merely have to ask." I thought over my words. Just how deep did I mean? Not willing to dip into my own subliminal thoughts I kissed her instead.

She kissed me back and all was right in the world. "The Spanish god wanted more than a sweet kiss, Henry, but I couldn't do it. Every time I considered it, I saw your face and I knew it would be a mistake I'd regret."

"Thank the gods for that. I don't think I could survive hearing you'd moved on from me so fast."

"I think you'll be a little harder to forget than you give yourself credit for."

"Well, I am trying." I stole another kiss, then another.

CHAPTER
Thirty

LONDON

I EXPECTED us to be staying at Henry's hotel in London, but again he surprised me. We drove through Notting Hill, the grounds of Kensington and the many gated mansions of international delegates passing us by, before our chauffeured car pulled into a gated Georgian mansion that sat directly on Notting Hill Road, the electronic gate closing behind us.

A servant waiting on the front steps moved forward and opened the door, greeting Henry and smiling politely at me. The house was three stories high, two large pillars framing the front double door, short box hedges running along the paved driveway oozed wealth and power.

I looked out toward the road, the six-foot fence with old hedging giving the house privacy from the public. A security officer was stationed at the gate for added security.

"We have your room ready for you, Mr. Fairfax. If you'll follow me." The older woman preceded them into the house. Henry took my hand, and we trailed her.

There were portraits of people through different periods of time lining the walls, diluted by modern images of contemporary art and family ones of course. I paused before a sideboard that had several images, one of Henry who looked to be a teenager in it.

"Is this you?" He was so handsome, and the naughty light in his eye was visible even then.

"It is. I just turned seventeen." He wrapped his arms about my waist and leaned his head on my shoulder, pointing to other pictures. "My mother and father, before his passing. And there is Sophia being a nuisance, which also hasn't changed."

"Our lives are so different. I struggle to comprehend how our paths crossed at all."

His hand dipped low on my stomach and he pulled me against him. "Well, if you need reminding should I tell you of the story of this super-hot, but innocent woman I spied in a nightclub and wanted the moment I did so?"

I faced him, wrapping my arms about his neck. "My nightclub knight in shining Armani as I recall. Who would have thought we would run into each other again. I'm pleased we did. I kind of like you."

"I kind of like you too." He kissed me, and I threw myself into his embrace. He made me want things, dream things I shouldn't, but I couldn't help myself. I was under his spell and didn't know how or even if I ever wanted to break it.

"Come, we'll freshen up and head out. I want to show you London. Have you ever been?"

"No, never, but I've always wanted to." Was this truly his house? I tried not to gape and look around like a starstruck poor person that I was, but I couldn't help it. Everywhere I looked there were antiques, beautiful flooring, history, and a bustling, busy city that had been around longer than my own country around me. How was one not to be impressed?

"Yes, our family has had it for about thirty years. I lived here on weekends when I went to school."

"You went to school in London?" We entered a room off the first-floor passageway. Fourteen-foot ceilings and curtains that ran the length of windows the same height greeted us. A large bed, opulent bedding, and a fireplace with marble surround finished off the beautiful space.

"Yes, Eton and then Oxford."

"You went to school where the future kings of England went?" I knew Henry was privileged, but to go to the same school as a future monarch was another whole level of wealth. The thought was a little humbling to say the least.

"Yes, but obviously the Prince of Wales is older and was a few years ahead of me. I don't actually know him personally." Henry pulled at his tie and tossed it onto the bed, before moving toward the walk-in wardrobe.

My backpack sat on a little trunk, and I didn't bother going over to it to change. It was warm in London today and my clothing was suitable for a day out sightseeing.

"I texted ahead, and the housekeeper has brought in some clothes for you if you want to change. Not that what you have on isn't perfect."

"I'll keep what I have on." Having more than what I brought would be handy. Hopefully I could get to the shops soon and buy more of what I need.

He stood shirtless before a full-length mirror and our gazes clashed. My attention dipped to his chest, the light feathering of hair that kissed his skin. He was a handsome man, hot as fuck and knew how to use that masculinity to his full advantage.

"Perfect."

Right answer.

I joined him at the mirror and pulled him close for a kiss, wanting his mouth on me. He was like a drug I couldn't get enough of. He picked me up, walking over to the bed before tossing me onto it.

"Take your pants off." Expectation ran through me, and I did what he asked without question.

He stood at the edge of the bed, his piercing eyes devouring me as I did what he ordered. He undid the button on his pants, slipping the zipper down with agonizing slowness.

I licked my lips, unsure what part of him I wanted

where most. He crawled over me, and I wrapped my legs about his waist. His cock pressed against my sex before he thrust into me, taking me, owning me, his thick, long cock fulfilling my every fantasy.

"Fuck me, Henry." I wanted him deeper, harder... more, just more.

He took me with a savagery that I reveled in. He pinned my hands above my head, our gazes clashed with each thrust. I wanted to hold him, reach for him, but he held me down, owning me, laying claim.

I didn't mind. I had claimed him too.

"Damn you feel good. Come for me."

I was already close, the delicious sensations taunting me before pleasure pulsated, fast and thorough through me, shattering me in two. "Henry." His name a plea on my lips. His eyes darkened with satisfaction. "Oh yes, I'm coming."

My body was not my own, nor was I responsible for the noises we made. He let go of my hands and I reached for him, holding him, kissing him as the last of orgasm rocked through me. His cock hardened further, my name a breathless plea against my ear as he came.

"Fuck, Maddie..."

After a few minutes, he slumped beside me. We stared at the decorated ceiling, both lost in our thoughts and aftermath of gratification.

"God damn it I lose all control when I'm with you."

His honesty caught me by surprise, and I rolled to face him, breathing deep his cologne. I ran my hand over his chest, his quickened heartbeat beneath my palm. "Is that a bad thing?"

"No." There was no hesitation in his response, and I released a breath I didn't know I was holding. "But it's different and not something I'm used to. But I won't run again, I promise."

"I'm glad to hear it."

Thirty~One

LONDON WAS EVERYTHING I HOPED. The city, a mix of old and new was never dull, full of history and culture that I'd never experienced before. Our days were spent visiting all the tourist hotspots, even though Henry had seen them before, or so he said, but he never once complained.

We took tours, rode the Uber boats on the Thames, Mudlarked with the society that allowed visitors to take part in the pastime. I never found anything but an old broken smoking pipe that I wasn't allowed to keep.

Henry promised to buy me a replica and later that evening there had been one on my pillow, tied up with a little yellow ribbon.

The art galleries and museums, the wheel, and the underground were all adventures I'd never had and would forever cherish. I'd never known a billionaire to travel by train and not complain, most weren't airconditioned after all…

We stood on Tower Hill, near the tube looking down at The Tower of London lit up at night, Tower Bridge behind it, one of the most well-recognized landmarks in the world.

I reached for Henry's hand, enjoying an ice-cream he'd bought me. How the hell was I here, with a man I was falling in love with? And there was no use denying myself. I was falling for him, falling in love, and there wasn't anything I could do about it.

I didn't know what he felt. He desired me, enjoyed my company and I made him laugh, which I adored, but did that mean he too was feeling more than he was willing to admit to just yet? There was no way I would spill those three little words before he did.

A niggle of fear tickled the back of my mind after being honest about my feelings before and I wouldn't make the mistake again. If he loved me too, he would have to say it first.

"Where to now, Miss Webb?" He dropped my hand to throw his napkin in a nearby bin. "The city is alive and I'm yours to command."

I thought about his question a moment, thinking of what we hadn't done. Which wasn't a lot. He'd indulged me in everything I'd wanted to see and been a good sport for it. I finished my ice-cream and wrapped my arm around his waist as we started to walk up toward St Pauls, the spire high in the city skyline guiding our way.

"I think we should return home. I'm a little exhausted."

He kissed my forehead. "We can do that." He pulled out his phone and texted someone, no doubt his driver who would come and collect us. Sure enough, within a few minutes a black BMW pulled up before us.

"Home, thank you, John." Henry pulled me close, and I snuggled into his arms. "Happy?" he asked me.

"I'm so happy. I never want this to end. I've had such a lovely vacation with you." The past two weeks in London had been some of the best times in my life and I never wanted our time to end. But of course it would. Summer would be over soon, and we were flying back to Sorrento tomorrow. The thought of Henry returning to work in Rome and not seeing him for several days made the breath in my lungs catch.

How the hell would I survive when I returned to New York? It could be months before we would see each other. How would I walk away from this enigmatic, kind man? A man who made me feel so many things I had only ever thought were found in romance novels, not real life. But he was real, and beside me, holding me, making love to me every night and I could no longer deny the fact.

I loved him.

Adored him.

As if sensing my distress he pulled back, a small frown between his eyes. "What's wrong? I can feel you're upset."

His phone chose to ring at that exact moment, and he declined the call, quickly putting the phone back in his pocket.

I refused to be the clingy girlfriend who didn't trust him. If we were to survive long distance, not just between Sorrento and Rome but New York and Rome, I had to trust. Put my hope in him and stop worrying about situations that may never happen.

"I'm just tired and overwhelmed. I don't want to return to Sorrento. I've loved our time here. London hasn't been bad either," I teased.

He smiled, kissing me. "I've loved it here too, but I have some disappointing news you ought to know of before we leave tomorrow."

"What is it?"

"I have some pressing business to attend to in Rome and won't be able to fly back to Sorrento with you."

That was disappointing, but of course he was a busy man. His job had multiple aspects being the CEO of a hotel conglomerate and so many people relying on him, I couldn't expect him to always be on vacation with me.

"How am I getting back to Sorrento?"

"The plane will drop me in Rome before returning to Sorrento right away. I'll have a car pick me up on the tarmac, so you'll not have to disembark and go through security."

His phone rang again, and a muscle worked on his jaw. "Is someone trying to get hold of you? Maybe you should take it. It could be important."

"It's not."

I didn't press him at his annoyed tone. The car pulled up before the Notting Hill home and we made our way inside. The butler greeted us in the foyer.

"Dinner is ready if you would like to make your way to the dining room, Mr. Fairfax."

"Thank you, we will."

I looked at Henry, not having known we were going to eat in this evening. We made our way to the dining room, and I paused at the door, seeing the table set with large candelabras and flowers that ran the length of the ten-person table. The lights were dimmed, curtains drawn, giving a cosy, yet romantic glow to the room.

"You've been busy when I've not been looking."

He laughed, and lifted my hand, kissing it old-school. My heart lurched and I fought to control my desire to crumble into a million pieces of love, all for him.

"I wanted to spoil you on our last night."

The words sounded final, a goodbye, but they weren't. He would return to Sorrento when work permitted. I was being paranoid.

"This is amazing. I've never had a dinner like this before."

Henry held out my chair and I sat, before he joined me at the table, sitting across from me. He reached for his napkin, watching me. "What do you mean? Not even at Christmas or special events like birthdays or anniversaries?"

I shook my head, reaching for my water. "We grew up vastly different, Henry. But this is lovely, thank you."

"But hang on," he continued. "What did you do at

Christmas then if you didn't have dinners? I don't understand."

The memory of being alone in a room in whatever latest family had taken me in floated through my mind. To celebrate Christmas or any special event was hard when one didn't know the people around them, to feel safe and comfortable, not to mention welcome. I rarely felt any of those things until college and I met Evelyn and Clara. "Henry, I didn't have a home like this growing up."

He stared at me as if I had grown a second head. "What do you mean?"

Clara and Eve barely knew much about my past, and I liked it that way. I hated people feeling sorry for me, seeing the pity in their gazes, treating me like the lonely orphan I was often irked. I wasn't a victim anymore and refused to be looked upon as one.

"I never knew my parents. My father was never listed on my birth certificate and my mother died a few days after I was born. She was a drug addict, and I went into the foster system before I was a week old."

The color drained from Henry's face, and I smiled, trying to lighten the mood.

"I can see I've shocked you." I paused. "Say something, Henry."

"But...don't people adopt babies more than any other age bracket? How was it you remained in the system for so long? I assume since you're saying you never had a home, or enjoyed such celebrations, that this is what happened to you?"

A staff member came in and poured us a glass of champagne, before leaving us. I picked up the champagne and took a fortifying sip. "I was a crack baby, Henry. No one wanted those problematic kids, and I was given a heart condition because of it. I was broken, and no one had the time or money to fix me, so I stayed floating from one house to another before college."

"What is wrong with your heart? Are you going to be okay?"

I reached across the table and took his hand. His fingers entwined with mine, and a little of the trepidation of telling my truth dissipated at his touch. "I had a heart murmur that I grew out of, thankfully. You don't need to worry about me."

"But I do worry."

He was so sweet and made me love him even more. "Being in the system made me work hard, to learn everything I could in school and make something of myself. I graduated and received a full scholarship to college in New York. I wanted to break the toxic cycle I was born into, and I think I have. I look forward to what my future holds."

Henry pushed back his chair and came over to kneel beside me. "I couldn't imagine what type of childhood that must have been. It makes me want to hold you, turn back time and pluck you out of there and save you."

I chuckled, knowing I had wished for someone to save me so many times, until I realized who that saviour would be. "I saved myself, Henry and please don't feel sorry for me. I'm fine now. Truly. I have great friends, a delicious, handsome summer fling that may eventuate to more and a bright future. I'm happy. Truly."

"It may have started as a fling, but I think we're past that now."

God, yes, that was true. "I think we're past that too."

CHAPTER
Thirty-Two

THE FOLLOWING AFTERNOON, forty thousand feet in the sky I watched Maddie sleep across from me, her pretty mouth open a little, her hand cushioning her head against the side of the plane.

She was an orphan.

A crack baby left defenseless and alone all her childhood.

A child who had to survive in foster care until finishing high school.

I took a deep breath, rubbing my spiky jaw. I should have shaved this morning, but I'd been distracted. Sadness, respect, and anger swirled inside me. How could people leave children so defenseless, care for their own vices more than anyone else who relied on them? Maddie was strong, far more than I had given her credit for.

Far stronger than myself.

She was an amazing woman. A person who probably should be mad at the world after how it had treated her, and yet she wasn't. She was caring, happy and loyal, had a positive outlook on life and gave people the benefit of the doubt maybe more than she should.

I grabbed a blanket and placed it over her, wanting her to be warm and comfortable in her sleep.

My chest tightened watching her and I couldn't stop staring. How could anyone desert her? Not love her as she deserved?

The word love reverberated in my mind, and I frowned… My phone buzzed and I glanced down, seeing it was another voice message from Margot.

The fifth in as many hours.

What the fuck did she want now?

Maddie stirred and slowly opened her eyes, stretching as she woke. She grinned.

Hell, she was beautiful, the cream Chanel suit pants and blue shirt I had gifted her in London brought out the dark blue of her eyes.

She encompassed summer and looked good enough to eat.

"You shouldn't have let me sleep. I want to spend as much time with you as I can."

I reached across and took her hand, playing with her delicate fingers. There was no denying what was happening to me. I had feelings for this woman that went far beyond like…

She occupied my thoughts persistently. For the first time in my life I wanted to push aside work to be with her as I had these past weeks in London. Out of character, I had postponed meetings scheduled months in advance. None of them more important than Maddie and fixing what I had broken. And now she was going back to Sorrento, and I wasn't sure when I'd get down there again. Soon, I hoped, but everything was up in the air.

"I was enjoying the view too much to wake you."

She chuckled and came to sit beside me. I tipped up her chin and kissed her. She kissed me back, playfully biting my bottom lip. My cock hardened and I debated if we had enough time to slip into the bedroom.

"Your kisses are wicked, Mr. Fairfax. What has come over you?"

"You, hopefully."

She bit her lip, understanding me completely. "That's very naughty of you."

I lost the ability to think straight and stood, pulling her toward the back of the plane. She hugged me from behind as we disappeared into the private suite. The moment I closed and locked the door I reached for her. We came together like two starved souls who hadn't just made love this morning. I kissed her with a need that fired my blood to scorching.

I picked her up and set her on the desk. She unzipped my trousers, her nimble fingers making quick work of my pants. My cock jumped into her hand, and I groaned when she stroked me.

"I want you, Henry. So much."

"I want you too." I pulled off her pants and thong.

There was no foreplay, no stroking, or prolonged agony, just sex. I thrust into her, taking her on the desk with a savagery I couldn't control.

Her nails scored my back, urging me on, denying me nothing.

"Fuck me, Henry. Harder," she demanded.

I gave her what she wanted, lost all sense of gentleness.

A paperweight and stapler tumbled to the floor, and we chuckled, neither of us caring how much noise we made. I pulled her close and she wrapped her legs about me and held on as we fucked toward orgasm.

I felt the first contractions of her orgasm and it was too much. "Maddie," I moaned, enjoying her orgasm as mine convulsed through me.

"You feel so good." Her legs dropped from about my waist. She watched me as we regained our breath, sated and satisfied. "You make me so crazy. What am I going to do with you?" she asked.

I didn't want to leave her. I didn't want her to go back to Sorrento without me. What the fuck was happening? Did I love Maddie and just hadn't admitted it to myself? I'd never been in love before, or at least I don't believe I had. Certainly what I'd only ever felt for Margot was vastly different to what was tumbling through me whenever I was around Maddie.

I was possessive and jealous with Maddie. Her happiness was everything to me, seeing her smile and enjoy herself was paramount. Being with her would upset my family, my mother in particular as she'd had hear heart set on Margot since we were children, but not even that was enough to sway me.

I wouldn't give her up for anyone, not even my blood.

"I'll be back in Sorrento in a few days," I decided, unsure if I could make that happen. "Any more time than that from you and I'll go mad." It was the closest I could admit to how she was making me feel. All of this was new and unchartered ground I'd never walked.

"You could just admit that you'll miss me."

She was right of course. I could stop being a coward and admit to what I was feeling. The seatbelt sign came on, saving me from having to man up. "We'll be landing soon. We better take our seats."

"You go ahead. I'll just clean up first. I won't be long."

I neatened up my attire as Maddie used the bathroom. Back at my seat I watched out the window and could see we were dropping altitude. Maddie joined me a few minutes later, buckling up before reaching for my hand.

Such an innocent gesture and yet, more personal than most.

"Promise you'll be back as soon as you can. There are only a few weeks left of summer. I want to spend as much of that time with you as possible."

"I'll be back before the weekend. I promise."

"I'll hold you to that promise, Mr. Fairfax."

I kissed her, unable to deny myself another taste of her. "No need for that. I'll be there, New York."

———

Four days later Margot sat before me in my office on the day I was supposed to fly out to see Maddie. I shifted in my chair, annoyance riding me hard at being held up from leaving for the airport. There was a lot of history between us, but we were over, she knew that. Why she was here was anyone's guess.

"Lovely to see you, Henry. I heard you were in London the last two weeks. See anyone I know?"

I took a calming breath. No doubt she knew exactly who I was in London with and wanted information on my time there. I wouldn't give her the satisfaction. For years she had cheated on me, said one thing to my face and then disregarded it the moment we were apart.

"Get to the point, Margot and tell me what you want. I'm flying out tonight and want to leave the office early."

Her eyes narrowed with annoyance before she shook herself and smiled, again the movie star with a poker face. "You can't leave tonight. We have Alessandro's birthday celebration you agreed to attend months ago, remember?"

"I'll have to give my excuses and apologies. I'll not be attending." I shut my laptop and filed several papers into a folder for my assistant to deal with later, the conversation over. Margot didn't move and my patience started to wane. "Is there a reason you're still sitting here?"

"Excuse me, Henry, but we dated for years, and I've

known you since we were children. How can you treat me with so little respect? As if our childhood and the friendship that our families share means nothing."

Her words would've once made me feel guilty. Our families had been friends for years and we were long-time friends before anything romantic occurred between us. Maybe I ought to give her the opportunity of friendship again, but there was something about Margot that was born out of years of unfaithfulness and underhanded antics. Like the one she pulled in Sorrento.

"Your antics in Sorrento and the paparazzi weren't what friends do. What do you have to say for yourself, pulling that shit?"

She leaned forward in her chair, her hands clasped innocently in her lap. "I'm sorry about that. Truly, if I had known you were serious about this American..."

"Her name is Madeline Webb, Margot. Remember it."

A blush stole across her cheeks, but she nodded. "If I had known it was serious I wouldn't have interfered. But it's Alessandro's birthday and he is one of your oldest friends. You must attend. Just postpone your trip one more day. I'm sure Maddie would understand."

Fuck me. I didn't want to go. I wanted to return to Sorrento. The thought of seeing her lightened any day and the dark mood Margot's visit had settled over me. But then, Margot did have a point. Alessandro had expected me to attend, and he was a good mate.

"I'll attend, but I'll be leaving early."

"Excellent." She stood and I was glad for it. "See you tonight, Henry."

The door closed behind her, and I slumped back into my chair, relieved to be alone. The woman was toxic and draining and old friendship or not, I no longer trusted her.

I reached for my phone, needing to let Maddie know I would be a day late.

Change of plans beautiful. An old friend is having his 30th tonight. I tried to get out of it but cannot. Better make an appearance. Will be in Sorrento tomorrow morning first thing to kiss you good morning.

Thirty~Three

I STARED AT THE WORDS, disappointed I wouldn't see him, or that he hadn't thought to ask me to join him at the event. I had a little money saved. I could have flown to Rome to see him, met his friends for the first time.

Was there a reason he hadn't introduced me to his mother or close friends yet? I know his sister didn't think much of me, but maybe she was a one off…

I shot a quick text back.

No problems. See you tomorrow.
Have fun!

There, I didn't sound like a jealous, nervous idiot who had fallen in love for my one-night stand and felt left out. I set my phone down on the coffee table in the lounge and moped into the kitchen. Clara was cooking fettuccine, or at least was attempting to. "You need to add water to that pasta, Clara."

"Oh shit, yes, water. Thank you! I was staring at the ingredients and couldn't remember what I was supposed to do next."

I had to give her kudos for trying to learn to cook delicious Italian food. I slumped onto the stool, bummed I wouldn't see Henry this evening.

"What's wrong? I can see your mood has changed after that text."

I picked up the cream that would be included in the recipe and pretended to read the label. "Henry won't be here tonight now. He's attending a friend's birthday. I'll have to wait for tomorrow to see him."

Clara leaned on the counter, ignoring her ingredients. "Why didn't he invite you?"

Trust my friends to always state the truth and voice the fear that I had asked myself only minutes before. I shrugged. "I don't know. Probably didn't think of it."

"Hmm." Clara went back to stirring her chicken. "How much does he know of your life and upbringing? Do you think that's why he's not invited you?"

Ouch. The thought hurt, and I hadn't considered that possibility. "I hope that's not why he didn't invite me. I was thinking it was merely an oversight. But he does know I was in foster care and never adopted and the reasons behind that."

"I'm sure he's just not thought about it." Clara

reached out and squeezed my hand. "You've turned out damn well for the shitty cards you were dealt at birth. It's nothing to be ashamed of, Maddie. You are not to blame for what happened to you."

"I know and I'm not ashamed. I was a good kid, even though no one would adopt me, and I worked hard to get my scholarship into college." I squeezed Clara's hand back. "You and Eve are my only family now. I hope you know how much I appreciate our friendship. It's everything to me."

"Oh, Maddie, we feel the same, babe." Clara came around the counter and pulled me into a tight hug.

I held on to her like a lifeline, my eyes unexpectedly stinging with tears. I'd never had real friends before college. It was hard to make connections in school when I was moved around so much between different houses and jurisdictions.

Clara sat beside me on the stool. "You really like him, don't you?"

I massaged the nape of my neck, nodding. I couldn't lie to Clara, never had been able to, she could always seem to pick up when I was skirting the truth. But I was also terrified of voicing how I felt. It somehow made it real, dangerous…to my heart.

"I do, more than I should considering we've not known each other long. We've decided to try long distance. Who knows how that will end."

Clara looked at me with concern. "Long distance is hard. Do you think he's worth it?"

"I think he's worth it, yes." Any issues we'd had

up until now had been forced upon us by other's reactions and meddling. But after London, the sheer enjoyment we'd had together, how easy we moved together through the day told me that we could work. Somehow, no matter how different our lives were, we fit.

"And how was London?" Clara asked, changing the subject. "You had a great time from the looks of your social media."

"It was amazing. He spoiled me and we visited every tourist location in the city, even though he'd been numerous times before. We had the best time. I didn't want it to end."

"We're only here a few more weeks, what does Henry think of you returning to New York? How is this long-distance relationship going to work?"

I shrugged, not entirely sure of all the particulars myself. "We'll fly back and forth as much as we can. Probably Henry will visit me more often since he has business interests in New York too and has the finances to do so."

"Well, you'll always have a room with me and Eve."

"I feel bad though about the rent." I loved my friends and their support of me, but I hated feeling like a financial drain on everyone. "I feel guilty I'm not paying anything."

"The flat is my father's, Maddie. I'm not even paying rent, a gift from him to me for graduating and joining his law firm. So stop worrying about money and just enjoy having a little good fortune for a change."

Clara raised the knife, pointing it at me as if she would prick me with it if I said no.

I held up my hands in surrender, chuckling. "Fine, but I'll cook as much as I can, and you'll not say a word about it."

Clara grinned. "Use this time living with us as a stepping stone, build up your bank balance while you can. It's the least I can do since you've been such a good friend to me."

I bit my lip, blinking back tears. "Thank you, Clara. Truly."

"What are friends for?" she quipped.

I smiled. "Perhaps to tell you your pasta is boiling dry again." I pointed to the stove top.

Clara swore, picking up the pot. "Fine," she sighed. "You can keep us fed and stop me from burning down the building."

"It's a deal."

Thirty~Four

I GLANCED at my watch for the hundredth time, the minute hand moving at a glacier pace from the last time I checked. The birthday boy, Alessandro stood beside his girlfriend, blowing out the candles on the three-tier cake.

I clapped and catcalled congratulations, but my heart wasn't in it. We were all turning thirty this year and I didn't care for it. In fact, I'd never been one who enjoyed my birth date. I inwardly swore as Margot sauntered over to me, swaying her hips in a suggestive manner she hoped would tempt me. Why she continued with these games when we had ended our fanciful relationship was beyond me. I was over her shit and starting to lose my patience. At this point, friendship would even be off the table if she didn't back off.

"Don't look so sour. Alessandro is one of your closest friends. At least pretend to want to be here."

"I'm happy for him, and he's having a good night, that's all that matters."

She leaned over the bar and ordered two bourbons, handing me one.

I took it and sipped. I should have flown Maddie here for the night. She would have enjoyed the party, and it would have been a good opportunity for me to introduce her to my friends. People I hoped would soon be her friends too, excluding my current company.

Only a few more hours before I'd see her again. I smiled at the thought and stilled when Margot draped against my shoulder.

"See, that's more the face I love and adore. I'm glad my being here and talking to you makes you happy."

I stared, dumbfounded she would stretch her imagination to think my happiness had anything to do with her. She was a serial cheater, mostly with her costars and liked to blame her infidelity on the distance so oftentimes inflicted on us due to filming locations.

Shame that most of her films were based in Europe and the last time I checked within a few hours flight. She cheated because she enjoyed being unfaithful and nothing more.

"I was thinking of Maddie, actually. I'm looking forward to seeing her tomorrow."

Her high-pitched laugh grated on my nerves, and I stepped away, not wanting to be near her a moment longer. "You're a fool if you think your family is going to accept an American and then on top of that, a woman who isn't from our world. You cannot be serious even considering making your one-night stand more than what it was. A quick fuck in a nightclub."

I narrowed my eyes. "Who told you I met Maddie in a nightclub?" I had only told my sister that information and if she had broken my trust, that wouldn't end well for her. We were already arguing after her antics in Sorrento.

"Sophia told me." Margot smirked. "Only whores give it up to guys they don't know in a club. You're more pathetic than I thought if you're going to run back to her like some pussy-whipped fool."

I let her words roll of my back, not willing to rise to her bait. She was pissed, jealous and nervous that I wasn't falling for her excuses and taking her back like all the other times.

"Maddie isn't the first woman I've fucked in a night-club, so you shouldn't throw stones while living in a glass house." I finished my bourbon, my eyes watering at the sour taste of my last sip. "Maddie and I have agreed to try long distance, see each other beyond summer, so you best start to learn to respect her, or our association is at an end."

"Well, good luck with that, Henry. But you'll be back, begging for another chance sooner or later. We're from the same world, literally made for each other. There is no room in our society for social climbers that have no pedigree."

I shrugged. "Like I give a fuck what you think."

I went over to Alessandro, unable to stomach Margot a moment longer. "Happy birthday, my friend."

I picked up a plate of cake and a small fork and dug in. Alessandro's latest squeeze excused herself, leaving us alone.

"I saw you speaking with Margot. She's still trying to get you back?"

"Yeah, and it's not happening. I don't understand her." And that was the truth of it. We hadn't been seeing each other for months, only pretending to, before the breakup in Paris, all staged and false narrative for the paparazzi. Why she was acting all pissed and possessive now that I was seeing Maddie made no sense.

"I've heard you're seeing someone in Sorrento. What's she like? I thought you may have brought her here tonight."

"To be honest I should have, and I regret not sending for her. It would've been good for you to meet." I glanced across the room and saw Margot speaking with a mutual friend, her mouth pinched in displeasure. "No doubt Margot is busy bemoaning I'm not falling to my knees before her yet again."

"You must really like this woman to throw a future with Margot away. Your mother has been planning your wedding for years."

I ground my teeth, rolling my shoulders to dispel the mounting pressure. "Margot ruined our future together. I should never have taken her back the first time she fucked up." A fucking chump was what I was, but not anymore. Nor would I allow her to dictate Maddie's future in our friendship group. If they didn't accept her, we would simply find other friends who would.

"Yeah, she's certainly had plenty of second chances. I'm surprised your mother has been more forgiving than you."

"So am I, but then mother has always worn rose-colored glasses when it came to Margot." I paused. "Mother will come around for Maddie, when she needs to. Everything is new right now, and I'm just enjoying our time together."

Alessandro clapped me on the shoulder. "Maddie sounds great, my friend. When are you seeing her again?"

"I fly out in the morning and as much as I love you and wish you a happy birthday, I really should get going."

"Wow, you really do like her to leave one of my parties." Alessandro laughed. "I'm happy for you. Truly. You deserve a good woman."

"Thanks, man. Have a great night. When I'm here in Rome again, we'll do dinner and I'll introduce you to Maddie."

"I'm looking forward to it."

I left, and within a few minutes was outside on the footpath, waiting for my driver who had been held up in traffic. Only a few more hours and I would be in Sorrento. Maybe I'd run the office from there next week and extend my stay beyond the weekend. I was the boss after all. I could do what I liked.

"Can I hitch a ride?"

I cringed at the sound of Margot's voice. She sauntered up to me yet again. Jesus, the woman never stopped. She pulled her thick fur coat about herself as if we were in the thick of winter instead of summer. Anything for fashion and lording it over everyone else.

"No, you can call your own driver."

"I gave him the night off." She slipped her arm about mine and I stepped aside, out of her hold. "What do you think you're doing? You don't get to do whatever you want with me anymore. We're not together."

"Please don't make a scene, Henry. There are paparazzi around who'll spread it across the papers tomorrow if you act like a bastard right now."

My attention slipped to the crowd gathered outside the venue, hoping to catch sight of the rich and famous at the birthday party. My driver pulled up and rushed around to open the door. I ground my teeth, not wanting to do the right thing, but unable to be such a bastard.

"Get in," I ground out.

She smiled to the crowd and slipped into the car. I followed and slammed the door, over her shit and being included in it.

CHAPTER
Thirty-Five

LIGHT PIERCED my eyes and I blinked, fighting to adjust my blurry vision. Pleasure rocked through me and I groaned, slipping my hand behind my head to enjoy the view. "Hmm, I could wake up to this more often."

"I love sucking your dick."

I sat bolt upright, scrambling out of the bed, ripping my cock out of Margot's mouth. She gaped at me on the bed, naked as the day she was born.

What the actual fuck!

I looked at myself, about the room, panic seizing me. Clothes were splayed over the floor, a bra hung from a lampshade, and my tie was tied to the bedhead.

What the fuck had happened?

I ran a hand through my hair, unable to reconcile getting into the car to drive Margot home and waking up with my cock in her mouth.

"What are you doing, Henry? You could have hurt me pulling your dick out of my mouth like that."

I swallowed the bile that rose in my throat. "Did we fuck?" I stumbled out the words, my stomach in knots, my mind racing as fast as my heart.

Fuck.

Maddie.

I looked at my watch. It was after lunch.

Fuuucccckkk.

"What are you doing in my apartment?" I spied my trousers and ripped them on, sitting on a chair as far away from Margot as possible, who continued to kneel on the bed, butt naked.

"In the car we had champagne, made a toast to Alessandro turning thirty. We spoke of your birthday later in the year and one thing led to another. We kissed, you told me you missed me, and we ended up here." She patted the bed and I wanted to vomit.

I wracked my brain, fighting to remember much beyond getting into the car. I wasn't that drunk. Why didn't I remember any of that? "Did you spike my drink?"

"What?" Her voice tipped to a pitch that screamed guilt.

"You did, didn't you?" I looked around for my shirt. "Did we fuck or are you just trying to frame me?"

"Oh, we fucked, and I fucked you good, Henry. You enjoyed it, and one drink in the car led to more. You were not drugged, but you were drunk by the time we reached home. I'm not surprised you can't remember."

I rubbed my jaw. This couldn't be happening. I'd lose Maddie if she ever found out. Maybe I had drunk more at the party than I thought and the champagne in the car tipped me over. Still, I've never not remembered fucking anyone in my life.

"You lie." I couldn't believe this was happening. "Leave."

I spied my phone on the floor and picked it up. One message from Maddie and a missed call, but nothing else and that was at nine this morning. When I had been due to pick her up.

Margot gathered her clothes and dressed, not bothering to hide her body from me. Any chance of us being friends vanished at her brazenness and underhanded actions of the night before. I may not remember what had occurred, but I couldn't believe I'd done anything with her of my own fruition.

"You'll regret this, Henry. Our families expect us to marry, and no matter what has occurred between us in the past few months, nothing will change the outcome. You will marry me, and our families will be connected just as they expect."

"We're not the fucking Italian mafia where we have to do what our families say, Margot. I'll not marry a woman who is unable to be faithful. Indiscretion in our teens is one thing, but you're far too old to be doing that kind of shit to a partner you're supposed to care about. You already tried to ruin what I had with Maddie in Sorrento with the paparazzi crap you pulled. I'll not let you do it again. You'll keep your mouth shut over what happened here, because as far as I'm concerned, nothing has happened. And if it did, it wasn't with my approval. I doubt the paparazzi would like to know what that makes you."

Margot gasped, slipped on her shoes and left, slamming the door on the way out.

I showered, needed to scrub away the idea, the feel of her mouth on me.

Jesus. What had I done?

Had I fucked Margot and cheated on Maddie?

How the hell was I supposed to tell her I'd fucked up yet again? She wouldn't forgive me and I couldn't blame her for that.

I quickly washed and dried before dressing and grabbing the bag I'd packed for travel to Sorrento the day before. I picked up my phone and read Maddie's text. My heart landed in my mouth at her sweet words.

I was going to lose her for sure this time and there would be no coming back from it.

> Hey, I hope everything's okay. Looking forward to seeing you. Xx

I looked at the missed-call notification, then quickly shot off a text, a lie that made my hands shake.

Plane issues. Will be leaving soon. See
you this afternoon. Xx

I was a prick. Possibly a cheating fucking prick. An hour later I slumped into the seat of the plane and ordered a water. Whether I slept with Margot or not was beside the point. I had woken up with her mouth swallowing my cock. How could I explain such a thing to Maddie and not ruin what we had started? And we had started something. What that was exactly I wasn't sure yet, but it was all-encompassing, thrilling, enjoyable, fun and loving, and I couldn't get enough of it.

I had a choice. I could either tell her what happened, and what I think had happened, or I could keep my mouth shut. See if Margot kept her mouth shut and let me get away with her antics.

My stomach churned and I sipped my water, eager to be in the air and away from Rome. Away from Margot. I wanted to see Maddie and no one else. We could hide away at the villa and forget about the troubles of the world.

My phone pinged and an image of me on my bed, Margot riding my cock, both of us smiling at the selfie.

WTF!

"Is everything well, Mr. Fairfax?" the flight steward Suzanna asked.

Had I sworn aloud? "Everything's fine. I'll have lunch now if it's ready."

"Of course, Mr. Fairfax."

I rubbed my forehead, unable to grasp I was in this position. However, not under my own steam I was sure of it. I looked at the photo again. I looked out of it, unaware of what was happening, while Margot looked far too sober and satisfied with herself.

What had I done?

Lost Maddie, that's what.

CHAPTER
Thirty-Six

I PACED near the window of our Airbnb, scanning the street, waiting for Henry to pick me up. He'd landed an hour before and said he was on his way. I couldn't wait to see him. I'd missed him and yet it had only been a few days since I'd returned from London.

I spied the black Porsche turn onto our street. Finally! "I'm off now. See you later!"

"Have fun," Eve and Clara shouted back.

I was out the door before anything more could be said, running down the stairs. I clasped my little bag in my hand, packed and prepared for our time together at the villa. The car pulled up just as I stepped onto the street. I didn't want to look like an eager, obsessed groupie, and yet I feared I did anyway. The car window slipped down, the sight of Henry leaning over, sexy as hell as usual, his mischievous grin making me inwardly sigh.

Oh man, I really liked this guy.

"Hi, New York."

I melted at the sound of his voice. I handed my bag to the driver, who placed it into the trunk of the car and jumped into the back with Henry. I pushed down the nervous jitters that always consumed me when having been away from Henry. Instead, I slipped my arms around his neck and pressed my body to his.

He was warm, hard, and all mine.

For now.

"Hi, handsome."

He kissed me, deep and long as the car took off, making its way through the town and toward the villa.

"I've missed you." He kissed me again and I drank him in. I'd missed being in his arms. The man made me feel things I'd never had with anyone else. There was an ease with him that I didn't think I'd get so soon into knowing him. But from that very first night we met in Ibiza, there had been an undeniable chemistry between us.

"I missed you too." I snuggled against him. "So, what are we going to do today?"

"Well, I thought we'd have a late lunch and then lounge near the pool. I need to relax after the couple of days I've had."

"Is everything okay?" He nodded, but there was a tension about his lips that said otherwise. I reached up and wiped my thumb over his bottom lip, trying to remove his concern. "Why do I get the feeling you're not?" When he didn't reply, I looked out the window, not wanting to pry. "You don't have to tell me if you don't want to."

"It's nothing." He sighed and pulled me tighter against him. I breathed deep his musky, vanilla scent.

"A day beside the pool sounds just the thing." I leaned up and kissed his neck, teasing the lobe of his ear with my tongue. A small smile lifted his lips and my mood lifted. It was what I wanted to see, Henry happy and unperturbed.

We had lunch outside as planned and after ended up on the lounges beside the pool, wide umbrellas shading us from the scorching Mediterranean sun. I turned, drinking in Henry as he sat, reading a book. He had a pair of reading glasses on that I hadn't seen him wear before and if I thought the guy couldn't get any more handsome, I was so fucking wrong. The man was deadly with spectacles.

As if he could sense me watching him, he grinned, laying the book in his lap. I figured a little grin was as good an invitation as any and joined him on his lounge, lying next to him. I entwined our legs and rested on his chest.

"You've been so quiet this afternoon. Did you drink too much last night at your friend's birthday and have a little hangover?" I teased.

"Sort of. I left reasonably early, not that it helped when I had plane issues this morning."

"So you've known Alessandro since childhood too? You went to school with him?"

"How do you know that?" Henry asked.

I raised my brow, not entirely sure why that question came out as harsh as it did. Was he angry that I knew something about his life he hadn't told me himself? "I wasn't prying on the internet if that's what you were thinking. The party was on the news, and it was mentioned on there that you would be in attendance and how long you'd known each other."

"Oh right. Of course. I'm sorry."

What was going on? There was a nervous energy emanating from Henry and it made me the same. I climbed off his lap, and averted Henry's attempt to pull me back onto his seat. I dived in the pool, my mind whirring with thoughts. Had something happened at the party? Why was he so touchy about it?

I came up for air and swam over to the infinity side of the pool, staring out over the ocean breaking against the cliffs below. The view was so utterly beautiful, and it was a shame more people didn't get to enjoy such locations of this pristine coastline.

I startled when arms wrapped about my stomach, before a warm, hard chest pressed against my back. "I'm sorry. I'm not being very fun today." He kissed my neck, before resting his head on my shoulder. "I don't want to lose you, Maddie."

What did that mean? I faced him, trying to read his expression, but as usual he gave nothing away, reading him impossible. "You're not going to lose me. Not yet. I have another few weeks left here."

"What would you say if I moved my office to Sorrento for the remainder of that time and we lived here? No distractions, no separation until you leave me."

I jumped into his arms, wrapping my legs about his hips and hugged him, kissing him all over his face. "I would love that. I was dreading you leaving on Sunday."

"Then it's settled. I'm not going anywhere. I'll notify the office later today and we can relax here, be together just as I'd prefer."

The idea of living in a bubble on top of this beautiful location with this sweet man was a dream come true. I ran my fingers through his hair, pushing his locks off his face. He watched me with his dark eyes that burned with need.

My body heated. "Are you ever going to touch me today, Henry?" The question was bold, but I was over waiting. I ached for him, wanted him so much.

Craved him.

Adored and yes, utterly loved…*him.*

CHAPTER
Thirty~Seven

"ARE YOU ASKING FOR SOMETHING, Miss Webb?"

Without shame I rubbed suggestively against him. My heartrate spiked and I gasped at the feel of his hard cock slicing between my legs. "Oh, I'm definitely asking for something."

He did not disappoint.

He slid his clever fingers over my bikini bottoms, teasing me. One finger hooked the material and moved it aside before he touched me where I ached.

"You're wet, Maddie."

I played with the hair at his nape, enjoying my view. "We're in the pool. Of course I am." I grinned. I knew that wasn't what he meant, but I couldn't help but tease him.

"Oh, I see how it is." Without warning he lifted me out of the pool and set me on the edge. He wrenched me to the side so my ass sat on the edge. "Lie down, Maddie."

What was he going to do? Surely he wouldn't do what he looked hell-bent on doing here. I glanced around the pool area, and although I couldn't see any staff, I knew they were never far away in case they were needed. But we couldn't do what he suggested. Christ, what if someone saw us? I'd never be able to look anyone in the face again.

"We cannot." I pressed against his shoulder, but he didn't budge. He stared at me with a determination that left me breathless. God, I adored everything about him. How could I deny him anything?

I shook myself back to reality and sense. "No, Henry."

"Do as you're told, New York."

Oh gosh, now he was being dominating. It suited him, which only made him hotter. I sighed and lay down, pretended to be annoyed, but really, my body thrummed with expectation, ached with need. Heat kissed my skin, and not entirely from the hot Mediterranean sky.

His arms wrapped under my legs and pulled me near his mouth. I watched, enthralled as he slipped the small piece of material aside and dipped his head. He groaned, the noise making me shiver. His tongue flicked out, teasing my clit, his eyes never leaving mine.

I almost came at the sight of him doing that deliciousness to me.

"I've missed you. All of you."

His muffled words teased my sex. His mouth expertly lathed my sensitive flesh, spiraling me toward ecstasy. I shut my eyes against the glaring sun and floated into the bliss only he could bestow. He fucked me with his fingers with an achingly slow, torturous rhythm.

"You'll be the end of me." I could feel my body coiling toward release. Wanton and without shame I undulated against his face, held his head against me as he fucked me with his mouth.

The orgasm ripped through me, strong and sharp, spiking through my sex and out through my body. He savored every tremor, before slipping my bikini bottom back into place and watching me with a self-satisfied grin that made me laugh.

"Did you enjoy that, Miss Webb?"

I couldn't move. I lay there, one arm over my eyes as I fought to control my breathing. After a few moments I sat up. Henry dipped a little into the water, watching me.

"You are a terrible example for me. Whatever will I do with you?"

His chuckle was deep and full of seductive charm. "Well, I could think of a few things."

I slipped into the water, throwing myself back into his arms. "In truth, Henry, how is this long-distance going to work? I'm leaving soon."

"Don't remind me. I'm going to miss you so much."

My head spun at the relief that poured through me.

Oh thank the heavens I wasn't the only one feeling what was growing between us. What I hoped wasn't just me wanting more from someone who was not on the same page.

"I'm going to miss you too." I kissed him and he spun me about in the water. I was giddy with relief. Did this mean we were officially a thing? Dare I think boyfriend and girlfriend?

"I'll come and see you as much as I can when you return to New York. I'm there a couple of times a year for business, but I'll make sure that's amped up to every quarter. And of course I'll fly you out to see me in Rome as much as possible."

"I can't ask you to do that. But I'll save what I can to see you often."

"Maddie." His tone was understanding, but firm. "A ticket to fly you out here is nothing to me. Let me do this for you. I want to see you as often as I can, and that's quite an investment on your behalf. I cannot ask you to do that. Let me pay for your tickets. Truly, I don't mind."

I wanted to argue, but then he was probably right. I could afford two, possibly three economy flights out to Europe a year, especially with Clara's father not expecting any rent from me, but even that would be a lot. I'll only be earning base level income for the first year, not enough to fund such lavish travel arrangements. And I really wanted to see Henry as much as I could. Already I missed him.

"Okay then. You win on this one. I'll let you pay for

some of my flights." I kissed the tip of his nose. "Thank you."

"You're very welcome, beautiful."

CHAPTER
Thirty-Eight

I SAT under the wisteria and pretended to reply to emails, but one in particular sat glaring at me in my inbox. Margot had emailed, explaining in great, damning detail what had occurred between us in Rome. I couldn't believe I had done what the image suggested. Out of it or not, drunk or not, I had fucked another woman.

How the hell would I tell Maddie?

I looked up, spying her in the pool, floating on the water, asleep on an absurd banana floaty Sophia had purchased last summer that no one used. Maddie had found it today in the pool house and thought it perfect to use.

I could lose her over this and just when we'd decided to be more than just a summer fling. I didn't want to lose her, but she deserved to know the truth. To decide if my indiscretion was too much to continue what we had started. I cursed knowing she was the first

271

woman I'd ever felt comfortable being myself with. There was something trustworthy about her. She wasn't false, or a woman who'd use my influence to further her career or lifestyle.

She was going back to NY to work, to save and fly out to see me. Not expecting me to help her with anything, wanting to go it alone and do it herself as much as she could. I couldn't help but admire her for that, even if I could send a private jet to her every week and it wouldn't dent my fortune.

She rolled off the banana into the water and I sat up, unsure if she meant to do that. But then she walked toward the pool steps to get out, wrapping the large, blue-and-white-striped towel around her before joining me at the table.

A servant placed a bruschetta with avocado and red wine on the table for a pre-dinner snack before leaving us be.

"Thank you, Maria. I'm starved."

I smiled, wondering when Maddie had come to know my staff's given names. "You're hungry? I would've ordered food earlier if I'd known."

"Swimming always makes me famished." She bit into a slice of bruschetta and her sigh of delight warmed the blood in my veins. Actually, there wasn't a sound that Maddie made that I didn't adore.

She looked all bedraggled and wet, her hair sticking to her slim shoulders and ample breasts that pushed up in her bathing suit. I placed a slice on a plate, needing to distract myself, and took a satisfying bite before pouring our wines. "Maddie, there's something that I need to tell you."

She set her food aside and picked up her wine. She looked relaxed and happy, and I hated that I was about to shatter the spell we'd been living in these past days.

Her eyes narrowed and a small frown settled between her brows. "What's happened?"

I ran a hand across my jaw, needing to prolong our time together, fear eating at me that she'd bolt as soon as she learned the truth. "You know I want a future with you, for as long as you'll have me, but you need to know something that's happened that may change your mind."

Her frown deepened and she played with the stem of her wine glass, her fingers shaking with nerves. "Okay…well, that sounds ominous. Why don't you tell me and then I'll decide."

I cringed and forced my mouth to move, to explain. "The birthday party in Rome I attended had Margot on the guest list. She spoke to me, was not approving of our relationship, and I threatened her that if she didn't stop, I would no longer be civil with her. That any chance of being friends would be out of the question."

"Well, that doesn't sound so bad." Maddie watched me with an affection I didn't deserve. I was a bastard who was about to break her heart.

"I left early, wanting out of Rome early the next morning, but when waiting for my driver, Margot joined me on, asking for a ride back to her apartment.

There were a lot of paparazzi around and not wanting to cause a scene, I agreed."

"Of course." Maddie sipped her wine, but her words sounded strained and unsure.

I couldn't meet Maddie's eyes, and like a coward, I stared at my laptop. "I woke up with her in bed with me the following morning. Its why I was late to the plane."

"What?"

I looked up at the sound of Maddie's chair pushing back. She stood, staring at me, her eyes wide and full of hurt.

"You slept with her?"

"Apparently yes."

"Apparently yes? What the hell does that even mean?" She gaped, her face paling and I stood, going to her. She pushed me away, holding up a finger to halt another attempt. "Don't touch me. Don't' even come near me. OMG…"

"I don't know when or how it happened." My heart raced, panic seized my stomach, making me want to throw up. "I woke up the next morning and she was there. She took photos of us and showed me when I didn't believe what I'd done. I'm sorry, Maddie. I'm so, so sorry. Please know I never intentionally wanted to hurt you."

The crack of her slap across my face stilled my words. I closed my eyes, savoring the pain, the least that I deserved. "I'm sorry, Maddie."

"Sorry?" She laughed, the sound mocking. "You're not fucking sorry. You're a using bastard who thinks only of himself. Clearly I've been deluding myself to think you're different from any of the other men I've known in my life, but you're not. You're an untrustworthy bastard who fucked his ex when seeing me. But then I suppose since I wasn't invited to your friend's party what should I expect? Just proves all along you never thought me good enough for you, your family, or friends."

"You are good enough, better in a lot of ways." I reached for her again and she pushed me aside, moving toward the French doors into the villa. "I only realized later that I should have asked you to attend the party. It was an oversight, nothing more. Even Alessandro asked why I'd not brought you."

"Well, we know the answer to that question don't we...because if I'd been there I would of cockblocked you from fucking your ex."

I shook my head. I was losing her, she was pulling away and there wasn't a fucking thing I could do about it. This had been my fuck up and she was paying the price. "Maddie please, I'm falling in love with you." Had I just said those words aloud? Shit. And now I was going to lose her. The thought made me crazy with alarm.

She stared at me, her eyes wide. "Love?" she scoffed. "You don't know the meaning of the word." She left me there, going indoors and I followed. She went upstairs and grabbed her small bag, throwing her belongings into it without care.

I ran a hand through my hair, not knowing what to do. I'd never said those words to anyone, and I also was clueless how to make her stay, to forgive me. Not that I deserved it, but the thought of losing her was too much.

"I didn't, I'll admit it. I had no damn clue what love felt like until I met you. I'm obsessed with you. I want to make you happy, spend every waking hour with you near me. I've never felt like this before."

"And yet you chose to fuck around. Well, now you're going to find out. Please order an Uber so I can leave."

"Please, Maddie. I don't want to lose you."

She stopped packing, hands on hips, glaring at me. "Well, you have lost me. We just don't work, Henry. We're too different, our lives, our upbringing. It doesn't work. That you sought to be with a woman who people warned me you would run back to eventually only proves this point to be true." She zipped up her bag and hoisted it over her shoulder. She tied a sarong about her waist and slipped on her flip-flops. "For days you've allowed me to stay here, make love to me, promise me a future that was worthless. I can never forgive such a breach of trust. I deserved the truth when you picked me up on the day you arrived. I feel used, like a fool, and that's because of you."

"Maddie...please."

"Please what, Henry? No." She shook her head, and

I knew it was over. She was immovable, as she should be. I wouldn't forgive either, if the roles were reversed.

"Goodbye and good luck. I think you're going to need it."

Thirty-Nine

I MANAGE to make it back to New York without losing control of my feelings. In the time it takes for me to pack up in Sorrento and fly across the Atlantic, Eve has managed to have everything for our new apartment unpacked and ready to move into. She texts me the code to get into our building and flat, and just like that, I can start my new life as a working adult.

Everything is sorted and wrapped up in a tight bow.

Except my heart and fucking life. That's a mess.

I hurt. So damn much. And there's one man I blame for that. Well, not just him—his ex too. What a fucking shit show.

I punch in the code to get into the flat and walk inside. An entire floor for three single women, overlooking Central Park. I go to the window and take in the million-dollar view and feel…nothing.

That's not entirely true. If I had to explain it, the feeling is numb—mind and body shut off from everything I see. Will I ever laugh again? Trust another man? Or even give any of them the time of day just to see if they aren't all made up of the asshole gene?

I go to my room. All new furniture has been bought for the apartment, and Eve—the best friend a person could ask for—has picked light-colored pieces, just how I like. The bedding is cream with large blue flowers, a happy, pretty duvet that does a little to cheer me up.

I smile. A small thing, barely there.

Hoisting my luggage onto the bed, I start unpacking. It doesn't take long. Once I finish, I place my laptop on my desk and open my emails, checking to see if my request to start early at York Advertising Firm has been approved.

The email is waiting for me. I open it, relief pouring through me. At least that part of my life isn't falling apart. I have a job. Friends who will be home in a few weeks. A roof over my head. Everything will be fine. My broken heart will eventually catch up to the new life I'm beginning here.

Another email catches my eye. The sender isn't one I recognize, but I open it anyway. A mistake.

The photo of Henry and Margot in his apartment stares back at me. Her sitting on his lap, Henry looking at her like she's the sun and the moon. The subject line reads: *Thought you'd like to see this.*

I shake my head. Margot is an evil bitch.

And no, I don't need to see that at all.

I slam the laptop shut and go to the bathroom, needing to shower and then sleep. I start work tomorrow and have to try to conquer my jet lag if I can. I have a life to make for myself. A future I worked damn hard to secure, and I won't let any holiday romance fuck it up.

Henry is a bastard. A cheating playboy who needs to grow the hell up. I don't need him, and I sure as hell don't need the fucking mind games that come with dating a complicated guy like that.

But I will use him.

I'll use the anger burning inside me to push forward, to make me hungry for what I want and what I can achieve—without any man's help.

Security under my own steam. Beholden to no one.

CHAPTER
Forty

Seven months later, Capri

MADDIE ISN'T HERE. I'd be lying if I said part of me hadn't been more excited at the prospect of seeing her again today—on the day of my best friend's wedding. Not exactly what a best man should be thinking about, but damn, I've lived in hope for months, and to have it dashed like this is a hard pill to swallow.

My duties are over—speech made, cake cut, enough pictures taken to last the happy couple a lifetime. I haven't moved from the main table. I danced with the maid of honor, ignored her fluttering eyelashes and perfected come-hither glances. They don't work on me. I only want one woman in my arms, and she's not here.

If disappointment were a person, I'd be it.

For a moment, earlier in the day, my heart lurched at the sight of her friends. Eve and Clara are here, enjoying themselves as usual. I held my breath, thinking Maddie would materialize behind them.

She didn't. Nor will she.

I down another scotch, my eyes watering. I should stop. I've had enough, and there's little point in drowning my sorrows. I've perfected that pastime over the past seven months—I don't need any more practice.

I debate going to speak to Eve, who, unlike Clara, hasn't glared at me every time she catches my eye tonight. I know what they think of me. What a cheating bastard I am. How dare I hurt their friend.

And I deserve their fury.

I did cheat. The photos proved it. Not to mention, I do remember waking up with Margot sucking my cock. I can't pretend that didn't happen.

Not that I can remember anything else from that night. No matter how much I try, the memory won't materialize of me fucking her. And that—more than anything—makes me feel like I'm being punished for a crime I didn't truly commit.

I blink, tired of it all. I haven't slept well in months, and today has been a big one. I rarely go out these days, preferring to stay home, throw myself into work, and avoid the world.

Eve saunters past not far from me, and I don't get up to speak to her. I'm a coward when it comes to Maddie's friends. Would they tell me anything about her if I asked?

Doubtful.

Margot, several months pregnant, dances with

Merrick, laughing and smiling in my business partner's —and ex-best friend's—arms. I grind my teeth, sipping my scotch. I can't stand the sight of either of them. Margot is trying to get under my skin, punish me because I haven't slept with her since Rome.

Why she thinks it's punishment is beyond me. I don't give a fuck who she's with. I'll raise my kid—preferably with joint custody—and have as little to do with her as possible.

She doesn't know it yet, but I've had my lawyers draw up the paperwork. I just need to have her served. Margot won't take it well. I'd be surprised if she doesn't do a tell-all interview, making me look like the biggest bastard to ever walk the streets of Rome.

Maybe I ought to tell the world what she did. I don't remember consenting to her fucking me.

I down the last of my scotch and stand. I'm going to talk to Eve. I tell myself it's just to make sure Maddie is doing well, moving on with her life. That she's not as wretched as I've been these past months.

"Eve." I smile, trying to be personable, friendly. I catch her at the bar alone, a stroke of luck since Clara clearly wants nothing to do with me. "It's good to see you."

Eve looks me up and down, all delight of the night seeping from her face. "I wish I could say the same, but I can't." She waves me off. "Off you go, Henry. I have nothing to say to you."

"I just want to know how she is." I don't need to name Maddie. Eve knows exactly whom I mean.

"She's better, no thanks to you. Not that I'd think you'd care after what you did to her in Rome."

I order a whiskey dry and rub the back of my neck. Remembering Maddie's devastation rips my soul in two. I don't know how to fix the fuck-up I made. But the thought of losing her—it's worse than death. She's the first woman I've cared for, deeply. So much so that I question if I've fallen in love.

I don't know what that emotion feels like.

I've lusted after women before, but with Maddie, it was different. Her happiness came before all else. I wanted to protect her from anything that could hurt her.

Including myself.

And what a piece of shit I am, because I'm the one who broke her heart.

"I don't know what happened." All true. I don't. The night still makes no sense to me.

Eve scoffs, looking at me like I'm garbage. I am. I can't blame her.

"Do you want me to remind you what Mads told me? Just to refresh your memory?"

"No." I hesitate, not wanting to sound desperate, even though that's exactly what I am. "Is she seeing anyone?"

I hold my breath as Eve digests my question.

"She's been out on dates, had a few flings. We urged her to get under someone else to get over you, and it seems to have worked. I think there's a guy now—Paul something. He's a banker and seems keen. We're hoping something will come of it for her. She deserves happiness."

I want to vomit.

I take a deep breath and reach for my whiskey. The image of her intimate with another man, a faceless stranger who makes her smile, laugh. Who takes her out on dates. Buys her a birthday present. A day I missed after we broke up.

Fuck.

I hate him, whoever he is.

"I guess I deserved that bluntness."

Eve sighs, shaking her head. "Why did you do it? What the fuck were you thinking?"

"I don't know how the fuck I ended up here. I'd do anything to go back to that night and change what happened. I miss her…"

"I'm mad at you, as is Clara, but I'm not going to keep punishing you. I wish you well, Henry." Eve steps away, but I go after her.

"Just tell me, did she land the job she had lined up in New York? Is she happy and settled there?"

"She is. York Advertising is very happy with her work so far, and she's already climbing the ranks. I think, for the first time in her life, she's not afraid of what the future holds because she knows she'll succeed on her own."

"She works for an advertising company?"

"Yes. It makes her happy and isn't far from where we live, so it's convenient. Maddie is working her way up, but we always knew she'd do well. She's smart as hell and committed to excellence. There was never any other outcome for her."

"Thanks for telling me, Eve."

She leaves, and I move back to the main wedding table, ready to see the night out, lost in my own thoughts.

York Advertising.

Interesting.

I wonder if they take on international clients…

Forty~One

New York

"CONGRATULATIONS, Maddie. You're now officially the advertising executive's assistant and intern. I'm pleased to have you on my team. I know you won't let me down."

I shake Catherine's hand, beyond pleased with myself—and honestly, a little surprised. "Thank you for the opportunity. I won't let you down. I promise."

I've done it. Somehow, with my last pitch and the successful advertising campaign for Bunkers Beer in Texas, I managed to outsell other indie brand beers in the state. Catherine had personally asked me to pitch for the position of assistant and intern to the firm's advertising executive—herself. Landing the job still feels like a dream. Someone needs to pinch me to tell me this is real.

"I know you won't set a foot wrong. Now, let me

show you to your new desk. It's closer to mine so we can work more closely."

I take a deep breath and follow Catherine, leaving behind the cubicles I've been working in for the past seven months. We step into the elevator and ride up to the next floor. This area of the building has more space, fewer desks. Catherine's office is a corner suite with windows that overlook the city skyline. One day, if I work hard enough, maybe that could be my view.

"This is where you'll be working from."

My new desk isn't far from hers, and thankfully, I face her. If she needs me, I won't miss the call. Nothing worse than having a desk where my back is to the boss.

"This is amazing."

Catherine smiles. "I remember when I was first promoted. I sat just over there, where Josh is now."

I glance over at Josh—a man I've seen around the office before. He's hard to miss. He often strides past us in the foyer, his tall, athletic build always a pleasure to view in those tailor-made suits. His long, blond hair falls over one eye, giving him an effortlessly rakish, almost-too-hot-for-the-office look.

Not that I approve of interoffice relationships, but there's nothing wrong with admiring a handsome man who's off-limits. Not that I'm looking for anything serious. I'm dating again, seeing Paul, a banker on Wall Street, more than anyone else. He's nice, tall, handsome —and very good in bed. He allows me to forget, for a few hours at least, the man who occupies far too much of my thoughts.

"You worked your way up through the ranks too. That gives me hope." I want to do the same—learn from the best and hopefully run my own accounts one day. Catherine is incredible—successful, independent, and beholden to no one. There's a good chance I have a little crush on her sheer ability to have it all.

"I did, and I even completed the same degree as you at NYU." Catherine gestures to my desk, and I move toward it. "If you work hard enough, the sky's the limit."

My new desk is large, with privacy screens on two sides—something I welcome. All my belongings from my old desk have been boxed up and placed beside my new Mac, work phone, and calendar.

"You get a company phone and laptop, which you can take home and use as much as you like. I only ask that if I need something, you're available to help if possible. I won't call on weekends unless it's urgent. There will be several international trips coming up, and I'll need you to accompany me. Is your passport up to date?"

I clear my throat, pushing away the memory of the last time I used my passport. "Yes, it's current."

"Great. We have a meeting in half an hour. The boardroom is at the end of the hall—you won't be able to miss it."

"Great, thank you again."

"You earned this, Maddie. No thanks needed."

Catherine leaves me to settle in, and I set about organizing my desk. I unpack my favorite pens, file away the accounts I'm currently working on, and place a framed photo of Eve, Clara, and me on the beach in Sorrento. A bittersweet image.

They aren't in New York right now. They're in Capri for Eve's cousin's wedding, which had been postponed after the bride broke her ankle skiing in Switzerland.

I set up my old laptop next to my new one, transferring files, making sure everything is in order before tomorrow. Only when I catch sight of Catherine heading to the boardroom do I grab a pen and notepad and follow.

The boardroom is already full—several advertising execs and their assistants. I take a seat next to Josh, knowing we hold the same level position.

"Hi. I'm Madeline Webb. Nice to meet you."

"Oh yes, Catherine's new go-to girl. Welcome."

Go-to girl? What the hell does that mean? I force a polite smile and ignore his quip, instead focusing on Catherine as she begins speaking about a new client.

"This is the biggest advertising budget we've ever had. This client, should we secure his company, has assured me the ongoing business will be extensive. It means, by the end of next week, I'm traveling to Europe to oversee the structure of Mr. Fairfax's businesses and what's been done in the past."

I freeze.

"Madeline and Josh, you'll both be joining me."

Josh sighs at the news. I, on the other hand, die in my chair. I can't move, blink, swallow—nothing.

Henry.

Henry has hired York Advertising to handle his new hotel's campaign.

What. The. Fuck.

I thought this might be an ad campaign for designer perfume, clothing, bags—something luxury. But a hotel chain?

"We'll have to make sure Mr. Fairfax is well pleased," one of the executives comments.

No shit. From knowing Henry firsthand, I already know he wants only the best for his business. But why the hell is he hiring my firm?

The meeting stretches on for another half hour, but my mind won't function.

How does he even know where I work?

Is he trying to weasel his way back into my life?

I scoff under my breath, and a few execs glance at me before returning to their discussion. Well, Henry won't succeed. He can go jump off a short pier for all I care.

"Maddie, a word, please."

Catherine's request catches me off guard. I blink up at her, my fingers gripping the pen too tightly. "Sorry, yes?"

Jesus, pull yourself together, Maddie.

Henry isn't here. He can't touch me without my permission. Other than working on his hotel brand and making sure his advertising is first-class, I don't have to have anything to do with him.

I straighten, pushing down my nerves. "Of course."

"Come into my office. There are some things I need to discuss with you."

I nod and follow her, my hands shaking, my stomach twisting into tight, painful knots. I don't know what she's going to say.

But whatever it is, I already know it isn't something I want to hear.

"You look very pale and shocked by this news. Is it the travel abroad that's worrying you? I can give you some Valium if you need it before flying, if you're nervous."

"Oh no, it's not that." I wave her concern aside. "But there's something you need to know before I come on this trip with you."

Catherine sits and gestures for me to do the same. I sink into the chair, relieved because I'm not sure my legs would hold me up much longer. I don't feel like myself at all. The thought of seeing Henry again— having to interact with him. How am I supposed to do that and not crumble into the heartbroken mess I've worked so hard to overcome?

"What is it?" she asks.

Damn it. I don't want to rehash old wounds, but I have no choice if I'm expected to work with Henry.

"I, um… I know Mr. Fairfax." I force the words out, hating how shaky my voice sounds. "In fact, I dated him for a month or so over the summer when I was in Sorrento. It's a long story how we met, but we ran into each other again there, and…well, we started seeing each other. But like most summer romances, it fizzled out, and I came home." I exhale sharply, the pain as raw as ever. Damnit, why couldn't I get over him? "I can't work with him, Catherine. At least, not in person. I think it would be best if I worked from the office here. I can adjust to European hours, always be on hand to assist, and send through anything you need."

I'm babbling, my words spiraling out of control. I clamp my mouth shut and let Catherine process what I just said.

She stares at me, shocked—her eyes wide, mouth slightly open—before she recovers and leans back in her chair. "Wow. That was not what I expected. I thought you were just overwhelmed by the idea of traveling so soon into the position."

"No, nothing like that. I'm thrilled about this job. But I need to make sure I didn't get it because of Henry —because he made it part of the agreement to work with this firm."

"Of course not. You earned your position on your own. I don't operate like that, Madeline. Please don't think that's the case."

I release a breath, nodding. "Thank you. I just needed to be sure. I don't want Henry Fairfax to have any influence over my career."

"I understand." Catherine's voice is firm, reassuring. "I'll send an email updating the travel team and find someone else to accompany Josh and me to Europe. I'll inform Mr. Fairfax's team of the change."

"Thank you, Catherine. I'm really sorry about this. I never imagined this would be an issue."

"No, it's certainly not a situation I've had to deal with before, but we will, and it'll be fine. I doubt he even knows you work here."

"I hope that's true." The idea that Henry hired York Advertising just to gain access to me makes my stomach churn. "I'd hate to think he's using this company as a way to track me down."

Catherine hesitates, studying me. "He wasn't violent, was he? If he was, I'll turn down the account right now and tell him to go to hell. I won't stand for that kind of business."

"No, nothing like that. Just the usual bullshit that happens in a holiday romance. He cheated on me with his ex. Nothing groundbreaking."

Disappointment flashes across Catherine's face, and I force a smile, wanting this conversation over. Even now, months later, saying the words aloud sends a lump to my throat and an ache straight to my chest.

"Was there anything else you needed from me?"

"No, thank you, Maddie. That's it for now."

I leave her office, checking my laptop as I pass my desk. The file transfers are complete, so I head down to the lobby café, grabbing a chicken roll for lunch before making my way back upstairs.

By the time I return, Josh is away from his desk, and Catherine is on a call. I eat while tidying my workspace, setting up for the accounts I've carried over from my previous position. The day flies by, and when I finally check the time, it's past six.

I pack up and catch the subway home.

The empty apartment feels hollow. No friends to welcome me. No laughter bouncing off the walls. I toss a ready-made meal into the microwave and settle onto the couch to watch a movie, exhaustion pulling at me.

Somewhere between finishing dinner and zoning out, I must fall asleep before the sharp ding of my phone jolts me awake.

I blink, focusing on the screen. A message from Catherine.

> Call me when you can. I won't be in the office tomorrow.

A sharp knot of anxiety twists in my gut. I haven't even done much today—what could I have possibly screwed up already?

I dial her number, pressing the phone to my ear.

"Catherine, it's Maddie. You wanted me to call?"

I hear papers rustling before she clears her throat. "Yes, thank you for calling back tonight. I'm sorry for the late message. I won't be in tomorrow, but you'll be working on the Fairfax-Dudley file, and there are things in there that won't make sense unless we discuss them first."

"Of course. I'm listening."

Catherine pauses. Why does she sound hesitant?

"Maddie, I received a call from the Fairfax-Dudley team in Rome. They've outlined stipulations for the firm securing this contract."

I sit up straighter. "Stipulations?"

Dread curls through me, settling low in my stomach. I already know where this is going.

"The client has specifically requested that you be part of the team traveling to Italy. If we're unable to accommodate this, they will reconsider working with us."

Silence fills the line. My heartbeat pounds in my ears.

That bastard.

Henry is pulling strings to force me back into his orbit.

I should message him—call him out on his bullshit. But that would mean giving him the ability to contact me on my new number. The number I changed the moment I landed back in New York.

"Wow. Okay. That's…a lot to take in."

"I'm really sorry, Maddie. I can assure you, as the head executive on this deal, that if you agree to go, I'll limit your interactions with the Fairfax-Dudley team— especially Mr. Fairfax."

I close my eyes, exhaling slowly. The thought of being near Henry again—hearing his voice, smelling his cologne, watching him—makes my pulse spike.

God damn it.

Why is he doing this to me?

I left. I gave him his freedom. Let him have his childhood sweetheart. Margot is pregnant with his baby, for Christ's sake. What the hell is he playing at?

Can I be professional? Can I resist the urge to slap Henry Fairfax the second I see him?

I inhale deeply. "Unlike Mr. Fairfax, I can be professional. I'll come, support you in any way I can. But I'd appreciate it if you limit my time around him. It didn't end well between us, and I have no interest in mixing my personal life with work. I know I'm being backed into a corner here."

"If you're uncomfortable, I can let the account go. There will be others."

"No, don't do that. I appreciate the offer, but this account is worth too much to the firm. Luxury hotel advertising is a niche market—I'd rather focus on that than my ex."

Catherine sighs, relieved.

I, on the other hand, feel sick.

"I'm sending the account details now. We fly out Friday. It looks like we'll be there for at least a month."

A month?

I swallow hard. "Okay. I'll pack accordingly."

We hang up, and I stare at my phone, debating whether to message Henry.

I don't.

I can do this.

I'm a professional.

Unlike some people I know.

Capri

I STARE at myself in the hotel bathroom mirror, smoothing down my long slacks and white silk shirt. It's professional, neutral—perfect for my first meeting with the Fairfax-Dudley team in half an hour. My stomach twists, nausea creeping in, and I clutch it, taking a deep breath.

I can't throw up now.

Henry probably won't even be there. He has a whole team working on this project—he doesn't need to be personally involved in the advertising. He could easily send his people to handle the campaign for his new hotel, which is almost finished and not far from the one I'm staying in.

"You can do this, Mads. You've got this. It's nothing. He's nothing to you. The bastard cheated on you— remember that if you have to see him today."

My phone dings.

Good luck today, babe.

I smile. Paul. Sweet, considerate Paul. It's nice he remembered to text me on my first international business trip.

Thanks. I'm excited for the opportunity, and Capri is lovely and warm.

Benign. Safe. I'm still not comfortable using endearments, but he doesn't seem to mind calling me babe, sweetheart…love. We haven't had the exclusivity talk yet, but something tells me he's not seeing anyone else.

I slip on my black shoes, grab my leather briefcase, and double-check that I have everything we've prepared so far for the new hotel's branding—concepts that tie into Capri's island atmosphere and its distinct appeal compared to a city like Rome or London.

I step out of the safety of my hotel room, fighting the overwhelming urge to turn around and lock myself inside. I've been avoiding going out, terrified I'd run into Henry.

What would I even say to him?

Nothing nice.

The elevator moves too fast, and before I know it, I'm stepping onto the second floor, making my way toward the conference rooms. Catherine is waiting for me, and the sight of her helps, just a little.

She smiles, no doubt noticing how much I'm dreading this. "How are you?"

"I'll be fine. I just hope he's not here."

Catherine hesitates. "Maddie…"

Oh God.

I recognize that warning tone.

He's here.

A sinking feeling grips me, like I'm a condemned queen walking to the gallows. Okay, maybe that's a little dramatic, but the last thing I want is to see Henry Fairfax. To remember anything about what we had.

The magic of London. The heartbreak that followed.

Months of crying myself to sleep.

Seeing social media headlines about Margot's most-welcome pregnancy.

The speculation that an engagement would be next.

I. Don't. Want. To. Know.

And yet, he's dragged me back here, forcing me to relive it all.

I latch on to my anger, using it as armor. Wrapping it around me like a shield, I steel myself as Catherine pushes open the conference room doors. I plaster on the fakest professional smile I can manage.

"Mr. Fairfax. Ms. Tonami. Mr. Rossi. Please let me introduce my advertising assistants, Mr. Josh Nankivell and Miss Madeline Webb."

I shake hands with the Capri team, keeping my focus on everyone except Henry. But eventually, I have no choice. I have to look at him.

"Mr. Fairfax. An honor."

A lie. And my voice drips with sarcasm.

He doesn't smile. Doesn't pretend to be professional. Doesn't do shit. Just stares at me with those damn fucking eyes that swim with emotion.

I rip my hand from his grasp and move to my seat beside Josh, thankful I'm on the opposite side of the table from Henry and not directly in front of him.

Catherine starts the meeting, and I focus on the file in front of me, outlining the concepts and strategy we've developed so far for the hotel launch.

The entire time, I feel Henry's eyes on me. Watching. Pleading with me to look at him.

I hate it. And worse, I want it.

I cave.

Fucking bastard, I cave.

A wave of emotion slams into me, and I blink rapidly, swallowing the lump in my throat. No. I won't cry. I stopped doing that months ago. I don't have any more tears left for him.

But Henry looks...broken?

Despite his cleanshaven jaw, his immaculate suit, the air of power and wealth that clings to him—he looks hollow.

Like the other half of me.

Breathing. Existing. But nothing song else.

No joy. No life. No laughter. Nothing.

"Madeline, could you pull up the presentation and put it on the screen, please?"

"Of course."

Grateful for the distraction, I open the PowerPoint

and begin discussing the campaign now up on the whiteboard. Josh jumps in to help, and the Dudley-Fairfax team seems impressed.

Henry, however, remains unnervingly silent.

Why the hell is he even here if he isn't going to contribute?

We wrap up the strategy discussion, and Mr. Rossi moves on to logistics. "We'll be having an event for the grand opening. You'll all be on the guest list, of course."

"We'd be happy to celebrate a successful business venture," Catherine replies smoothly.

I glance at her. I'm not sure I will be happy to celebrate. I'd rather just return home.

"Which brings us to our next agenda item. Would you like a tour of the hotel? It's in its final fitting stages —tiling, painting, flooring. It's only a short walk from here."

"We would, thank you." Catherine stands, signaling the end of the meeting.

I pack up my files and laptop quickly. "Are we all required to go?" I whisper to Catherine.

"Yes. Everyone," Henry answers before she can. His tone is sharp.

My stomach clenches. We make our way out of the conference rooms, stepping into the elevator. Somehow, I end up standing directly in front of Henry.

Everything within me stills.

I can't move.

I can't breathe.

I can feel his body behind me, tall and imposing, far too close.

We've stood like this before—except last time, he wrapped his arms around me, kissed my neck. The memory crashes into me, sharp and unexpected. I need to get out of here.

The second the doors slide open, I rush forward, moving to walk beside Josh. As far away from Henry as possible.

There is a limousine van waiting outside for us at the valet area, and we climb in. This time, I make sure I'm nowhere near Henry. I take a seat beside Josh, look out the window, and pretend the island views from the hotel are too breathtaking to ignore.

Which, of course, they are. Capri is stunning, and I've only been here once before—for a single night, nightclubbing with my friends.

The morning after, Henry whisked me away to London and made me fall in love with him.

Damn man.

How could he have been so cruel?

I shiver, knowing he's watching me, trying to read into every emotion that crosses my face, every tiny movement.

He shouldn't bother. He's happy, isn't he?

In every article I've read, he and Margot certainly seem to be. They even did a *European Vogue* cover and a ten-page spread about their lavish lifestyle and her pregnancy.

I don't think I've ever torn up a magazine so fast in my life.

The people on the subway that day had kept their distance from me. Probably thought I was a crazy person.

And I was—for about ten seconds.

The limo van pulls up in front of the new Dudley-Fairfax Capri hotel. We step out, and I glance up at the Neoclassical-inspired architecture. The elite hotel is utterly breathtaking. I turn to take in the view of the Bay of Naples, the deep-blue ocean so aqua and still, the sky competing with it for attention.

"Do you like it?"

I don't look at him. I can't—not yet. I need to gather my wits, my gumption. "It's a beautiful location. I imagine many people will want to come and stay here."

"Would you?"

The longing in his tone almost breaks me in two.

Why is he speaking like this? What does he mean by that? There has to be an alternative meaning behind those words, because it bloody well sounds like there is.

"No. I wouldn't. I couldn't afford it, for a start." I smile, that fake-ass smile I've perfected this morning. "Shall we go in?"

I walk away, needing distance, but he catches my hand, pulling me to a stop. "Maddie. Damn it, Maddie, look at me."

I rip my hand from his, glare at him. "Do not fool yourself into thinking my being here has anything to do with our past. I'm here to do a job—one you forced on me when you threatened my firm to lose the account if I wasn't in Capri with Catherine and Josh."

"I knew you wouldn't come if I didn't stipulate those terms."

"You're right. I wouldn't have."

I leave him and join my team waiting in the foyer, ignoring the curious glances from the Dudley-Fairfax team after my exchange with Mr. Fairfax.

Not everyone needs to know our past. The fewer people who do, the better.

Maybe Henry doesn't usually bother with little people like me. I wouldn't be surprised if he doesn't.

Nothing surprises me anymore.

"Are you okay, Mads?" Josh asks, leading me away from the foyer to follow the others, his hand lightly against my back.

"I'm fine. I know Mr. Fairfax from a past life."

"A past life?"

"Yes. And one I want to forget."

We tour the hotel, and I'm thankful that Henry doesn't follow me into the foyer.

Good. He needs to get a grip and read the damn room.

We are over.

I will not be his fuck buddy, or the woman he cheats with on his pregnant girlfriend—fiancée—whatever the hell they are these days.

Hell no.

The meeting ends after we view the swimming and gym facilities. I go back to my room at the other hotel, wanting to catch up on work I left back in New York and continue refining ideas for the Dudley-Fairfax hotel. The hotel team seems to like the direction we're going in, so barring a catastrophe, I should be out of Capri by the end of the month as planned.

I pick up my phone and shoot off a text to Eve and Clara, who are now back in the States.

> Saw Henry today at the meeting. Awkward as fuck. Looking at him made me want to smack his handsome face off.

Not my best text, and violence isn't necessary—no matter how mad or hurt someone makes you. I can handle smugness, indifference. But the longing I read in his eyes? That, I did not expect. And it makes me mad as hell. Even now, my fingers shake as I hold the phone, waiting for a reply. Why is he upset? He's the one who slept with someone else. Put his pecker where is wasn't meant to be. How can he pretend to care about me when he did that?

My phone pings with Eve's reply.

> Oh, Mads, I'm so sorry. That would've been hard. Did he say anything to you?

> He tried. I shut him down. It's going to be a difficult job. Looking forward to when it's over.

> I bet. Sending hugs.

I throw my phone onto the bed and head to the shower. The workday is over, and I've finished everything I planned.

After changing into a black, short-sleeved dress, I decide to go into town near the port for dinner. I need to get out of this hotel. A change of scenery will do me good.

The hotel orders me a taxi and drops me off near the ferry docks. I walk along the paved foreshore, taking in the marina. Some superyachts—similar to Henry's—are berthed there.

I find a small, quiet pizza restaurant, order a chicken BBQ pizza, and sit near the window, people-watching while I enjoy the ocean view.

With the new Dudley-Fairfax hotel, the island will be busier. More jobs, more money for the locals—but also more challenges, especially for those trying to afford homes here.

A young man, no older than sixteen, sets my pizza before me.

"Thank you."

It's huge—far more than I can eat. After three slices, I push my plate back. "May I have a takeout box, please?"

He quickly grabs one and brings it over. "Here you are, miss."

"Thank you. The pizza was delicious."

He grins, his face lighting up. "You're welcome."

I leave the restaurant and stroll along the marina pier, lost in thought. The ocean is impossibly clear, calm. The Mediterranean is perfection—warm and inviting.

"Madeline?"

I stop. Freeze.

Fuck.

Of all the people to run into…

I turn toward the voice, immediately recognizing the yacht. How did I miss Henry's boat docked here earlier?

He descends the stairs at the back of his yacht, jumps onto the dock, and stands before me. He's all casual elegance, gone is the suit, and in its place is the guy who spent days at the beach, swimming, playing, loving me…

"Mr. Fairfax." My voice is stiff. "I didn't think to, um…"

Ugh. How do I say I wasn't looking for you without sounding like I was?

Which I most definitely was not.

"Don't call me that, Maddie. It sounds so clinical."

I grind my teeth, fighting the urge to say something snarly.

Be professional. Be professional. Be professional.

"I'd prefer to remain professional. Please, use Miss Webb when addressing me."

He steps closer, towering over me in that stomach-clenching way of his.

I force myself to look toward the town, hating that I can smell his hotness—that same intoxicating cologne that once made me weak.

Not anymore.

"Come on, Maddie. You'll have to talk to me eventually."

I laugh. I can't help it. Does he actually think I owe him a conversation?

"Actually, no. I don't have to talk to you at all. Outside of the hotel launch, you don't exist to me."

His eyes darken. "How can we fix this? You must know how much I miss you."

"I'm sorry for you, then."

I walk away.

Because hell will freeze over before I let Henry Fairfax break my heart a second time.

Forty~Three

OVER THE NEXT WEEK, we make strides in the advertising for the new hotel. The opening gala is planned for the middle of next month, and if everything goes to plan with the finishing touches, the launch and opening will be a success.

I sit with Catherine and Josh in the boardroom, working. I sip what feels like my tenth coffee, desperate to stay motivated while being closeted in our office space instead of outside enjoying the island's sunshine and stunning vistas.

With Henry back in Rome this past week, work has been enjoyable. I can almost pretend he doesn't exist—or that he isn't the reason I'm here at all.

Maybe after our conversation at the dock, he's finally decided to leave me the hell alone.

I can only hope.

"Right, I think that's enough for today. Any plans for tonight?" Catherine asks as she packs up her desk.

"I'm going out with a friend who's visiting the island," Josh replies.

I smile at him. I still don't know if he has a girlfriend or partner—he's so quiet and rarely speaks about anything but work. Which is fine with me. I prefer it that way.

"I'm having dinner in my room, then probably hitting the gym before bed."

"Well, you both have a great night. I'll see you here tomorrow at nine."

Later that evening I decide to hit the gym before dinner after all. As soon as I get back to my room, I change into workout clothes, grab a bottle of water from the mini-fridge, and head down to the third floor where the gym and pool facilities are.

I'm relieved to find the gym empty.

With an island this beautiful to explore, I suppose working out indoors isn't a priority for most of the hotel guests.

I lift a few dumbbells before jumping on the tread-mill, slipping my earbuds in and blasting my exercise playlist. Sweat pours off me, and I already know my gym wear will need to be sent for dry cleaning after this.

"Well, well, well… if it isn't the chick who blew me off last summer."

I blink in surprise.

Merrick Dudley.

He grins at me, dressed in gym wear, looking totally hot while doing so.

Not that I see him that way, but he's nice to look at when there's nothing else around.

"What are you doing here?"

The stupidity of my question hits me the second I say it. I switch off the treadmill, jump down, and walk over to him, giving him a quick hug. "Forget that. I know why you're here. I suppose I should be asking how long?"

He flips his workout towel onto his shoulder, his grin widening. "Just a few days. I came down to check on the progress of the hotel, but I heard you were here and wanted to catch up. I'm glad I came to the gym now. Must be fate…"

I laugh and ignore his insinuation. "Yeah, good timing."

He nods. "What are you doing for dinner? Want to join me?"

I reach for my towel and water, considering his request. "Why not? That sounds lovely. Beats having dinner in my room alone, which was the plan."

"Oh, hell no. We can't have that."

"You just starting your workout?"

He moves over to a treadmill, setting his water and towel down. "Yeah. You just finishing?"

"I will now that we're going out for dinner. Where should we meet?"

"We can eat here, if you like. The restaurant is great —beautiful views. And we can share a bottle of red without worrying about getting back to the hotel in one piece."

"Sounds great. I'll see you at seven in the restaurant."

"I'll be there."

The sexy smirk he throws me—I ignore.

I haven't been on a dinner date with Merrick, and I push down the prickle of guilt at the thought that it might hurt Henry.

Not my problem.

Back in my room, I text Paul.

> Heading out to dinner with a friend from last summer, he's staying at the hotel. I'll call tomorrow night.

Have fun, beautiful. I hope he's not as handsome as me. I smile and decide to lie to Paul. No point in mentioning that Merrick has Italian godlike features.

> He's handsome, but just a friend. You have nothing to worry about.

Good. I'd hate to have to fight off Italian men.

> A gladiatorial fight to the death is not required. Talk later.

I shower and dress in black linen pants and a white shirt. I didn't bring a lot of casual clothing since this is a business trip, but looking at myself in the bathroom mirror, I decide I look fine for dining out.

At seven, I meet Merrick in the hotel restaurant. He's already waiting for me at the bar, his suit just as impeccable as Henry's always is. These men know how to dress well. They are so privileged, and yet probably don't realize just how much compared to everyone else who works hard to make something of themselves. A lot of their wealth has been inherited, not earned.

I try to stop myself from feeling bitter about that thought.

I'd been given nothing from my parents—besides withdrawal to crack at birth and years of shitty foster homes with people who never cared for me.

"Hey," Merrick says when I join him. He kisses my cheek, and the waiter shows us to our table.

"Thanks again for dinner. It'll be nice catching up."

"I haven't seen you since the night of the rave in Sorrento. I heard what happened between you and Henry. I'm sorry."

Is he, though?

I sit, slip the napkin onto my lap, and reach for the water. "It is what it is. We never suited each other anyway."

"Do you truly believe that?"

Merrick orders the best red on the menu, and the waiter leaves to get our wine.

I think about his question—about my time with Henry. Everything that was different between us. My upbringing compared to his. His social status. My lack of family.

I only have two real friends in the entire world.

"I do think that. As much as the chemistry between us was there, more is needed for a relationship to work. We fell apart in that sense."

The wine arrives, and I'm glad for it. I pick up my glass and take a sip. It's delicious and smooth.

"What really happened? I've heard conflicting stories."

I look out at the view, the ocean in the distance, a little choppy today, white caps cresting now and then. "Umm… Well, he slept with Margot in Rome after a friend's thirtieth birthday. Alessandro someone…"

"I was there that night. Alessandro is a mutual friend. I saw them leave at the same time but didn't think she'd end up in his bed."

The thought still makes me want to vomit. Seven months later, and the idea of them being intimate makes my stomach churn. I can't get the picture Margot emailed me out of my head.

"I should've known I'd be played in the end. My friends had suggested that their relationship was on and off for years. I chose to ignore the warning signs. I was just a temporary clog in Margot's life plan with Henry."

Merrick rubs a hand over his stubbled jaw, studying me. "He's back here tomorrow. We have some paperwork to sign off before I head back to Rome."

I fight to look indifferent, but I know I fail. I fumble for my wine and finish it off.

"Great. Something to look forward to."

My sarcasm isn't lost on Merrick.

"How is it that you're here anyway? I was surprised to find out you were working on the Capri hotel project."

"Long story, but let it be known that I was left with no choice."

"I'm sorry, Maddie. It seems like Henry is using his might to get you to do what he wants. Want me to have a word with him? I don't mind. You know we don't shy away from arguing these days. He's no friend of mine— just a business partner. If it weren't for our inheritance, even that wouldn't be a reality."

"No." I reach across the table and clasp his hand in thanks. "There's no need to say anything. I'm working with my team, and I'm not having much to do with him. I'm a big girl. I can handle it."

"Well, just let me know if anything changes and you feel uncomfortable."

"I will. Thank you, Merrick."

The waiter returns, and we place our orders. I choose lobster with spiced carrot and lemon verbena sauce for my starter and veal filet with white asparagus and lovage sauce for my main.

"Now, tell me—has anyone managed to tie down your bachelor lifestyle yet?"

He throws me a cocky grin, shaking his head. "Absolutely not. Although there was a woman who couldn't make up her mind, so I ended things myself. I shall see soon enough if I win her in the end."

I pour more wine into my glass, digesting his words.

Does he mean me?

I hope not.

As much as he's eye candy—his dark features, olive skin, perfect bone structure—I feel nothing but friendship toward him. I want him to find someone who makes his heart race the way mine once did with Henry.

Like it still does.

Damn it.

Even though I try not to let myself get pulled into Henry's orbit, it's impossible. Not that I'll ever let him know how much I still struggle around him.

"Well, good luck with that. Is she anyone I know?"

I met some of Henry's friends in London—not many, but it's possible the woman Merrick is talking about is one of them.

"You know her quite well."

Thankfully, our entrée arrives, saving me from questioning him further.

"This looks amazing. Thank you again for taking pity on me and inviting me out. It's nice to see a friendly face."

"It's nice to see your beautiful face, too."

I shake my head, hoping the heat creeping up my skin isn't obvious.

Jesus, the man is a flirt.

And as much as he may hope it will lead somewhere, it only makes me uncomfortable. I can't see him that way. Not anymore. Not after Henry.

"And you?" Merrick asks, sipping his wine. "Is there anyone special back in New York?"

I smile, thinking about Paul. "I'm dating a banker. He's very serious and has already had me invest some of my income. He's nice, and I like him." I shrug. "I'm hopeful this one won't end as badly as my last relationship, even if we don't go the distance."

Merrick laughs. "Whoa. Does Henry know you're seeing someone? He will not be pleased."

He downs the rest of his wine, grinning. "If I were spiteful, I'd text him right now and tell him the good news."

"Don't do that. What he doesn't know won't hurt him, and Paul doesn't need to get mixed up in this messy business trip. I only have a few more weeks here, and then I'll be going home."

"True." Merrick sighs. "What a shame, though. I'm fond of you and hoped I'd be seeing you around more. New York is so far away."

"You can always call me when you're in town. I'd love to catch up if you're ever over my way."

"I'll do that. You can count on me."

Forty~Four

THE FOLLOWING MORNING, we are called into a meeting with the Dudley-Fairfax team. I'm not sure what the emergency meeting is about, but Catherine sounds a little flustered on the phone when she calls at six.

I rush into the boardroom, ten minutes late—thanks to getting locked in my bathroom and having to use the emergency phone to call reception to let me out.

The sight of Henry catches me off guard, and I fumble with the door handle before finally slipping inside. I take a seat across from him. "Sorry," I whisper to Catherine. "I'll explain later."

"In the future, if there is a meeting, I expect my team to be on time, Miss Webb."

Henry's cutting, hard words slam into me, and I freeze.

I've never heard him sound so distant. So cold.

His eyes are ice—unfeeling. A shiver runs down my spine.

"Of course. Apologies. I got locked in my bathroom."

"I thought it might have been the late night," his colleague murmurs, smirking.

I don't respond. I just take out my laptop and files, preparing to update them on the advertising team's progress.

Conversation and ideas flow for the next hour, but the meeting is anything but pleasant.

Why the hell am I being called out in such an unprofessional way?

I've done nothing but work hard for the Dudley-Fairfax team—and for Henry, despite our differences and past issues.

This is uncalled for.

"Thank you. We'll meet again in a few days."

Henry stands.

"In the future, excuses such as being locked in one's bathroom won't fly. If you're going to lie, make sure it's believable."

And then he leaves.

I narrow my eyes, snapping my mouth closed when I realize I'm gaping.

Where is he going? His room? Is he staying here again, or somewhere else? Maybe he's flying back to Rome.

The hell he's getting away with that shit.

Without thinking, I stand and go after him, catching him just as he steps into the elevator.

His eyes widen in surprise before he schools his features, slipping back into that arrogant, annoyed expression he's held the entire meeting.

The doors close.

"What the hell do you think you're doing calling me out like that in the meeting just now?" I demand. "Don't forget that I don't want to be here. You forced my hand, and now you're rude because I got locked in my bathroom?"

"Was that really why you were late?"

"What?" I shake my head, trying to make sense of his tone. "I don't understand where this is coming from. Are you calling me a liar?"

He presses the emergency stop button, and the elevator jerks to a halt.

"I don't appreciate my advertising staff being late to important meetings. Your excuse doesn't hold up. Do better."

"Do better?" I bark out a laugh. "You must be kidding, right? Do better?"

The man is absurd.

"Perhaps you ought to do better than blackmailing me into being here. Threatening the company I work for just to get me back in your vicinity. But for what, Henry? Why force me to be near you again?" I my chin, my anger bubbling over. "Were you hoping I'd crack under the pressure and fuck you? Is that what you want?"

His jaw tightens. His breathing turns ragged. Good. Let him feel something.

"We're no longer friends, and there's certainly nothing between us. You made sure of that, Henry."

His eyes flash. "Unlike what's between you and Merrick."

I blink. "Merrick?"

How does he know I saw Merrick? Is that what this anger is about? He's jealous.

"I went to dinner with him. So what? What's it to you? I can see whomever I please when I'm not working."

"Are you fucking him?"

I gape. "That's none of your business."

"It is my fucking business. You're my business."

I go nose to nose with him, over his shit and high-handedness.

"No. I'm not." My voice shakes, but I don't back down. "You fucked Margot, remember? I've seen the pictures, Henry. She emailed them to me. Not sure why —maybe just to dig the knife a little deeper. To twist it and ensure ultimate pain."

I pause, inhaling sharply.

"I saw you on the bed with her on top. I saw your cock in her mouth, you fucking prick."

His expression shifts. "I don't remember any of that."

I stumble back, my breath catching. "That's your excuse? You don't remember?"

His hand clenches at his side. His jaw tightens. And

his eyes—his fucking eyes—glass over. Is he...teary? I still. The sight of him hurting infuriates me more. He doesn't get to be hurt.

"Are you going to see Merrick again?" His voice is low.

I hold his gaze, wanting to hurt him. Wanting him to feel the pain he's inflicted on me for the past seven months.

"I don't know." I my chin. "If he asks, I'll go out with him again. Sure." I watch his shoulders stiffen.

Good.

"But I won't fuck him, if that's what you want to know."

I let the words hang there, deliberately drawing out my next sentence.

"I'm seeing someone back in New York. And unlike you, I won't fuck an ex just because my current boyfriend isn't around to scratch an itch."

Henry's nostrils flare. "Merrick's a prick, and you're weak for falling for his charms."

He takes a step toward me, forcing me back against the elevator wall.

My heart pounds.

"And who's the guy in New York? Have you been seeing him long?"

I grit my teeth. "Paul is none of your business. And I am not weak." I snap the words at him, matching his intensity. "You, however, have proven to be less than complimentary."

"Merrick always wants what's mine. Ever since we

were children. It started with toys—taking mine, playing with them rough before handing them back broken. Of course, toys were soon replaced with women. I won't let him break you, Maddie. No matter how much you may hate me for saying so."

I swallow. "Well, you can't break something that's already broken, Henry. Merrick had no hand in that."

His eyes darken. "And does Paul make you feel everything I know you felt with me?"

Henry's hand slips against my hip, his fingers tightening on my waist. I loathe the man before me, glare at him, want to spit in his face—and at the same time, I want to sit on it.

He makes me want him with just a look, a touch. His anger spikes mine, makes me want to punish him. Taunt him with sex, then rip it away before following through.

I smirk, tilting my head. "He makes me come so hard. His mouth is as wicked as his large cock that fills and pleasures me most nights. Mmm, even now, thinking about him makes me wet."

A lie.

I can count on one hand how many times we've had sex. And while it scratches an itch, it has nothing on what the damn man before me makes me feel.

A muscle works in Henry's jaw, his grip tightening. "Is that so? Maybe you should let me test that theory— to see who's better at it."

I swallow hard and slam my hand against the button to start the elevator.

Henry is on me before I can react.

He presses me against the wall, his hard body flush against mine.

My mind screams to hurt him. To slap him, scratch his beautiful face—and at the same time, to undulate against him. To soothe the ache between my legs.

How can I hate him and want him at the same time?

Damn him.

"No," I say through gritted teeth.

His eyes burn into mine. "I want you back, Maddie. And I'm not the kind of man who likes to lose."

And there it is.

The words I've longed to hear for the past seven months.

But I won't be his plaything. Not again. Once was enough.

I lift my chin. "Go back to your life, Henry. Back to your perfect domus with your beloved Margot. And leave me the hell alone."

The elevator doors open. I shove past him, striding toward the bar—anywhere but near Henry. My hands shake. My blood is hot in my veins. I need a drink. But if I think I can escape him, I'm dead wrong. I skid to a stop near the bar door. Inside stands Margot. Sophia. And an older woman I've never seen before. I don't need an introduction, the resemblance is enough. Henry's mother. Their lively conversation halts at the sight of me.

Henry reaches for my hand, still oblivious to them. "Maddie, wait—"

Shit.

I rip my hand free, but it's too late. His mother and Margot have seen. Neither of them misses how it looks —as if Henry is chasing after me around the hotel. My stomach twists. I turn on my heel and leave without saying a word. What the hell is there to say? We just gave them a fucking show. I don't talk to anyone until I'm back in my room. I lock the door, flop onto the bed, and stare at the ceiling.

What the hell was that?

So unprofessional. Too emotional. I sigh, reaching for my phone.

> Hi Catherine. I'm really sorry. I'm not feeling well. I think I better take the day off if that's okay.

> That's fine, Maddie. We'll see you tomorrow if you're better by then.

> Thanks. I'm sure it'll pass.

But will it? My illness is six-foot-two, a hot pile of man goodness that I cannot seem to get over. I've tried. So many times. I even pretend that the thought of him no longer hurts.

All bullshit.

It hurts.

It hurts so damn bad.

I'm so mad. At him. At Margot. At the fucking world for giving me a glimpse of what life with him could have been—then ripping it away. A life that always guarantees I don't get anything.

Not love.

Not even respect.

From the moment I was born, that lesson was hammered into me every day.

I. Am. So. Fucking. Over. It.

I want more from my life. I deserve it, don't I? I'm not an awful person. I try my best to be friendly, to do what's right. When will I be treated the same way? It better be soon. Because I am on the verge of losing my shit. And for the first time in my life, I just might do something for myself—not for the greater good.

CHAPTER

Forty-Five

"I DIDN'T EXPECT you until next week."

I kiss my mother's cheek, and no one else's who is present. I don't feel particularly congenial for socializing now—not after my argument with Maddie.

The sight of Margot, her smugness at seeing Maddie upset, is too much for me to even pretend she isn't malicious incarnate.

Over the past months, she's become worse. So far removed from the woman I used to care for and date. From the childhood friend I once adored. All those emotions are no longer there. They are gone, long gone. Had been well before Maddie entered my life.

Not that it matters now.

We are having a child, and I will be there for that child, but pretending that everything is fine, that we can live happily ever after, isn't something I can do. Not even for my family.

"We want to inspect the new hotel before it opens. As a shareholder, it's only my right."

"And mine," my sister adds, looking past me to where Maddie just turned and fled. "Was that Madeline Webb I saw just before? What's she doing here?"

"Oh, didn't you hear, Sophia? Your brother hired her advertising firm in New York to handle the new hotel's PR."

Sophia looks at me as if I have lost my mind. And perhaps I have. For the past months, I haven't been myself. A shadow of what I once was. I go through the motions of everyday life, keeping the business profitable and running like a well-oiled machine. As expected from the Dudley-Fairfax luxury hotel chain.

But none of it makes me happy. Not anymore. If I am truthful, I am the unhappiest I have ever been in my life. I don't want to be resentful toward Margot, but I am. I don't want her near me. She continues to live in her apartment in Rome, but seems to think that when the baby comes, she will move in with me.

I will have the baby, but not her. Not that she seems to understand those rules.

"I can hire whomever I want since I'm the majority shareholder of the Dudley-Fairfax hotel chain, Margot. Just for clarification, in case you have forgotten."

"A word, Henry."

My mother links our arms and guides me out of the bar and toward the entrance of the hotel. I escort her outside, and we start to head in the direction of the new hotel, which isn't far.

"What's going on, son? Why is Miss Webb here? I thought it was over between you two."

"It is over."

I hate saying those words. They rip my guts out every time.

"I fucked up, Mother."

She doesn't say anything, merely looks forward, like she always does. Strong and ready to face whatever challenges come her way.

"I have nothing against Miss Webb personally. I'm sure she's a professional woman. I'm glad that she's no longer working as a waitress, at least."

"That was only a summer position, Mother."

"In any case, there will always be a divide between you. You're from a family of great wealth and privilege. You've grown up with expectations and the weight of the company that you now run on your broad shoulders. As much as I can see why you enjoyed Miss Webb's company and may have even fallen for her a little more than the other women in your life, she is not the same as we are. She doesn't have the social cues you have perfected, there is no family supporting her. From what I know of her, she has her two college friends and employment and not much else."

"She's an orphan, Mother. How can that be her fault?"

"So you know of her past?"

Something in my mother's tone gives me pause, and I pull her to a stop. "I know enough." Her pain and shame, that I did not think Maddie ought to carry. She had never done anything wrong.

My mother purses her lips, and I can tell she is debating whether to continue this conversation or not.

"There is no record of her father at all. People presumed he was addicted to drugs just as her mother was and has fallen off the earth, but that's unknown. The mother we do know passed a few days after Miss Webb's birth, but the child was a crack baby, Henry. What if that news came out in our social sphere of friends? What would they think of us? Of her, should you pursue your obsession with this woman? They will always look at her as someone who is broken, possibly someone who is inherently likely to become addicted to drugs herself. Her life would be made harder if such information became public, and if you pursue her, it's certain to come to light. Someone will dig up the dirt, and we'll all be left looking muddy."

I watched my mother, wondering when she became so cold and unfeeling towards those less fortunate. "I don't care what people think. Let them say anything to my face and see what they receive in return. I will not have her name sullied by a situation that was not of her making. Shame on you for thinking this is all somehow her fault."

"I do not think that, but these are facts. Margot, darling, is from our world. Yes, she's been a little naughty, much like yourself, but that only means she will be ready to settle down. She's pregnant, with your child, my first grandchild. Please give your love to her, which I know you once had. Everyone deserves a second chance."

More like a third or fourth chance. I've lost count of how many times she's cheated. "A child is no reason for a couple to be together if they're no longer in love, Mother. That is a recipe for disaster, and you know."

My mother's lips press together before she speaks again, her voice softer, but firm. "Well then, let me put it this way, Henry. And know that I do not say this lightly, but if you continue to pursue Miss Webb, throwing your obsession in Margot's face, then I will be left with no choice."

I still. "What do you mean?" I stare at my mother, having never heard her speak words like this before.

"If you do not marry Margot and make my grand-child a Fairfax—a legitimate heir—I will sell my shares to Merrick Dudley and make him majority shareholder."

I blink. What?

"He is like a son to me, and if I believe your obses-sion with this American jeopardizes the business and our family name, I will do all that I can to remove you as the face of the Dudley-Fairfax brand. Do you understand?"

I take a step closer, towering over her, my blood running cold. Never has my mother dared to threaten me in such a way. I fight to control my anger, my disap-pointment in her. Who is this cold, heartless woman standing before me?

Uncaring. Threatening.

Well, two can play at that game.

"You would cross your own son—your blood—for a man I lost respect for long ago?"

She doesn't even flinch. "What Merrick did with Margot was a childish, spontaneous mistake they both regretted. You must let it go, Henry."

I scoff. "I will block you from selling those shares. You forget, as majority shareholder, the clause my father put into the contract states that I get first bid against anyone wanting to sell."

Her eyes widen, her lips parting slightly.

Did she not know this truth? Satisfaction runs through me. I've bested her and her judgmental ways.

"To ensure such outcomes as the one you threaten me with can never be enforced on the rightful heir. Me."

She inhales sharply. "Henry, dearest, please, think of the family. Think of your child."

I shake my head. "I am thinking of the family—and what is best for me. Which, in the long run, is what will be best for the child. I will not raise my child in a home empty of love and affection. I do not love Margot. I tolerate her at best."

"That is a cruel thing to say."

I round on my mother. "No. What is cruel is a parent who sides with people she knows have wronged me in the past. I do not recognize the woman you are today." My voice lowers. "I'm ashamed of you."

I turn and start back toward the hotel, no longer willing to escort her to the new build.

If she wants to look at the hotel, she can do it herself.

Alone.

I DON'T SEE Henry for the rest of the week, nor do I see his family anywhere around the hotel. I'm grateful to avoid them. It's no secret they dislike me—have from the moment they found out I was seeing Henry. I stepped into the middle of a situation, and somehow, I was blamed for why Henry was no longer willing to give Margot another chance.

Not that it lasted long. As far as I know, they've been seeing each other in Rome these past months. The tabloids certainly suggest that when the baby arrives, they'll move in together. None of it makes sense after my run-in with Henry the other day. He didn't seem interested in Margot, but maybe I'm reading him wrong. I haven't seen him in almost a year.

Things change. And Henry can be very closed off emotionally when he wants to be. Seeing me again may have triggered something unfinished, nothing more. He said he misses me. I miss him too. But that doesn't change what happened.

I stroll through the streets of Capri, weaving my way through the narrow paths, catching breathtaking glimpses of the sea. When I spot Henry's yacht in the marina, I can just make out the crew going about their jobs.

I stop, looking out over the water, my mind restless. What do I do with him? We have to work together. We can't keep fighting like this. There's too much tension, too much anger—and too much love still lingering in me to let us stay at each other's throats all the time.

I shouldn't still care. I should hate him to the end of my days.

But I don't.

Not that there's any future to be had, but we could at least be civil. Friends, even. Until I return to New York, where I'll probably never see him again after that. I exhale and start down the steep hill. I'll see if he's on the yacht. We need to talk, away from everyone.

I thought he returned to Rome—maybe he took a helicopter off the island or used his private airport and plane—but I don't think so. It doesn't take long before I'm walking up the dock toward his yacht. I slip off my sandals and step on board.

"Miss Webb, welcome. It's very good to see you again," Owen, one of the crew, says with a smile.

I return it, even as nerves coil in my stomach. Is this a bad idea? Maybe I shouldn't be here, shouldn't be trying to fix things. Maybe I should leave things as they are. "Hi, Owen. It's good to see you too." I swallow, clasping my hands together to stop myself from fidgeting. "Is Mr. Fairfax on board?"

"He is. If you'll come up to the next deck, I'll go and see if he's free."

"Thank you." I follow Owen and settle onto one of the outside lounges upstairs. My gaze drifts to the spa I once enjoyed, to the table where we used to have breakfast. I tear my eyes away from the past, forcing myself to look at the ocean, at the town—anywhere but the memories that haunt me.

"Maddie, what are you doing here?"

I turn as Henry strides toward me, his steps purposeful, his tone hopeful.

For a moment, I can't look away. He wears a black shirt and white shorts—so different from his usual immaculate suits. He reminds me of before. Of the villa. Of when we were happy and relaxed, enjoying each other's company. I ignore the pang of loss and gesture for him to sit.

"Can we talk?" He sits beside me, eyes searching, hopeful. Why does he have to look at me like that? Why can't he be angry like the other day? It's so much easier to stay irritated with him when he is.

"Of course. Is everything well?"

"Yes, nothing's wrong. I came here because I think we need to be more professional and not let what happened at the hotel happen again." I take a deep breath. "I didn't like what we said to each other. And while I know we're done, there are clearly feelings we both harbor that sometimes raise their ugly, jealous heads. And they shouldn't."

He watches me closely.

I hold his gaze and push on. "I'm not sleeping with Merrick. I do not see him that way. He's a friend. You know I'm seeing Paul, and he's who's helping me move forward with my life."

His jaw tightens.

"That is the last time I'll tell you anything about my personal life. You don't get to have a say, Henry. You know that, don't you?"

He massages the back of his neck, exhaling. "No matter what you've seen in the papers, I'm not with Margot. I haven't touched her since that night..."

He cringes. "Fuck, I'm sorry, Maddie. I don't know what happened. I don't remember any of it, and so it feels like I lost you for no reason."

I hesitate, the old question rising again. "How drunk were you?" I've wondered about it so often. I've never been so blind drunk I didn't know what I was doing.

And I can't picture Henry being like that, either.

He frowns. "I didn't think I was that drunk. It's odd...it's like I've blanked it out somehow. I woke up and found her in my bed. It makes no sense to me how she got there."

I inhale sharply.

Had Margot done something to him? No. I can't believe she'd stoop that low. Not to a man she loves, a man she's known since childhood.

"No matter how it happened, maybe you'd be better

off making it work with her," I say carefully, even though it cuts me to my core to voice those words. "You did have feelings for her in the past, and sometimes love can return." I shake my head. "In any case, I didn't come here to talk about Margot. Or last summer. I just want us to be civil—to be friends, if we can, in some strange, exes-who-don't-want-to-kill-each-other kind of way." A small, wry smile tugs at my lips, but my chest aches. "Whether we like it or not, there's jealousy between us whenever we're around each other. And it has to stop."

Henry exhales. "I know…" He reaches for my hand, and weak-willed that I am—or maybe I just want to feel him one last time—I let him. He traces his fingers over mine, the warmth of his skin sending a shiver up my arm.

"I miss you, Maddie." His words soft. "I don't know how to move forward after having you in my life. I've lost something I know I can't replace, and it's killing me."

I swallow past the lump in my throat and gently pull my hand away. "I'm not immune to what happened between us. But I can't keep working here if we're going to be at each other's throats over something we cannot change."

His voice is rough. "I wish I could change it."

I stand, breaking free of his hold before I do something stupid—like lean into him. Like let him win. Let him kiss me like I can see he wants to. Like I want to.

"I'll see you at work, Henry."

I leave him there, walking along the pier. The ocean sparkles under the afternoon sun. The island is breathtaking—unforgettable. Only three more weeks, and I can return to New York. Move on. This time, I will move on. A pang of sadness grips me.

I wish I was enough for him.

I wish he hadn't strayed.

I wish. I wish. I wish.

Hindsight is a fucking bitch.

IT'S odd being civil with Henry after we've been at each other's throats for so long. The meetings are much more productive, and I find that working with him—without holding on to my hurt—is a much healthier way to live. Better for my mental health. That's not to say I don't still look at him every now and then and wish I could go up to him, wrap my arms around his waist, and hug him. Kiss him. Tell the world he's mine.

But I can't.

He isn't mine.

He's Margot's, who—right at this moment—sits across from him in the restaurant, eating dinner. Her baby belly is showing, but then, with only eight weeks or so to go, I suppose it's understandable that she's getting big.

"Madeline, come, our table is ready."

I follow Catherine, and a waiter escorts us to a table near the window, overlooking the ocean. Catherine sits, giving me the view of Henry. Should I ask her to swap places? I think better of it. I can ignore them, ignore their cozy little meal, and remain professional. Everything will be fine.

Right?

Catherine thanks the server who hands us our menus. "Is everything okay, Maddie?"

I force a smile. "I'm fine."

But am I? Being friendly with Henry again makes me confused. Do I hate him still? Or do I feel sorry for him because he can't remember cheating on me? What kind of fucked-up thought process is that? It doesn't matter if he remembers or not—the end result is the same. He broke my heart. I need to remember that part of the story.

Catherine studies me, skeptical. "You don't look fine. You look like someone ran over your cat."

"I don't have a cat." But maybe I should get one. A little company. Something just for me. Something that would love me—and something I could love back as much as I wanted. A cat wouldn't cheat with its ex.

Catherine gives me a pointed stare. "You know what I mean."

She glances around the restaurant, and I see the moment she realizes what's sullied my mood.

"Is that the woman who he…you know…"

"Cheated on me with? Yes, that's her. The European movie star and childhood friend."

Catherine smirks. "Tell us how you really feel."

I cringe. Was my tone of loathing so obvious? "I

don't mean to sound so toxic, but I've been thinking about something Henry said. Something I only just recently started to consider because I wasn't really listening when he first told me last summer."

"What is it?"

I exhale, pressing my fingers against my temples. "I went to see Henry the other day. He's staying on his yacht, and I wanted to clear the air. Make sure our interactions are more professional and not tainted by our past while I'm working here."

"Probably a good idea. Our meeting last week was certainly interesting."

"Exactly." I take a sip of water, shamed on our cattiness that day. "Henry mentioned he doesn't remember anything from the night he strayed. He remembers offering Margot a ride home from the birthday party they were at—and then waking up with her in his bed. Nothing in between."

Catherine frowns. "And do you believe him? He could just be saying he has memory loss. I've had exes who tried to use the amnesia excuse. I never bought it."

I shrug. "I don't know if that rings true for Henry. I think he truly doesn't remember."

She lifts a brow. "What are you thinking happened then?"

I hesitate. Can I even say it out loud? I exhale. "I think she drugged him and staged it."

Catherine gapes. "No. Who would do that?"

I shake my head, my own words sounding ridiculous. "I don't know. Maybe Margot would. I was the first woman Henry had seen exclusively since they broke up. He pursued me hard, and I think she felt threatened. In the past, he was always waiting in the wings, but after me? He wasn't. He moved on—for good, I thought—and she didn't like it." I swallow. "So she tricked him to make sure we'd break up."

Catherine sighs. "You'll never prove it if it's true."

"I know."

She orders a red from Penfolds, and I order my entrée and second course. I shake my head. "I could just be grasping at straws. Wanting to believe that people can't be that cruel. I thought he loved me. And for the first time in my life, I thought I was in love too."

Catherine studies me for a long moment. Then she sips her wine and raises a brow. "I think he still does."

I blink. "What?"

She smirks. "I've seen how he looks at you in meetings. Like he's memorizing your every feature, drinking you in like we're drinking this delicious wine."

I laugh, liking this side of my boss—the out-of-the-office, fun, wine-drunk Catherine.

She grins. "You know what we should do? We should go dancing. It's Friday night, work is over for the week, and I could use a night out to let our hair down."

I arch a brow. "Should we invite Josh?"

"No, he's off the island. He caught a ferry to Naples this afternoon to explore for the weekend."

"Oh, that sounds nice." I consider her idea. A night out does sound fun. "You know what? Let's do it."

"Absolutely."

We finish dinner and head straight to a nightclub, where we dance for hours, drinking far more vodka than we should. We aren't just work colleagues anymore. We're friends. Over vodka shots, Catherine manages to pull a hot Australian guy, and I know it's only a matter of time before she leaves with him.

"I'm going to head off," I yell over the music. "You have fun and get home safe. I'll see you Monday."

"Be safe! See you then." Catherine winks, smirking like the cat who got the cream.

And I suppose she did. The Aussie is godlike. I stumble outside, the air warm, the scent of the sea drifting in the light breeze. I hail several taxis, but every one of them is occupied and drives right past me. I sigh and start walking in the direction of the harbor. There are coffee houses near there—some probably opening soon. Maybe I'll have better luck finding a taxi or Uber there. After walking another five minutes, I pull out my Uber app and frown when it says an hour wait time.

I could walk back to the hotel myself by then, but it's a terribly long hike, especially drunk, but not impossible. I cancel it and keep walking. My feet start to sting in the heels I'm wearing. Probably not the brightest idea to leave the club before securing a ride… I walk several more minutes before realizing something. I don't recognize where I am.

Shit.

I stumble into a narrow alleyway. A dead-end street. I exhale, my pulse kicking up. I'm lost.

Fuck it.

How did I manage this? I reach for my phone, swallowing my pride as I text the one person I don't want to —but the only one I know will come get me. The one person who knows his way around, unlike me.

Henry.

Forty~Eight

THE PING of the text wakes me, and I sit up the moment I see who it's from.

> Can you come get me? Sorry, I know it's late…

A pin drops with Maddie's location, and I blink, trying to make sense of where she is. I'm out of bed in seconds, grabbing my discarded clothes, shoving them on as I rush up the dock toward my car. I punch her location into the GPS, my grip tight on the steering wheel as I speed toward her. Fifteen minutes. That's how long it takes me to find her, standing on the outskirts of town, in some dark alley no woman should ever be alone in.

Relief pours through me when I spot her, leaning against a wall. Safe. Unharmed. The sight of her in that short black dress, dark makeup smudged from the night, reminds me of the first time we met in Ibiza.

Hell, she looks good enough to eat…

I pull up and get out, moving to her immediately. "Are you hurt?" My voice is sharp with concern. If something had happened to her, I'd kill whoever was responsible.

She shakes her head. "No, just lost. I'm sorry, Henry. I would've called my work colleagues, but Josh is off the island, and Catherine hooked up with a guy at the club. I couldn't get a taxi, and then I got lost. I know I shouldn't have messaged you, but I didn't know who else to call."

"No, you should have messaged me. Of course, I don't want you out here on your own."

I wrap my arm around her waist, guiding her toward the car. The feel of her against me is like coming home. I miss being this close. Touching her. I open the door, and she climbs in. The drive back to her hotel is silent, the air in the car thick with unspoken words.

"You were heading west," I finally say, breaking the silence, the scent of alcohol heavy in the car. How much had she drunk tonight? "You weren't heading toward the harbor at all."

She exhales, looking out the window. "I must be more drunk than I thought."

I want her to look at me. As much as I want to look at her, but I can't. Pity he didn't wake his driver so he could be sitting in the back seat with her right at this moment. "Don't feel bad about messaging me. You know I'll always come to you if you need me."

She bites her lip, and I stifle a growl of need. The

action reminds me of post-coital euphoria and my cock twitches.

"It doesn't change the fact that I'm sorry I had to." She sighs. "I'm normally better at looking after myself." A pause. "I know you were with Margot tonight. I hope I haven't ruined your evening."

I tense. "I don't want anything to happen to you, Maddie. I would never have forgiven myself if you hadn't asked me for help and something happened." The thought alone sends a chill through me. "And Margot has already left the island. We had dinner to discuss the baby, nothing more." I glance at her quickly —probably too quickly—but I need to see her. Drink in her beautiful face.

She's stunning.

Her hair falls around her shoulders, her slip dress barely reaching her knees, showing off those long, damn legs. Everything about her makes me want things I know she'll never give me again.

Her.

"I was in bed, pretending to sleep," I admit. "I don't sleep well these days."

She scoffs. "Really?" Her question is laced with disbelief. "I would think you sleep better than most people."

"Because I have no financial concerns, you mean?"

She shrugs, not denying it.

I nod, eyes back on the road. "Money isn't the problem. It never has been. But that doesn't mean I'm immune to everything else that causes pain." I grip the wheel tighter. "I haven't slept well since we broke up."

Her eyes widen, but I don't see the point in hiding it anymore. "You're surprised?" I glance at her. "That since you went back to New York, I struggle to sleep?" I exhale. "The guilt eats me alive every day, Maddie. And it doesn't help that I got used to you being by my side. I miss you."

She shifts in her seat, looking anywhere but at me.

"Henry...you shouldn't say things like that. You have a baby on the way with a woman who clearly still loves you. Never stopped, if I'm right." She swallows, straightening in the seat. "You should give her a chance. Stop pining for someone who's not coming back."

I pull the car into the parking lot just before her hotel, away from the valet. I don't want her to leave just yet. I need more time. She unclips her seatbelt, but doesn't move to get out.

"I can still be a good father and not marry Margot." My voice is firm. "We weren't together when it happened. She can't expect me to switch on feelings I don't have."

Maddie stares at me. I hate the pain in her blue eyes. I never wanted to be the cause of that kind of emotion in her.

And yet—I am.

Just another person in her life who's disappointed her.

She exhales. "We wouldn't have worked." Her voice is quiet.

I clench my jaw. "That's not true."

"It is." She hesitates. "My life was the opposite of yours, Henry. My upbringing left us with nothing in common. You're better off marrying a woman from your world." She laughs, but it's bitter. "Just think…if you'd ended up with me, I probably would've only embarrassed your family."

I reach for her hand, needing to hold her, needing to touch her, even in this small way. Her fingers wrap around mine, and I never want to let go.

"You are not to blame for your childhood," I tell her. "And I would never let anyone talk down about you if you were mine." I turn her hand over, my lips brushing against her palm.

Her breath catches.

"I'm still in love with you, Maddie," I whisper, lifting her hand to my cheek. "I want you with every breath, every waking hour of my life. I dream of you. I dream of us. And I want it back. I don't care if it's selfish—it's what I want."

She exhales shakily, her fingers twitching against my jaw. I hold her there, longing for the touch I haven't felt in months. For a moment, I think she might let me in.

Then, softly—so quietly I almost miss it—she whispers, "You broke my heart, Henry." Her voice cracks. "And now it's too late."

She pulls away, slipping out of the car. Her steps toward the hotel are uneven, the alcohol still in her system. I jump out of the vehicle and follow her, and when she stumbles again, I catch her. My arm tightens around her waist as I guide her inside, unwilling to let go.

Not yet. Maybe not ever.

"Let me help you get back to your room."

"No, you shouldn't touch me. I don't trust myself around you when you touch me."

I stop breathing at her words. I've wanted to hear her say something like this for months. To have the smallest sliver of hope that we aren't over. That there's a crack in the armored wall she's put up around herself, a chance for me to break through. To win her back.

"I just want to make sure you get back to your room safely. That's all. I'll leave straight away."

Maddie glances up at me, her eyes a little unfocused from all the alcohol she's had. The night staff at the hotel smile as we walk into the foyer and wait for the elevator. Maddie sighs and, without warning, slips her arms around my neck, leaning into me.

I close my eyes, savoring the scent of her sweet perfume, the fruity shampoo she must have washed her hair with earlier today. She smells good enough to eat.

The elevator dings, and the doors slide open. I guide us inside and hit the button for her floor, forcing myself to keep my hands around her waist—only her waist—to not slide them lower over her pert ass and lift her against my already hardening cock.

"Hmm, you smell so good, Henry."

Damn it. That sensual tone does things to me. I grind my teeth, count to ten, and stare at the ceiling of the elevator. A mistake. The mirrored panel gives me a perfect view down her dress.

Fuck.

"You smell good too," I rasp, not lying. She does.

I keep my arm firmly around her waist, making sure she stays upright. The idea of her wandering the streets of Capri in this condition sends ice through my veins. Then, she presses the stop button on the elevator. I barely have time to react before she shoves me against the wall, her hands cradling my face as she looks at me, her eyes clouded with regret and longing.

I know that look well.

"Why did you do it to us?" she whispers, shaking her head, our lips only a breath apart.

My throat tightens. "I don't know what happened. I never wanted to hurt you."

"But you did hurt me. You ripped out my heart."

Her fingers glide over my cheek, her nails running through the rough stubble of my jaw almost painfully, punishingly. Heat licks at every part of my body. Our breaths mingle, my heart races.

"Give me another chance," I beg, voice raw. "Please, Maddie. Let me prove to you that you can trust me."

I'd do anything to get her back. I can have it all—my business, my responsibilities as a father—and be happy with the woman I love. If only she'd meet me halfway.

She swallows hard. "I shouldn't be here with you. You have a woman who's carrying your child, and I'm all over you like some desperate ex—a homewrecker."

She pulls away, but I wrench her back. Her breasts

press against my chest, and instinct takes over. My hands slide lower, gripping her hips as I hoist her against me, pressing my hard cock against her warm center.

She gasps, her pupils dilating with need.

"You're not a fucking homewrecker," I growl. "There was never a home to wreck. My life—my home—was with you."

I drag a hand up her back, my fingers pressing into the soft skin at her nape. "I made a mistake, but I won't make another by letting you go without a fight."

She exhales shakily. "I have a man waiting for me in New York. I can't do to him what you did to me."

My blood boils at the mention of him. "The fuck you can't," I snap. "I had you first. You're mine, and I will win you back, Maddie."

She bites her lip, and it's too much.

Raw desire licks up my spine, and I grind against her, taking what little pleasure I can while she's still in my arms. Her hands slip around my neck, her hips rolling—grinding—against my dick.

"Maddie…" I don't sound like myself. My voice is a plea, a desperate cry for her to give herself to me.

"Mmm," she moans softly, shifting against me. "That feels nice. So fucking good."

I grab her ass, squeezing tight, pulling her flush against me.

I need more.

I bury my face in the crook of her neck, breathing her in before I lick the sensitive skin under her ear. She shudders, tipping her head to the side, allowing me access.

I take it.

I kiss down her throat, every press of my lips laced with months of longing.

"Henry."

Our eyes lock.

I'm barely holding it together.

She can shatter me instantly if she chooses. Only with Maddie am I this vulnerable. This open. I lay my heart at her feet, praying she doesn't stomp on it.

"Yes?" I whisper.

She doesn't say anything for several heartbeats.

Then…

"What I want, I can't have."

My mind races. I feel her pulling away. "One last time," I blurt out. "Just tonight. We forget everything and do what we want—for ourselves."

She hesitates.

My pulse pounds, desperate for her answer. But I see it in her eyes before she even says the words. She presses a hand against my chest, gently pushing me back.

I let her go.

"No. I won't do it."

She turns, pressing the button to restart the elevator.

The doors open on her floor, and I step aside, my body still burning for her.

Her sharp gasp makes me look up.

"Paul?"

I tear my gaze from Maddie to the man standing in the hall. Dressed in a tailored suit, arms crossed, wearing a fucking puppy dog smile.

"Mads," he says, stepping toward her. "I thought I'd surprise you."

She lets out an awkward laugh, stepping out of the elevator.

I don't follow.

I can't.

I simply press the button to go back down, my jaw tight as the doors slide shut.

The last thing I see is him kissing her.

Fuck the New York banker.

He looks like a good guy. Looks like he cares about her. But I love her. And that has to mean something. I won't give up. Not a chance in hell. Even with Paul here or not—Maddie is mine.

And I'll prove it to everyone.

Including her.

CHAPTER
Forty-Nine

I HUG PAUL, the sight of him sobering me instantly. Does he suspect anything from seeing me in the elevator with Henry? No. He doesn't even know who Henry is. Not yet, at least. I haven't introduced them and never mentioned my holiday in Sorrento or the history Henry and I now share. The chemistry between us, however, is undeniable. No matter how much I try to mask it or ignore what Henry continues to make me feel, it's there. It's like an invisible red string that links us together, no matter what distance separates us in the world.

Even Catherine has noticed. She often asks if I'm okay, if anything is wrong.

Everything is wrong. Everything is so messed up.

"I didn't think you were coming to Capri. What a surprise to see you," I say, squeezing Paul tighter.

He hugs me back, kissing my shoulder. "I had some holiday hours available and thought I'd come see you.

How have you been? It's been weeks. You look great, by the way."

We stand there, looking at each other. My mind goes blank. What now?

"Is this your room?" he asks, motioning to the door beside us. "I got the number from the front desk. I wanted to surprise you."

Wow. So much for security. Paul could've been some random guy off the street. I need to have a serious chat with the front desk about their lapse. Not that Paul is a threat, but they should never have taken him at his word.

"The front desk gave you my room number?" I ask, arching a brow. At least he has the decency to look sheepish.

"Yeah. I hope you're not angry." He clasps my hands, giving them a light squeeze. "Don't make an issue out of it. I don't want anyone to lose their job."

"Yeah, well, I don't want any woman getting raped and murdered by some random either." I sigh, swiping my keycard. "This is my room."

We step inside, and suddenly, I feel torn with Paul here. I've been seeing him in New York. I thought we were doing fine. Until I saw Henry again. Until I was back in Henry's orbit, where he always seems to pull me in, no matter how much I fight it.

Paul looks around, his expression unimpressed as he takes in the basic layout and amenities.

"It's not a very good room for someone who's the advertising executive's assistant in a big NY firm," he mutters. "I thought they would've put you up in better digs than this."

I cross my arms, already feeling defensive. "This is fine for me. I don't need much. A bed, a shower, and a desk. It works."

Paul stops his inspection and turns to me. "Do I get any more hugs and kisses, or was what you gave me in the hallway it?"

I hesitate for a fraction of a second before stepping into his arms. Why am I hesitating? I need my head read. Paul is too much of a good guy for me to be so lukewarm toward him. He'll tire of me if I keep being this way. Not that we had talked of what this relationship actually was or if we were exclusive. I lean up, wrap my arms around his shoulders, and kiss him.

Like always, his kiss pulls me out of my lull, dragging me into lust. Paul is a damn good kisser. His hands slide down, grasping my ass as he pulls me flush against his body. I can feel him harden against me, wanting more.

Panic twists in my stomach. Can I sleep with him and not feel wrong? Not feel like a tease, a user? I haven't seen Paul in weeks, and after what happened in the elevator, I could use the relief. But it wasn't Paul who sparked my need. It was Henry. And that makes everything feel wrong.

I'm not cheating on Henry, I remind myself.

I pull away and busy myself with slipping off my shoes. "I suppose you're tired after flying all day. Did you want to have a shower?"

"Actually, what I'd really like is to hold my girl in my arms."

I freeze. "Am I your girl, though?" I ask, forcing a light tone. "We really haven't had that chat."

Paul smiles, but I can see the nerves in his eyes. "Well, while I don't want to put an official title on us just yet, I will say that I want to see more of you. I'm not sleeping with anyone else, and I'd like to think you aren't either."

His hold tightens when I don't answer right away. Do I want to be exclusive with Paul? What I really want is Henry. But I can't have him. Well, at least I shouldn't have him. I should let him go. I should give Margot the opportunity to salvage their relationship. I should stop wishing for something that will never be mine.

"Maybe I can shower with you?" I suggest, my voice coming out a little too airy. Paul's eyes darken, filled with desire. He likes that idea. But I can't answer his real question. Can't tell him the truth.

I'm a terrible person while he's being so sweet. I should tell him I'm conflicted, that I don't know what I want, that even when the better choice is right in front of me, I can't seem to choose him.

Henry has a lot to answer for.

"A shower sounds great," Paul says, his voice husky.

I smile and busy myself around the room, achieving nothing.

"It's Saturday tomorrow," I say. "What would you like to do?"

"How about you show me around the island? It'll help with my jetlag."

"I'd be happy to. Capri is beautiful. We could even catch a ferry to the mainland on Sunday if you want to do a day trip."

Paul rips off his tie and tosses it onto a chair, then unbuttons his shirt, revealing his chiseled chest.

The man is hot.

I should be all over him.

I should be excited.

Instead, I feel nothing.

Jesus, I have serious problems.

"So, who was the guy in the elevator?" Paul asks, unbuckling his belt. "Anyone you know? He looked less than pleased to see me talking to you. In fact, he looked pissed."

Shit. He noticed.

I force a casual shrug. "Oh, yeah. He's the owner of the new hotel being built on the island—Henry Fairfax, from the Dudley Fairfax hotel chain."

Paul's brow furrows. "And?"

I exhale, keeping my voice light. "We had a bit of a disagreement regarding an advertising idea." Lie.

The truth is burned into my mind. Henry's hands on me. His lips at my throat. His need pressing against mine. And my weakness to want him back.

"Wait, that was Henry Fairfax from the Dudley Fairfax hotel chain?" Paul whistles low. "Shit! Do you think you could introduce me? If I picked him up as a client, that could be huge for my investment portfolio. I didn't know you knew people like him. That's amazing, Maddie!"

Know him? *If only you knew how well I know him.*

"I can introduce you," I say slowly. "But I don't think you should bring up business. That seems…a little weird."

Paul grins. "Oh, come on. These billionaire types are used to people talking shop. It won't be a problem."

I shake my head, but he just kisses the tip of my nose.

"Don't worry about it," he murmurs. "Now come on, it's time for you to wash me…"

Oh, joy.

I let him lead me into the shower, my stomach in knots, my mind torn in two.

CHAPTER
Fifty

I SEND an email to the team, inviting them for a day on my yacht as a thank-you for all their hard work these past weeks. I include the New York team, wanting Maddie on the boat where I may get to speak to her again. Alone this time. Without interruptions from Paul.

Who the fuck is this twerp, anyway? Some banker from New York?

The moment I return to the boat, I look him up, check out his bank, his deals, his net worth. Unfortunately, his socials check out, and he's even posted a couple of pictures of Maddie on their dates back in the States.

The sight of her, cuddled up to him, looked down upon in adoration, sends a dagger through me. That should be me. I'd once been that man—until I fucked it up.

I run a hand through my hair and grab my radio. "Lisa, meet me in my office."

She knocks on the door a moment later. "May I come in, Mr. Fairfax?"

"Yes." I gesture for her to enter. "Tomorrow, I'm hosting a group of business colleagues on the boat. It's a casual day—we'll head out, dock near the island somewhere. Get the water toys out, give them lunch and afternoon tea, plenty of wine. Make a day of it. Do you think you can have everything organized by ten tomorrow morning?"

"Of course. I'll order provisions straight away."

"Thanks."

My phone pings, and I sit up, surprised to see Maddie's name come up.

> Hi. I hope it's okay to text you. I won't be at work tomorrow. We're off the island, visiting the mainland for the day.

I grind my teeth, stare at the text, debating how to reply. I don't want to force her hand. I've done that once, and she's still pissed at me. But the idea of her sightseeing with anyone other than me isn't on.

> I'd hoped you'd be able to attend. It's a thank-you from the Dudley-Fairfax group to the advertising team. You've all worked so hard. I wanted to do something nice for you all.

There. That isn't too guilt laden. Not a straight You have to come. No excuses, which is what I want to say.

> Can I bring a plus one?

I down my whiskey and snatch up my phone. Fuck that bastard New Yorker.

> Of course. I'd like to meet your boyfriend.

> ...

Those three little dots. She's typing…thinking… debating. What is she thinking? Is she pissed? About to give me an earful? I want to say more. To text her back and tell her Paul isn't welcome. That I don't want him anywhere near her.

> He's not my boyfriend…nothing official yet. And anyway, that's none of your business. We'll see you for lunch.

I lounge around the boat for the rest of the day, drink far too much whiskey, and pass out early. When I wake, the sun is already up, and my phone reads 10:00 a.m.

Fuck.

How the hell did I sleep this long? I jump out of bed, rush to the shower, and try to ignore the pounding in my skull. I don't need a hangover today.

The team arrives on time at noon. I greet them, welcome them up to the top deck where the dining table is set beneath the canopy, laden with food. Crew stand ready, serving drinks and canapés.

Maddie is late.

I walk to the side of the deck, pretending to look out over the water, but my eyes flick toward the dock.

And there she is.

Hand in hand with her non-boyfriend.

She looks happy, smiling, relaxed.

I grind my teeth, swallow down a growl of irritation. Why the fuck did I agree to let her bring him? If the bastard puts his hands on her all day in front of me, I swear to God, I'll rip his fucking arms off.

I sit at the table before she sees me watching. The last thing I need is for her to think I'm waiting for her like some desperate idiot.

"Hi, everyone." Her voice—light and airy—rolls over me like a balm. I push back my chair and stand. I have to do the right thing. I invited everyone here, after all.

"Miss Webb, thank you for coming. And this is?" I keep my tone even, but the moment I stand eye to eye with Paul, I feel my mask slip.

Paul thrusts his hand out before I offer mine. "Mr. Fairfax, an honor. True honor. I've followed your business for years, and I can't tell you how pleased I am to meet you. We must discuss investments. Maddie suggested you may be interested."

Maddie what?

I glance at her. Her eyes are wide, her expression mortified.

Oh, this is interesting…

I smirk and clasp his hand, squeezing harder than

necessary. "I'd be happy to listen to any of your pitches. If Maddie believes I'd be interested in what you have to say, then I will be."

She shoots daggers at me, but I just drink her in, fighting to swallow down the need that overcomes me every time she's near.

"Please, join us."

The crew begins serving lunch. Conversation flows, light and easy.

Until—

"And what about you, Maddie? Where's your family from?" one of the executives asks.

Maddie stills, her eyes flicking to mine. I want to reach for her, tell her she doesn't have to answer. But she does.

Her voice is even, but there's an edge to it. "I...I don't have any family. I never knew my father, and my mother passed a couple of days after I was born. I was raised in foster care."

Paul laughs. "Seriously? You were raised in foster care? Ouch."

I glare at him. The blind dick doesn't seem to notice.

Maddie keeps her tone light, but I see the shake in her hand as she reaches for her wine. "Yes, I was. Although I have no blood relatives, I do have my two best friends in the US—Eve and Clara. They're my family now."

"Was it hard in foster care? I've heard horror stories, even in Italy."

Maddie nods. "It was difficult. You're vulnerable to

everyone until you're old enough to leave. I fought for where I am today, and I'm determined to never be beholden to anyone again."

"Good for you," Catherine interjects, running a supportive hand along Maddie's arm.

Paul, oblivious as ever, grins. "There was a kid in middle school who was in foster care. His clothes were always dirty, and he stank. Had no friends. I wonder what he's doing now."

Maddie's jaw tightens. "He's probably dead."

The table falls silent.

Paul forces a laugh. "Well, let's not bring down the vibe, Mads."

I clench my wine glass, tempted to throw it in his face.

Fucking prick.

I clear my throat. "I wanted to thank you all for your hard work. The new hotel is already booked out a year in advance, no doubt thanks to this team's talent. So please, enjoy today—once we dock off island, use the water toys, the salon, the spa, stay for dinner if you'd like. The boat is yours."

One of the executives beams. "That sounds amazing. Thank you, Henry."

Maddie's eyes flick to me. I know what she's thinking. I know she's regretting staying. I smirk. She can't avoid me forever. Not out on my boat. It's only a matter of time…

Fifty~One

HENRY HAS his staff bring out a two-seater kayak after the boat anchors not far from the Grotta Azzurra.

"Would anyone like to see the cave? It's beautiful inside and worth the visit."

Henry slips on a life vest, and the sight of him in his swimming trunks—shirtless, toned, tanned—is enough to send my mind into a spin. He meets my eyes, a knowing light in his. I know what he's doing. He's showing me what I'm missing.

"Can we swim in there?" Catherine asks, lazing on a daybed with a round straw hat covering her face. She doesn't look the least bit interested in visiting the cave.

"You can, but I think by small boat is best. You can float and take it all in. It's truly beautiful."

Henry climbs into the kayak and waits for whoever is joining him.

"I can't swim, so I'll stay on board and enjoy the champagne." Paul kisses my cheek and pushes me toward a deckhand holding life vests. "You go, Maddie. The sooner you leave, the quicker you'll be back."

Henry clears his throat, lips twisting into a sarcastic smirk. "You should join me first, Madeline, so I can return you ASAP to Paul."

I glance back at Paul, certain he must have heard the mocking in Henry's tone. But Paul is already sitting beside Catherine, taking another glass of champagne from a stewardess, completely unfazed.

"Okay, I've heard of the cave. I'd like to see it."

A deckhand helps me into a life vest, and I move toward the kayak. Henry holds out his hand, and I hesitate for a second before taking it. His touch is firm, his skin warm—it sears me where we connect. I sit quickly, not wanting to prolong the torture. Henry takes an oar from a deckhand, and they push us off. He starts to row toward the cave entrance.

"Is it safe to go in there? It won't collapse, will it?"

"It's perfectly safe. It's checked by skippers each morning. My crew was notified that it's safe to enter and that I could take anyone who wanted to visit inside."

We row closer, the towering cliffs growing larger as the little boat glides toward the cave's opening. Then, we slip inside.

I gape at the crystalline blue water with silver reflections, glowing from beneath the surface. "Oh my God, Henry. This is spectacular. It's like another world."

"My thoughts exactly."

Heat rises to the back of my neck. I feel him looking

at me instead of the water. I turn to face him, and sure enough, he's watching me.

"Paul seems nice…"

I roll my eyes and turn back to the cave, deciding to take in its beauty instead of engaging with Henry's obvious bait. "You should bring the others in here and show them. They'd love it." I pause. "How is the water so blue?"

"I'll have the crew bring the others. But I only wanted to be the one to show you this hidden gem."

Henry sets the oars inside the boat and looks around the cave. "The water looks this way because the cave's entrance extends beneath the surface, allowing sunlight to filter through. It creates the blue glow. They found Roman statues in here once—now they're in a museum in Anacapri. But for centuries, sailors avoided the cave, believing it was cursed by evil spirits."

"There can never be anything evil in a place of such beauty."

"How long have you been seeing him?"

I sigh. "Henry, you can't ask me those questions. We agreed to be professional. I don't ask you about Margot."

"That's because I'm not with Margot."

"She's having your baby." I bite my lip, lean over the boat, and pretend to focus on the water. But I see nothing except everything I've lost.

"I can be a good father without marrying a woman I do not love."

I hear shifting before Henry moves closer. Suddenly,

he's right before me, his hands gripping my upper arms, hauling me forward until I have to look at him.

"I want you back, Maddie. I want you so much I fucking break in two every time I see you."

"You can't say that to me."

"I can, and I will." His hold tightens. "Get rid of Paul. Send him home. You don't want him here. I know you don't. I feel it every time we look at each other."

I shrug, not wanting him to continue this train of thought. "You're a handsome man, Henry, and you're good in bed. Of course, I'll look at you—and any man who's of similar aesthetic perfection—but that doesn't mean I'm going to fuck all of them."

His jaw flexes. "I don't want you to fuck any of them except me." He pauses. "Tell me now, to my face, that we're through. That you don't feel what I still feel for you. I fucked up, I know, but I want a second chance. I won't fuck up again, I promise you that."

"Henry, stop."

"Tell me, and I won't bring it up again."

He lets me go, and I stare at him. My throat tightens. I prepare myself to say the words aloud. The words I know I don't want to utter. Words I don't believe.

But it's the right thing to do.

He made a mistake, and that mistake now includes an innocent child who deserves a family. I can't deny a baby that—not when I know what it's like to not have one.

I swallow. "We're over, Henry. We can be friends, at

best. I like Paul. I want to see where it goes with him. I'm not going to give you another chance. I'm sorry."

A muscle ticks in his jaw, but he says nothing. He moves back to his seat, picks up the oars, and rows us out of the cave. As sunlight blinds me for a moment, I pretend to take in the view, my chest aching with the weight of my own words. It doesn't take us long to make it back to the yacht, and I can't get off the kayak fast enough. It's torture being around Henry when we're alone.

"Is it alright if I use the guest bedroom to clean up a little?"

Not that I need to clean up—I just need a moment to breathe.

"Of course. You know where the guest rooms are. Use any you like. They're all empty."

"Thanks."

I leave Henry, climbing the stairs to where Catherine, Paul, and the others lounge with their champagne and sun hats.

"I'll be back in a moment. Just freshening up."

Paul doesn't even blink. "Alright, babe."

I move inside the boat and head downstairs to the guest quarters. As soon as I step into one of the rooms, I shut the door and slump against it. My heart races. My mind whirls.

Damnit, Henry Fairfax. I won't let you break me a second time. I won't fall at your feet like a sad little puppy who's been kicked to the curb.

I won't.

———

I knock on the cabin door and hear Maddie's sharp gasp behind it. "Let me in, Maddie."

"No."

Impatience eats at me at her denial. She doesn't mean it. I won't let her mean it. I will remove anyone who gets in the way between me and Maddie, including the absurd banker upstairs who seems more interested in my money than his girlfriend.

My girl.

I try the door and it's unlocked. I step inside, closing and locking the door behind me. Maddie stands in the short hallway, arms crossed, her glare slicing into me.

"How dare you. Get out."

"No."

"Yes," she repeats.

She's mad as hell, practically vibrating with emotion. I stride up to her, and she backs away, her ass hitting the small hall table.

I clasp her face, fingers pressing into her skin like I need to hold her, need to remind her who she belongs to. I already taste her on my tongue. I ache to have her in my arms, and I won't be denied. Her hands press against my chest, a half-hearted push—before her fingers seize the material of my t-shirt instead.

"I hate you," she seethes.

She's mine. No one else's. "No, you don't."

I grip her waist and lift her onto the table, stepping between her legs and pressing my body against hers.

Damn, she feels good. Like home. I ache, my cock rigid. I want her. She bites her lip, watching me. I can't tear my eyes from her, she is so damn beautiful. I take my time leaning in, savoring every second I have her in my arms, mine to enjoy, to love, to win. Her fingers move up my chest and slip about my neck.

"This is wrong, Henry."

"No." I breathe. "It's not."

I dip my head and brush my lips against hers. Fire ignites within me, and I take her mouth in a kiss that sends my wits spiraling. She opens for me, her tongue tangling with mine. I moan, reaching under her dress, stroking her sweet flesh that is wet and ready for me. She lets out a sweet squeak, almost making me come. "Fuck, I've missed you."

I kiss her harder, the tone punishing. Both of us punishing the other for everything we've done to each other. Myself more than her. I kiss her hard, knowing she has a boyfriend, wanting to wipe the bastard from her memory. Get her to send him away. Her fingers clasp my hair, pulling, searing pain through my scalp.

I slip a finger into her warm, tight cunt. She wraps her legs around my waist, undulating against my hand. It isn't enough.

"Fuck me."

My stomach clenches, tightens at her plea. Her fingers rip at the ties of my shorts before she wrenches them off my hips. I haul her to the edge of the small table, clasp her hips, and pin her to take me.

I won't be gentle.

I press the tip of my cock at the core of her heat. She throws her head back, her feet against my back pushing me into her. "Fuck me hard, Henry."

"Maddie?"

What the actual fuck.

I still at the sound of that fucking loser Paul on the other side of the door. I meet Maddie's eyes, wide with alarm, her cheeks flushed, her lips swollen from my kiss.

I kiss her again, ignoring the man who dares to touch what is mine before Maddie pushes me away, her eyes heavy with need.

I know the feeling well. My cock is harder than it has ever been in its life.

"Get off," she mouths.

I move away, righting my pants. I watch her climb off the table as quietly as she can, quickly checking her dress and hair. She points toward the bedroom.

"Hide," she whispers.

Hide? Seriously? I sigh, but do what she asks, going into the room and entering the walk-in closet, closing the door behind me. I hear Maddie open the door.

"Paul, I was just coming up."

"Everything okay? You were taking a while, and I grew concerned."

"Everything's fine. I just needed a moment."

I hear the cabin door close, and I stand, looking at myself in the mirror for several breaths.

Have I seriously just hidden from a man in my own boat? Who the fuck have I become?

. . .

Several hours later everyone was gone. I stood at the side of the yacht, watching Maddie leave with her boyfriend. She is right, as much as I don't want to admit it. I have to stop obsessing over her. It isn't healthy, and it doesn't help our situation. She won't forgive me for my indiscretion, and I can't change what I've done. I'll make myself sick if I continue the way I am.

My phone buzzes, and I groan, seeing Margot's name light up. I answer and pull out onto the road.

"Yeah, is everything okay? It's late, Margot."

"Henry, you must come to Rome tonight. I'm in labor."

"What?" I turn, ready to instruct my cabin crew to pack my things. "But you're two months early. Can't the doctors stop it?"

"No, it's too late for that. My water has broken."

"Alright. I'll be there soon. I'll take the helicopter."

"Hurry, Henry. I'm scared and don't want to do this on my own."

"I'll be there." I hang up and call everyone required to get me off island ASAP. I wake my pilot and inform the captain to prepare the boat for the helicopter to travel to Rome. Within half an hour, I'm in the air, flying away from Capri.

I'm about to be a father. A child will be wholly dependent on me. I run a hand through my hair, fighting to stop the panic that assails me. I've never overseen such a precious living thing before in my life.

I hope I do a good job at being a parent.

I text Margot that I'm in the air and email my Capri hotel team about what's happening. As much as a child wasn't planned, I'm excited about the prospect of raising my son or daughter to run the company one day. To be a good person, an honest, caring human being who helps those less fortunate than they are.

A selfish part of me wishes the woman birthing my child is the same one I just left in Capri.

I push the awful thought away. That's cruel and unkind, and I don't like thinking like that. What has happened can't be changed.

But I can do better.

And I will.

For everyone.

Fifty-Two

"DID YOU HEAR THE NEWS?" Catherine joins me just as I walk out of the elevator, heading toward the offices we are assigned to use during our stay in the hotel.

"No, what news?" I'd been pretty hungover on Sunday and stayed in my room all day, deciding to order room service and watch television, even if it's all in Italian and I can't understand much of it.

"Margot Hathaway went into labor Saturday night, and it looks like she's going to have the baby early."

"Oh no, I hadn't heard. I hope everything goes well for her." And of course, I do want that for Margot, no matter what has happened between us. Or how much we loathe each other.

Henry is going to be a father.

I need to get over him, let him go, and stop hoping for a different future than the one playing out before us.

I push the doors open to our shared office space. "Hi, Paul. I hope your weekend in Naples was good."

"It was, thanks. Naples is worth visiting if you have a spare weekend before we head back to New York."

"Speaking of which." I sit and open my laptop. "Everything is in hand now for the opening of the hotel. It looks like it'll open on time, and the advertisement has already brought in bookings, so it'll be full for the next twelve months. That brings me to my next question."

"Shoot." Catherine sits back in her chair, giving me her full attention.

"Well, everything is in hand here now, and I was hoping to return home. Do you think I could leave earlier than planned? I'm not needed for the opening gala event, and considering my history with Mr. Fairfax, I wouldn't feel comfortable attending."

"You shouldn't let what happened between you and Mr. Fairfax jeopardize your career, Maddie."

"I don't want it to, of course. But...it's complicated." More so after our interaction on the boat the other day. How close I was to fucking him. Breaking my own rules to not be a cheating asshole like Henry. I don't trust myself around him. I want to shout to the world that I don't care who I hurt as long as I get what I want.

Henry.

"I think we can accommodate the request. You were coerced to be here after all, and you've done a wonderful job for the past few weeks. Say another week to finish up anything you have outstanding. We have the classical music concert celebration to attend and then you can return to New York?"

"Thank you. I appreciate your understanding." At least in New York, I won't be tempted to do something that could hurt so many people. Myself most of all, when Henry runs back to Margot yet again. Not that I could blame him, not now that he is going to be a father. The child deserves a chance at a happy home. God, I know what it's like not to have one of those, and no one deserves such an unfortunate upbringing.

"Well, if you're going back to New York, we need to go out and celebrate." Paul grins, and it's the first time he's offered to do anything with the people he works with. Even Catherine looks surprised.

"What do you have in mind?" Catherine asks.

"Dinner and clubbing. This Wednesday is a public holiday here, no one will be working, so I say we go out with a bang on Tuesday. What day are you thinking to return to the States?"

"Probably Saturday so I can finish off the week."

"Catherine, thoughts?" Josh asks.

"Gosh, we just had an entertaining Saturday night. I'm not sure I could endure another one midweek."

"You only live once..." Josh grins, and I laugh. He makes a good point.

"Sounds good to me. I'm in. I can recover Wednesday."

"Fine." Catherine groans, opening her laptop. "But you guys have to make sure I return to the hotel alone."

I grin. Catherine had been very cozy with the Aussie

the other night. Obviously, she had regrets the next morning. A shame, because he did look like a lot of fun and certainly seemed to be enjoying his time with my boss the last time I saw him.

"We can do that." I start to work, but my mind won't concentrate, too preoccupied with what's happening in Rome right now. I suppose Henry's mother must be over the moon to learn of her first grandchild's birth. They will push even harder for Henry to marry Margot now.

I force myself to think of something else. Anything but the continued merry-go-round that is Henry Fairfax.

"Oh, I see here the breaking news that Margot has given birth to a boy."

"The baby was early. I hope everything is well with the child. I've heard preemies can have issues when born too early." She is only seven months along, eight weeks early. A little part of me feels nauseated that perhaps the stress of me being in Capri could have been a factor and brought the child on early. God, I hope that isn't the case. I don't need to feel guilty about that too, on top of what I wanted to do with Henry Saturday night in the yacht's cabin…

"It doesn't say there were any complications. They haven't announced a name yet."

I pick up my phone. Should I text Henry, congratulating him?

I throw the phone down on the desk. No. Absolutely not.

Do not do that, Maddie. Stay out of his life and this happy time.

"What a life that child's been born into. The little boy will want for nothing," Josh says.

"A pity all children didn't suffer the same fate." I don't want to sound spiteful, but I also can't help but notice the gap between the wealthy and the poor. The children who are born with everything and those like me, who fight every minute of every day to survive. To not become a statistic of abuse, in whatever form that comes in. Children who fight to get out of the poverty they were born into, to make something of themselves.

"I second you on that." Catherine throws me a small smile. "Right, back to work, people. We have a lot to get sorted before Maddie leaves. This week is already shorter as it is."

I settle down and work through lunch, finishing early and making sure everything needed for the day is done. I stroll back to my room, checking my phone for the hundredth time. Still no message from Henry.

But what do I expect? We've ended as friends. Put a full stop behind our past. His future is with Margot, whether he thinks so now or not. I have to let him have a chance at happiness there, with a family of his own.

It's the least I can do for that child. A shame no one had done the same for me.

CHAPTER
Fifty-Three

MARGOT LIES in the hospital bed, and like her, I can't stop staring at our son. The sweet little guy is wrapped up in a white blanket and looks content to sleep the morning away.

"What should we call him?"

Margot purses her lips, thinking. "A family name. Maybe after your father. What was his middle name?"

"Aldo." It's a strong name and not too old and stuffy that it isn't still commonly used today. Does my son look like a Fairfax? I stare at him, the urge to pick him up and kiss the little guy overwhelming. I don't think I'd feel so in love with another person so quickly, instantly, but I am. People are right about the changes that happen when you become a parent. Your love is instant and overwhelming.

"I'm tired. I'm going to take a short nap while the baby is asleep."

"Very well. I'll come back later. I have some work to

finish off at the office anyway. I shall return in an hour or two."

Margot nods and huddles down in the bed, pulling the blankets over her shoulders.

I frown and leave. Is she okay? There's a quietness about her since she gave birth only hours before that I've never seen in her before. Maybe she's just feeling as overwhelmed as I am.

I catch sight of the doctor and hail him down. "Dr. Costa, a word if you have a minute."

"Of course, Mr. Fairfax. And may I say congratulations again? A fine son for you and your family."

"Thank you." I move away from the hospital room to allow Margot to sleep. "I just wanted to ask to settle my concerns about our child. Being that our boy is eight weeks early, is everything well with him? He's sleeping and doesn't seem to have any issues that premature babies can have, and I just wanted to make sure that he's not in distress or we're not missing anything that should be done."

"Premature?" The doctor frowns, clearly confused. "The child isn't premature, Mr. Fairfax. He's right on time." He goes over to a nearby computer and pulls up Margot's records. "Yes, Miss Hathaway was due last week, in fact, so she's a week late. We would have induced had she not gone into labor naturally, but she did, so no need to interfere with nature."

I swallow the lump in my throat. What... "So, to confirm, Margot's due date was last week? The child isn't two months premature?"

"Yes, that's right, Mr. Fairfax. No need to worry at all." The doctor pats my arm and heads off on his rounds.

I stare after him, watching him walk away. My mind spins. The child is on time. The child is not premature. The child is therefore not mine. And Margot damn well knows it.

All this time, these months of pressuring me to marry her. My family growing more and more excited about the impending birth of my mother's first grandchild. And the kid isn't even mine.

Couldn't be. The dates don't add up to when I was in Rome and with Margot that one night.

I stumble to the wall and lean on it for support. The room spins, and ringing explodes in my ears, deafening me. The boy isn't mine. The little lad I already love can't be my child.

My heart lurches, my eyes sting.

How could she?

I walk back into the hospital room, almost in a daze, and close the door, sitting on a chair beside the bed. "Margot, the doctor tells me the baby isn't premature. Please explain to me so I understand what the hell is going on here when you've led me to believe you're only seven months pregnant."

She mumbles something under her breath before stretching and blinking her eyes open. Is she at all concerned that I've found out something that was possibly always meant to be kept from me? Has she been playing me for a fool this entire pregnancy? What the hell is wrong with her that she would do that to someone she supposedly cares for?

"Sorry, what are you asking?" She sits up and clasps her hands in her lap, giving me her attention.

I take a deep breath, my mind racing. "I'm asking whose child it is that you birthed today. Our interaction in Rome and the birth of this child is out by two months, and the baby isn't premature. The doctor just told me that truth. So explain that to me so I can understand what the hell kind of game you're playing."

"What?" Her voice trembles, and I know she understands the game is up. That I know the truth and want her now to confirm it.

I remain calm, keep my voice low but firm. "I spoke to the doctor just now. I wanted to make sure the child was well considering he was born eight weeks early. You said you were only seven months, which lines up with our night in Rome, but that's not true, is it? You were already pregnant when we slept together in Rome. Who's the father of your baby? Because it sure as hell isn't me."

The words hurt to say. I clear my throat, aching from the lump that won't dissipate.

I have claimed the child as my own. Loved him as any father should. But he isn't mine, and another man deserves to know the little boy, raise him right, and do the best for his future. But who the hell is the father? Who the hell plays such a cruel game on another person? It seems Margot Hathaway does.

I should have known her hatred of Maddie has no

bounds or morals. Even pretending to fall pregnant by me to get what she wants isn't beneath her jealous rage.

"You're being absurd. Of course, the baby is yours. Do not say such awful things, Henry."

"We hadn't slept together for six months before I met Maddie in Sorrento. Other than the night in Rome, we hadn't been intimate. So unless you carried this baby for over a year, that sweet boy isn't mine." I take a calming breath, not wanting to lose my cool. "Who's child is it, Margot? I'll not ask again."

She looks at the baby and sighs. "Fine, the baby is another man's and not yours. But he's not suitable to be a father, and I cannot trust him. So it doesn't matter who it is because he wants nothing to do with us."

"So you just decided to make me the father instead?" I stand and pace before the windows, looking out over Rome. People go about their busy lives, the streets full of tourists and cars.

"Was that the plan in Rome all along? Get me drunk, sleep with me, and play off your pregnancy as my child?" It can't be true. She can't be this awful. "Who are you? I don't recognize the woman you've become."

"It would seem I do." She shrugs. "My career would be tarnished if I had a child out of wedlock. It would be scandalous and all over the papers. The paparazzi would have a jolly good time with this story. I didn't want that for my family and certainly not for the baby."

"This isn't the dark ages, Margot. No one would care if you had a child on your own or not. What makes you think what you did was in any way appropriate?"

"I was desperate, and I have always cared for you, Henry. I wanted you to be the child's father. You are more settled and suited for the role."

"We weren't together. What makes you think I'd then want a child with you? You must tell the real father the truth."

Margot's face twists in irritation. "And what are you going to do? Run back to your poor little American girl? She's nothing, Henry."

"This has nothing to do with Maddie. This was your choice." I glance at the little boy, used as a ploy. My heart clenches. I run my finger along his soft cheek. "How dare you do this to me. I've known you all my life and this is the repayment of that friendship. I had hoped we could be amicable, part ways, but you refused to let me go and now I know why. It was just to save face and use me." I shake my head, heading toward the door. I stop, and turnback to look at her. "I would have found out eventually. Years from now perhaps, and your son would have grown to know only me as his father. An unbreakable bond, that was based on a lie. How could you think that was in any way okay?"

She rolls her eyes, shaking her head, clearly unmoved. "I do what I have to when the need arises. Do not be so dramatic and emotional, Henry. Just spare me the lecture and leave."

"I am. Do not ever contact me again." I blink, hating the emotions coursing through me, the hurt and anger.

Hating Margot for the pain she inflicted on my family. Everyone will be devastated by her lies.

I've been so blind, so forgiving and I should never have been. I've been used and because of another's choices lost my first child, and the one woman I ever loved. But at least with Maddie I could get her back.

There was still time to remedy that at least.

Fifty-Four

AS PART of the celebration for the new hotel opening, the island is hosting a classical music evening. I stand with Catherine, Eve, and Clara, who have flown in for my work milestone. I've never been in charge of the advertising for a new hotel in such a beautiful location before, and I have to admit, this is a big deal.

Even with everything that has happened between me and Henry, the shit he's put me through, I have succeeded here. The hotel is fully booked and ready for guests. Everything is perfect, and the advertising has been mint. No one, not even Henry's mother or the shareholders, can be displeased.

Paul stands before us, talking to Henry's mother, who is here to support her son, no doubt. I don't attempt to speak to her—we are hardly friends—but I'm silently amused that she is speaking to Paul, my boyfriend of sorts, without even knowing it.

The prickling of my skin tells me, even before I turn and look, that Henry has arrived.

Why I am so in tune with him, I do not know. Especially now, when there is nothing between us. He is a father now and should be there for his new family. I could not get in the way of that child's happiness.

An acrid taste enters my mouth at the thought of him and Margot together, creating a family and being happy when I am not. And that is the truth of it—I am not happy with Paul. Since being in Capri, he has turned into a man I hardly recognize, obsessed with those I may know, the contacts I could possibly have made to strengthen his banking portfolio. He's turned into a man obsessed with his next big deal.

"Good evening, ladies," Henry says.

I stifle a sigh, hating myself for relishing the sound of his voice as it flows over me like a Mediterranean wave. The man is too charismatic for his own good, and the way he is looking at me right now isn't fair.

"Eve and Clara all but spit like kittens, their lips turning up in distaste before Eve gives Henry her back and walks off in the direction of the bar.

Clara meets my eye, and I smile, telling her without words that I will be fine if she wants to escape this awkwardness. She, too, turns on her heel and leaves, leaving me and Henry in a sea of guests as they move about to take their seats before the Symphony Concert starts.

"The opening celebration with his concert is a marvel, Maddie. I knew you would not disappoint me."

I sip my champagne, attempting—and failing miserably—not to roll my eyes. "Really, Henry? I don't need your praise. I did my job, which I am capable of. I'm glad you're happy with the service and how the hotel has been advertised, but I don't want you praising me unconditionally. I wasn't the only one who worked for you."

A muscle works in his jaw, and he glances at the stage before his eyes move over to Paul, still speaking with his mother.

"We need to talk."

"What about?" I adjust my tone after catching the attention of those around us. "We have nothing to say outside of work," I whisper.

"The hell we don't."

There's something wild in his eyes, and my stomach twists. I hate and love that feeling he evokes in me. It's like a drug I want a hit from over and over again, but also want to be free from—a cage my heart continues to hold me in.

"We can't talk here. The concert is about to start."

Without asking, he grabs my hand and drags me away. I look back at Paul, and seriously, the man has no idea that I have even left, still perfectly content talking to Henry's sister. I will have to break up with him. I am not his ticket to more lucrative clientele.

We exit through a side door of the makeshift stadium, and Henry slams the door closed behind us. I glance at the door, noting there is no handle on this side.

"Henry, we can't get back in this way." I start back toward the entrance. I hear Henry coming up fast behind me, and a little part of me loves that he is chasing me, wanting me as desperately as I still want him—damn him to hell, the cheating piece of shit.

"Stop, for Christ's sake." He grabs me around the stomach and whirls me about. "I need to speak to you, and you need to listen."

I still.

Being in his arms again isn't a good idea. I shouldn't have let him chase me so he could grab me like this. God, my body melts at the feel of being in his arms. I want him still, crave his touch, his kisses.

Will I ever get over this man? I so need to get back to New York and away from him.

What's that saying? Out of sight, out of mind crap.

"What is it you want to say? Hurry, or we'll miss the start of the concert."

"Fuck the concert." Henry runs a hand through his hair, pacing before me. "Something happened in Rome, and I need you to let me tell you so you can choose what to do with that information."

I cross my arms, wary. "Okay, what happened in Rome?" Other than him becoming a father…

Do I really want to hear about the happiest moment in his life? Anyone's life, I'd assume. As much as I love babies, the fact that Henry has one with someone else hurts my heart. I want to be the mother of his children. I want to be his wife and have his babies.

Selfish thoughts I need to stop.

"You know Margot had the baby."

"Yes, congratulations, by the way. I should have said it earlier. I'm sorry I didn't." Shame washes over me, and I fight not to hate myself more for being jealous of an innocent child.

"The baby wasn't premature as I believed him to be, which made no sense. So I questioned the doctor, who was under the impression the child was born when he expected him to be—not premature."

My mind races as I try to understand what he is saying. "Well, that's good, isn't it? Better not to be a premmie baby, yes?"

"Well yes." He paced some more, a frown between his brows. "It made me question the time of conception, and when I pushed Margot, she admitted the child isn't mine."

I gape at him, then realize I am staring like an idiot and shut my mouth. What the hell? Not his? "What?" I manage, still unable to comprehend what he is saying.

"Margot admitted to lying about the child. I believe the baby to be Merrick's, but Margot wouldn't admit to that. But when she said he doesn't want anything to do with the child, I knew who she'd slept with. I'll make sure his opinion on becoming a father changes if he wants to keep his reputation and family on his side." He pauses, meeting my eyes. "But the baby isn't mine, Maddie."

I nod but don't say a word. The baby isn't his. I do not know what to feel. Relief yes, but also pain. "I'm so sorry, Henry. That must be painful for you."

"I will not abandon the child. I will ensure he is cared for and looked after very well and I will have care in place to ensure he's never forgotten by his selfish mother and absent father."

I remain silent, unsure where we go with this new information. "Are you still engaged?" I blurt before thinking better of it. I don't want him to think I'm selfish, but I need to know if he's truly broken from Margot. For good this time. Dare I hope that he isn't? Am I a bad person for hoping that he's single? Should I loathe myself for feeling relieved that the baby isn't his?

Yes, I should feel bad about that. The poor child is innocent in all this crap his mother has already put him in.

"I was never engaged, no matter what the tabloids said. I can't believe you still believe that. I've been trying to tell you for weeks." Henry grabs my hands and starts rubbing his thumb over them. I don't pull away. "The child isn't mine, and I'm not engaged, but that's not all Margot admitted to."

"There's more?"

A small, lopsided smile lifts his lips, and I fight to concentrate on his words.

"The night the child was supposed to have been conceived, Margot spiked my drink. The emailed photos—everything—was staged. I never slept with her. She admitted that I could barely speak, let alone get a hard-on, but she pretended we did to hurt you, to trap me."

"Because she knew you would do the right thing by the child."

He nods. "She told Merrick about the pregnancy, and he did a runner. Fearing her reputation as Europe's sweetheart, she ensured I was put in a compromising position that she could use against me. She was already pregnant when she staged those photos, almost two months along in fact."

"So…" I swallow, hope welling up inside me. "You didn't cheat, you're not a father, and you're not engaged."

He smiles then, pulling me closer still. "No. I'm not any of those things."

I don't know what to do or say. Emotion wells up inside me, and the sight of Henry blurs.

His warm thumb swipes a tear off my cheek before he pulls me into his arms. I fall into him, holding him tight, never wanting to let go. I breathe in the cologne he wears, relish the beat of his heart against my chest.

I've missed this. I've missed us.

"I love you so much, Maddie. I want you back."

I press my head into his shoulder, the lump in my throat too big for me to speak through. His hand rubs along my back, warm and comforting. "I love you too. I thought you were lost to me."

He sighs and holds me tighter. "I was never lost to you, but I would have done the right thing by that boy. But I would have fought for you. My heart broke each time I had to look at you and the pain I caused. I want you to marry me. Tomorrow isn't soon enough, but I want you to be my wife, my future—before anyone else tries to rip us apart."

I pull back to look up at him. "You're asking me to be your wife?"

He smiles, kissing the tip of my nose. "I am. What do you say?" His devilish grin is back. Oh, how I missed seeing it. "Yes, I'm hoping."

What do I say? Is he mad? "I say yes!"

He kisses me then, and everything is right in the world at this moment. I kiss him back, all the past months apart, the longing, the dreadful, horrible idea that I would never be with him again like this—without hurting others in the process—dissipates as we kiss.

He pushes me up against the side of the makeshift stadium. The classical music of the concert starts, muffled as we devour each other, drinking in and savoring all that we've missed.

He grabs my ass, lifting me and stepping between my legs. I hook them around his hips. Henry reaches for my underwear, ripping it in two and tossing it aside. I reach between us, unzipping his pants and freeing his cock. I stroke him, having forgotten how much I love the feel of him—hard and big and all mine.

"God, yes, touch me."

I shiver, stroke his cock, making it even harder. I can feel my own wetness, my need making me ache. "I want you. Don't make me wait."

He brushes his lips over mine before pushing my hand away and hoisting me higher. He closes the space between us and fucks me—takes me up against the wall like there is no tomorrow.

But there is a tomorrow. And a day after that.

We have forever.

We move together, his cock stretching me, taking me, owning me. I hold on to Henry, lost in the feel of him filling me. It feels so good, his cock teasing the ache within me until I want to shatter into a million pieces.

"I love you. So fucking much."

I kiss him, try to show him how much I love him too. Love everything about him. "I adore you."

Our eyes lock as he pumps relentlessly into me. "Come for me. I want to watch you shatter. I've missed us so much."

I roll my hips and take him deeper. His eyes flare, and I am so close I can taste it. He jerks inside me, and that is all it takes. I shatter, come apart in his arms. My orgasm rips through me, teases and satisfies every part of my soul. "Henry," I gasp, our eyes locked.

"I love feeling you come." His kiss is brutal as he spills inside me.

No protection this time. No barrier between us. No need.

We are going to marry, and what does it matter if we have babies?

I want to be the mother of his children just as I want nothing but his happiness—and in turn, my own.

We stay locked together for a few minutes, both catching our breath before Henry lowers me to the ground.

We look around and settle our clothes. I reach down, picking up my ripped underwear and shoving them into Henry's pocket. "Better not leave these here."

He chuckles. "No, probably best."

"What now?" I ask.

Henry takes my hand and kisses my fingers. "Now, we go home to Rome and we marry."

He pulls me down the side of the building. I glance around, hoping no one saw what we've been up to.

"You cannot mean right now?" I try to pull him to a stop, but there is not stopping him.

"Right now. I'm not waiting another minute."

And we didn't. Not a second more.

WHAT HAPPENS IN

What Happens In Sorrento

About the Author

I'm GILLI BRADLEY, the author behind steamy, high-stakes billionaire romances. I write sizzling, jet-setting love stories where passion meets power, emotions run deep, and the chemistry is off the charts. With a love for luxury, high society, and captivating characters, I create worlds where ambition, desire, and romance collide in unforgettable ways.

Get ready for love that's Filthy Rich and Fiery Hot.